Thicker Than Water

Isabel is the unwanted daughter of charming but irresponsible people who married in haste, divorced just as quickly, and distanced themselves from one another—and from her. Left to her grandparents' care, longing for her elusive, glamorous mother and for a father she barely remembers, Isabel's agony erupts into perverse and dangerous rebellion. A compelling novel that lends new meaning to Freud's "family romance," *Thicker Than Water* brilliantly illuminates how fragile is the line between family love and the darker sides of passion.

"Dazzling...stunning...
almost perfect in its conception and execution.
It is a tragic, darkly aberrant story,
but it is human, occasionally bitterly funny,
sometimes beautiful,
and steadfastly proud and uncompromising."
—*Hartford Courant*

Other Avon Books by
Kathryn Harrison

THE KISS
POISON

Thicker Than Water

KATHRYN HARRISON

AN AVON BOOK

AVON BOOKS, INC.
1350 Avenue of the Americas
New York, New York 10019

Copyright © 1991 by Kathryn Harrison
Front cover photograph by Christine Rodin
Inside cover author photograph by Marion Ettlinger
Published by arrangement with Random House, Inc.
Visit our website at **http://www.AvonBooks.com/Bard**
ISBN: 0-380-73156-8

The Random House edition contained the following Library of Congress Cataloging in Publication Data:

Harrison, Kathryn.
  Thicker than water / by Kathryn Harrison.
    p.   cm.
  I. Title.
  PS3558.A67136M68 1991   90-38317
  813'54—dc20

First Bard Printing: December 1998

BARD TRADEMARK REG. U S PAT OFF AND IN OTHER COUNTRIES, MARCA REGISTRADA, HECHO EN U S A

Printed in the U.S.A.

OPM 10 9 8 7 6 5 4 3 2 1

FOR COLIN

*"The happiest women,
like the happiest nations,
have no history."*

—GEORGE ELIOT

Acknowledgments

I wish to express my gratitude to James Michener and the Copernicus Society for their generous fellowship in support of the writing of this novel.

I am indebted also to Nan Graham, to Amanda Urban, and to Kate Medina.

Thicker Than Water

In truth, my mother was not a beautiful woman. She told me so one day—certainly no one else had ever said such a thing—when we were driving on Sunset Boulevard on the way home from a shopping trip. A half hour before, our heads had been inclined together over a makeup counter in I. Magnin's department store, discussing blusher and the thickness of my eyebrows; she was all for having them waxed. Her own were cosmetically symmetrical, twin brush strokes of derision, purposefully countering the undisguised melancholy of her large hazel eyes. I had asked her as the car swept smoothly through the canyon, past the long stand of eucalyptus outside the entrance to UCLA, and through the tall black gates of Bel Air, "But don't *you* think you are beautiful?"

I believed, of course, that she was—it was one of our family's most cherished myths, my mother's loveliness. "Isabel," she said, "my nose is too big, my face is too thin, my mouth is too small."

On that afternoon I was stunned by her assessment, and by the speed with which she reported her flaws, as if too many times she might have rehearsed those shortcomings as she looked at herself in the mirror while dressing for a date. But as I look back through the surprisingly few photographs that I have of my mother, I see that she was right. She was not beautiful.

There is one picture, though, of us together in my grandfather's garden, each with fruit and flowers in our arms—the photograph a testament to the garden's generosity. We are standing before the flowering peach tree, the sun is on our faces, our slender fair arms. In that picture she is breathtaking.

Young—twenty-two, white skin, rich dark hair, her small mouth slightly open and her lips flushed crimson. Her nearly green eyes wide and solemn. Even when she laughed, my mother's eyes did not accompany her in mirth; they were unflinchingly sad, and dry, as if they did not recognize the use in weeping.

My mother was not yet eighteen when she and my father married. They were totally unsuited to one another. In one of those metaphorically apt instances that fate provides, they met at an amateur production of Oliver Goldsmith's *She Stoops to Conquer, or The Mistakes of a Night.* They were teenagers, each attending the play with his and her high school English class; each reinforced in their flirtation by the presence of giggling, envious friends; each, at heart, lonely.

My father had been living in Los Angeles for only a few years. From September to June he attended a preparatory school for boys located in the Hollywood Hills; summers he worked as the institution's groundskeeper in exchange for room and board. His father, a man who made his living as an exterminator and drove a panel truck with sombreroed cockroaches stenciled on its sides, sent his favorite son to this school which he had read about in *Look* magazine. He intended to reimburse my father for a miserable childhood of abandonment and philandering and spent what was for him a small fortune on my father's high school education, forcing the boy to emigrate from Douglas, a small, dusty and predominantly Hispanic town on Arizona's border with Mexico and a twin to the southern country's town of Agua Pieta, to Los Angeles, a much greater city and one that my father did not understand. Because travel was expensive—to drive the 576 miles between Los Angeles and Douglas required, in the days before steel-belted radials, a new set of tires which would be ruined, used up, on the desert highways—my father was not encouraged to spend summers at home. In any case, his old room had been taken over by one or more of his four brothers. There were two sisters in Douglas as well; my father was the middle child of seven—eight, if his identical twin, born dead, was numbered among them. It was expected that among this brood my father, at least, would make something of himself, that he would transcend his heritage of Catholic poverty, of desperate, drinking missionaries and senseless, pretty girls who were pregnant at the altar, of car clubs and knife fights and sweltering summer nights when young men were killed in the streets of Douglas for rash words or acts, for making a pass at somebody's sister. The more urban environment of Southern California, the company of affluent boys with whom he ate and showered and shared his dorm room, and with whom he played a more civilized version of football than the one to which he was accustomed, was undoubtedly a shock. Surely he found himself out of place and time and feeling. But he was determined to earn the respect of his father, to succeed, however that was accomplished, and to go to college as no one else in his family had done.

Probably my mother seemed, on the appearance of things,

to fit in with those aspirations. Not that my father's attraction to her was so calculated. No, I think that she must simply have represented all that was so nearly out of reach for him: wealth and culture and, yes, breeding. And of course, even if she was not actually beautiful, she did have that ineffable, incalculable something that made us all believe she was.

When he was older, my father would describe my mother in those years of her late adolescence as a sleek cat, feline of eye and grace, and mysterious. She was able to convey her essentially empty heart and mind as unfathomable, deep rather than depthless. She was fashionably voluptuous and small-waisted. She came of old money, and her parents were British subjects, a fact not without moment to a boy of humble Irish origins: peat bogs, potato famines. My father was always hungry, and there was a lot of food in my grandparents' house: a pantry crammed with things he liked, some of which—the pickled herring, the matzoth and fish balls and little packages of kosher soup mix—he'd never before encountered. For, of course, my mother was Jewish. But this was more curiosity than impediment; after all, her parents, and mine, since they later raised me, were not orthodox: they weren't even practicing beyond their habitual, reflexive observance of the Day of Atonement. Still, she was probably one of the first Jews he ever met.

They found one another at a play, my parents, my mother and my father, whom I recall seeing together on less than ten occasions, their last encounter being when he was simply an observer and she the observed, a body in a casket. It seems appropriate, their meeting at a play, because my parents were actors—not in the vocational sense, but in that neither subscribed to any honesty of heart. They were the kind of people who fooled themselves even as they fooled others. They came together briefly for their own drama, and then separated, leaving a mystery that tormented my family for years. What had

6

happened between them? Who had they been together that so ruined them when they were apart? We never spoke such questions aloud, but they were fodder for years of private, anxious speculation.

On that night long ago, during that play, after that play, perhaps in some way infected by the romantic intrigue of lovers long dead, my teenage father and mother embarked on a fateful, irreversible flirtation that culminated in pregnancy, wedlock, divorce and perhaps, ultimately, death. At least while she was dying, my mother was not above accusing my father of torturing her. She said that it was because of him that she no longer wanted to live, and that during the last years of her life he had taken his revenge on her, had sullied everything she valued: their love and their only child. But, then, my mother was not a woman who could ever accept responsibility, not for herself or her fate, and certainly not for me, whom she gave to her own mother, but like an Indian gift, one she constantly threatened to take back.

My mother and my grandmother fought. The earliest years of my childhood, when the three of us, the women who determined the ugly, angry dynamic of our family—leaving my grandfather to his own gentle arts, his gardening, his reading— when the three of us lived under one roof, it seemed the very beams and bolts of the house would break apart for the fighting it contained. The sound of my mother's and my grandmother's caustic voices, of their pitched, vicious battles, is my first memory. Probably my mother never won any of these fights; my grandmother was not a fair adversary. Her physical presence alone—six feet tall and big-boned with hair that was absolutely white and eyebrows which remained strikingly black—was enough to discourage most contenders. For anyone who persisted beyond the warning arch of those eyebrows (and, of course, my mother always did), her style of argument—to abandon any pretense of rational discourse, to dredge up her own past victories and introduce irrelevant but affecting memories of her opponent's many trespasses, in short, to do whatever would ensure her triumph—was unnerving. And she had no pride in this endeavor; she would say anything.

It was my father who was the focus of my mother's and her mother's first truly divisive and destructive arguments, and my father about whom they argued until my mother died. Whether overtly or in desperate sub-rosa disagreements characterized by a knife striking a plate too loudly during dinner, a meal left untouched, a chair empty, they fought forever over him.

Initially, at least, it was that my grandmother could not stand to have her only child make such an ill-advised match. It was long past the time for an abortion when she discovered that my slender, secretive mother was pregnant—five months—and in any case, Mom-mom valued children too greatly to push her daughter to that solution. So she gritted her teeth for the marriage, a civil ceremony attended only by my parents, two silent friends and my grandparents. It made quite a picture, that unfortunate wedding, with my tall, snow-capped grandmother like a forbidding peak in her brown tweed suit, my grandfather the game explorer by her side. Smaller in stature than his wife, and given to wearing walking shorts and a Tyrolean hat, when standing next to Mom-mom, Opa sometimes seemed as if he were about to ascend to her summit, discover the secrets of her dark eyes, steal a kiss, perhaps. Even on this day, the one photograph taken by my father's best man reveals Opa's sporting presence between the frightened bride and her mother. My parents wore casual clothes to their wedding, as if to avoid calling further attention to their folly, as if the marriage were incidental, an errand accomplished between other chores. My father, so blond and thin, his blue eyes rendered blank and red by the flashbulb, has his hands placed one on each of my mother's shoulders, a bold gesture and perhaps one he dared make only for the moment of the photograph. My mother's eyes reveal no more than his, for they were shut at that same instant; she blinked, I guess. Her friend, the maid of honor—and the only person dressed in white—stands off to one side. Diminutive, especially in contrast to my grandmother, she looks like a child in her first communion dress, as if she had wandered, lost, into the wrong ceremony. It is not so much a sad picture as it is inauspicious. And, though I am not much visible, it is the first photograph of me.

After the wedding, thus recorded, my grandmother allowed my father to move in with his young pregnant wife. Better to have the boy in her daughter's bedroom than to lose her to the marginal existence of a seedy apartment on the outskirts of the city. At the time of my birth, my father had graduated from high school just four months previously and, having postponed unaffordable college, became a floorwalker for Bullocks Wilshire's downtown department store. His new employer provided him with Bally shoes and a tailor-made suit, a selection of silk ties—surely the most expensive clothes he had ever owned—and it was his job to supervise sales personnel, assist customers and keep an eye out for shoplifters, all while wandering decoratively through the various departments on the fifth floor. He was a conscientious and hard worker—punctual, polite and dandyish in the care of his new suit—but my father lost that job within the year. He was handsome enough, with a voice that was sonorous and deep for so young a man, but one of his very blue eyes had the unfortunate tendency to wander, which might have aided him in surveillance; but it made the ladies who asked direction to the powder room or shoe department very nervous. He looked good from a distance, but the intimacy required by even an abbreviated conversation was unsettling.

By the time he was asked to resign, my father had used his

employee discount to purchase a ridiculous amount of toiletries for my mother who, even in her extravagance, was unable to make use of all the perfumes and creams and bath crystals. Unopened, the innumerable bottles of Guerlain and Dior and Chanel, all grown stale and worthless, gathered dust on my mother's closet shelf throughout my childhood. Had I known from where, from *whom* the perfumes had come, perhaps I would have taken more interest in them, examined and claimed them for myself, looking for some clue, some hint of the always elusive past of my mother. But, as it was, they collected dust for years until someone chanced to mention their origin and until it had become necessary—more than a childish amusement—to discover all that I could about my parents, my father particularly, as he was to become my tormentor, my Svengali, my ruin.

He disappeared before he could leave any imprint upon my childish memory. By the time I was walking, my father was gone, asked to leave by my grandfather, whose words, softly spoken, were supported by the bitter anger and determination of my grandmother. While it was never discussed—that last confrontation between my parents and grandparents—I learned years later that my father had left meekly at my grandfather's bidding. He hadn't seen my mother for two days. She had, not unusually, I was told, and perhaps anticipating some cataclysmic outcome, locked herself in her room, hidden under her bedspread. Suffering from fits of agoraphobia—either that or cowardice—my mother periodically took to her bed like a neurasthenic Victorian lady. She did this many times as I grew up, but this instance, the one that preceded her divorce, was the inaugural episode and lasted for five weeks.

My father, the story goes, knocked repeatedly on her door; he rattled its brass handle and slipped notes through the crack underneath; he sat, waiting, on the floor in the hall outside my mother's room, and my grandmother stepped over him when she had the occasion to use that passage. But this humiliation was to no purpose; no answer came; and so he gave up, finally, and left. Left his clothes, his few books, and all that he owned, and drove off in his old car, the rattletrap coupe he'd brought with him from Arizona.

For months my father lived in his car on the streets of Los Angeles: slept in it, ate in it when he could panhandle a dollar or two, drove it when he had a few cents' worth of gas, combed his unruly blond hair in the rearview mirror. Perhaps he might have embraced such an existence altogether had his older brother not come from Douglas on a Greyhound bus, taken the keys from his pocket and driven him back home. I never did learn how he found him.

Eventually my mother came out of her room, and even left the house. She went to secretarial school and taught herself to type with great and accurate speed. She wore her long curling hair in a chignon and got a job, and she started dating other, more suitable young men. Her divorce was accomplished within a year—papers returned to her lawyer with an uncharacteristically faint and crabbed signature from my father—and she was proclaimed, by the law, free.

But my grandmother never allowed her much liberty and never restored her faith in my mother's taste in men. Mommom loudly challenged her every choice until, finally, my mother moved out of her parents' house and kept her romantic life a secret.

My mother once told me this story about a date that my grandmother tried to sabotage. Unable to convince her daughter beforehand that she ought not to leave home that night, my grandmother took her revenge. Oh, I can picture my mother at nineteen, lovely and lithe in her yellow silk dress, its narrow skirt defining the length of her legs, her slightly knock-kneed grace; it must have been worth any price to escape that house of heavy antiques and heavier burdens: parenthood, divorce.

That night long ago, she simply walked out of the impossible argument with my grandmother—she *would* go out no matter what.

And so my grandmother waited. When the young man came to the door, when he stood on the Bokhara rug that covered the cold flagstone floor of the foyer, waiting for my mother to pick up her coat and say good night to her father, my grandmother began to scream. She was in her bedroom down the hall from the young couple, and the door was closed. But my grandmother was always a good screamer. Her shrieks filled the house and created the impression that a madwoman was incarcerated on the premises. And she did not stop after a minute or two, but continued to call steadily out in the wild indecipherable language of animals and infants. Her howls continued as the young couple bid my grandfather a good evening, rather ironically under the circumstances. They were audible as my mother stepped into her date's Thunderbird convertible and as she carefully smoothed her skirt before sitting. The couple heard the screams as they cruised slowly around the circular drive and headed down the steep, winding incline of Stone Canyon onto Sunset Boulevard. My mother remembered that neither she nor the young man mentioned the incident all evening. They ate at a restaurant on the beach; they danced; they were relaxed and fluid in their movements even without the encouragement of alcohol; he brought her home at a respectable hour, which then must have been no later than midnight, and he never called her again.

But my mother never gave up, or at least, even as she slowly lost the battle to escape her mother and be her own person, she did so noisily; the two of them quarreled until years later when my mother was too ill to lift her head or move her arms or her hands while she spoke. While arguing, my mother had always punctuated each comment with some dramatic and improbable gesture, like a crazy woman taking swings at unseen assailants, and her angry stillness in that bed was the final defeat for my grandmother, who retreated into her own silence.

But that was years later. Until then, the fights continued. They are the one constant memory of my earliest years, the years until, finally, my mother moved out of her parents' home and into a studio apartment somewhere in the vicinity of the firm where she worked as a legal secretary. She spent most of her days there transcribing long, tedious documents, a dry occupation that could hardly have satisfied her love for art and music, for drama. Her high school yearbook page had listed Broadway Actress as her aspiration.

I must have been five when she moved out, and from then until I was eleven and she invited the three of us, Mom-mom, Opa and me, to eat Thanksgiving dinner at her apartment—an epochal occasion and one which I am at a loss to explain—I did not know where my mother lived. I saw her each day, but she was so protective of her privacy, her fragile illusory freedom, that not until years later did she reveal her address, or even her phone number. She moved fairly often, living sometimes alone, more often with a girlfriend, but she never told her parents or her child where it was that she slept, parked her old blue Pontiac, kept her clothes and her food, and her small, private life.

*I dream that my mother and I are brides in a double wedding.
I have insisted upon wearing a totally inappropriate, short, red
dress. I know that the dress is wrong and am afraid that my
groom's parents will hate me because of its vulgarity, but somehow, I have been unable not to wear it.*

*Mother, in the traditional white, has baked a number of very
curious pies for the reception. They turn out to have nothing
under their flawless crusts but small sewing notions: little buttons, thimbles, needles, thread. I realize I could never have
baked such wondrous pies, and I grow afraid, and fear that I will
be discovered as a sham, not a real woman.*

*Contemplating the pies, I am filled with awe. Their golden
crusts flake with cosmetic, commercial perfection, and underneath there are tiny icons of feminine virtue.*

It was my father who commented on the ironic collection of men who served as my mother's pallbearers. It was I who invited them to the task. They seemed, each one of them individually, if not together as a group, a natural and appropriate choice. But I knew what he meant. By then I understood what I had not as a child; I had been forced to study my father and his passions, his unreasoning love for my mother and the depths to which it would ultimately drag him, and me in his grasp. The planning of my mother's funeral had fallen to her only daughter, and I had obeyed convention by selecting those closest to her among family and friends. To a casual observer, all looked as it should. After all, by the time she died, I was well practiced in making things look normal, in clothing what was unnatural with a facade of respectability.

At her right shoulder was my father himself, the man to

whom my mother was married for less than a year, the man with whom she was obsessed, if not in love, for most of her life, the man whom she saw only infrequently, even as they shared their seasons of impassioned phone calls, their cyclical plans for reunion.

Her left shoulder was born up by Albert, a man small in stature if not in heart and the lover with whom she had lived for the last seven years of her life. Had it been asked, common law would have declared them man and wife the week before she died. It was Albert who had stayed at her side while she was ill, who with me had changed linen, administered morphine, and who finally, on that afternoon when she discovered she could no longer get out of bed and walk to the bathroom, gently took his credit card from her hand after she had ordered seventeen pairs of shoes over the phone—pumps, loafers, flats, sandals, one pair of evening slippers—from Bloomingdale's, Neiman-Marcus, Saks, I. Magnin. He stopped her at seventeen. No one else had dared come near the bed, catalogs and blankets all heaped together at the foot, myself and my usually imposing grandmother hiding with the physical therapist in the kitchen, listening to her dial and redial, ordering more than two thousand dollars' worth of shoes when she didn't have the money to pay the therapist, who couldn't get her out of bed any longer. No insurance either: she had stopped paying the premiums months before the fateful diagnosis. Six weeks after she ordered them, the shoes began to arrive, sometimes three pairs in an afternoon, and I was at the post office each day, returning the unopened boxes, which we never showed her. She didn't ask where the shoes were or even seem to notice that they hadn't come. Albert: also the man who drove her to despair with his drinking, his nostalgic inability to divorce his wife, his fey, introverted Gallic charm.

At her side, by her waist, was Albert's son, Christophe, the boy she never had—I was her only child—although my mother should have had boys, and only boys. She was a woman who could never befriend another woman of her own blood. One night in the hospital, Christophe read her the whole of *The Old Man and the Sea* while she wept. I cried too, but with envy, for only that afternoon she had pushed me away with my book, my offer to read. She listened to the story of Santiago while she pulled her hair out in fistfuls, refusing to let it drop out in its own time. Behind the battle of the marlin was the steady drip of Cytoxan, slow, each clear drop hanging for a moment before slipping down the tube and into her ruined vein.

Walking in pace with Christophe, the both of them tall and solid men, was Grant, the man my mother almost married time after time. Grant met my mother when she was nineteen; he was a clerk at the law firm where she worked—an ambitious young man with dreams of one day being a Supreme Court justice. As it turned out, he became a divorce lawyer, and then a palimony specialist, a divider of goods for people whose hearts had already parted company. He told me after the funeral that when he came to our house on Sunset Boulevard to pick Mother up for their first date, the door was opened by my grandmother, who had an infant—me—in her arms. His story ended there: I am not sure if my grandmother surprised him with a scream or something worse.

Each foot was held aloft by a cousin, one of the Davids, my grandfather's brother's children, Daniel David and David Solomon, but each, confusingly, called simply David. They were already men, or nearly so, when my mother was born in 1942. There are pictures of them in their World War II uniforms, ready to kill Nazis, defend the motherland, stand up for their faith. They were big men, muscular; in the pictures each balances an infant, my mother, in his arms; each poses awkwardly as if practicing for parenthood, my mother's white lace dress and bonnet starkly outlined against the uniform coat. The occasion was her christening, one of many Gentile traditions my grandmother would not forgo. After the war, in the fifties, when my mother was a teenager, the Davids, now in their thirties and still unmarried, would take my comely mother out on a Friday when she had no date. They took her to dances at the VFW Hall, they shared her pretty company. So much older than she, they were like indulgent bachelor uncles and sent her chocolates and flowers, birthday cards with checks enclosed, invariably the same amount from each. Now the Davids, men in their sixties, held her aloft for this last ceremony.

My mother, who had married only once and disastrously—a civil service in the dirty downtown courthouse—was thus escorted down the aisle for the first and only time by six strong admirers. Surrounded by men, with Vivaldi's "Winter" played above our heads, she would have liked the service, I think. She was a vain woman, and a woman dependent upon the attention of men. She had female friends, but she held those at arm's length; and while she loved her mother and daughter, it was with a love that was paranoid and destructive. She never really trusted us, Mom-mom or me: she never shared herself with us. Either she was complete, psychologically, without the interference of others of her sex, or she was too fragile. She was secretive; we never understood her; and after her death, it was necessary to select and painstakingly re-create events long past in order to discover whom it was that we had lost.

Were my grandfather still alive, he would naturally have taken a place around that casket, and someone would have had to yield a place for him. But we could think of him as represented by his brother's sons, and as it was, it worked out neatly, the six men handsome, if grave, in their dark suits. Only my father's still bright blond head struck a discordant note among the family of dark Jews. Not one of them cried as he carried the coffin; sitting in one pew at the front of the church, their faces were wet together by one flick of the priest's wrist during the blessing at the end of the requiem. Water from the tiny golden bucket in the altar boy's hand fell on us all, and it was cold water. It had been a cold day for Los Angeles, February the seventeenth, three days after her death on St. Valentine's Day. My mother was sped on her way to the underworld by Catholicism, the faith she took when she was thirty. Her conversion had been a passage influenced by the romantic image of my grandmother's sister, who turned coat and became a Catholic during the occupation of France; whose lover, a woman, a Catholic nurse, had saved her from the Nazis and then taken her to bed. A passage aided also, perhaps, by the revelations of Edna, my mother's psychic, a "white witch" whom she paid over the years an astonishing sum of money for her potions and consultations, all the transactions recorded in a little leather account book. Edna told my mother that she had been a nun in a past life. And, of course, my father had been a Catholic.

I have not been in a church since my mother's funeral; even from the outside they frighten me. The only truthful ones were those I saw in Mexico: Christ awash in blood, the gore spilling from his side. Such a primitive faith, trading one man's anointed blood for other men's sins.

When I was confirmed—not because I believed, but because I wanted to follow my mother into that stone building, sit dressed up beside her in a pew, sing with her—I had to wait a year behind the other little girls because every time the father tested my catechism, I said that bread and water, prisoner's fare, was the stuff of miracles. I could not seem to remember that it was bread and wine that fueled the Eucharist's fire; and while the priest could excuse my lack of faith, he couldn't allow my memory lapses as well. When I was four and a Christian Scientist, also in the perfumed wake of my mother's skirts, I was at the head of my class and knew the ten synonyms for god before any other child. Being held behind by the father, as a dunce, was new to me, and to my mother, and it made us both dislike me.

Finally, though, I was there beside her in the sanctuary, a Catholic. She picked me up at her parents' house each Sunday at ten minutes before eleven, so we would arrive just a little late for the eleven o'clock high mass, the noise of her heels on the stone floor echoing around the great alabaster crucifix and freezing more deeply the stunned faces of the angels as we walked before the entire congregation to our seats. This same church where my mother's soul was beckoned to its final reward had a crucified Christ bigger than any man, and more beautiful. I used to stare up at his exquisite, almost sexual torment, the blood on his brow and from his side spilling discreetly in two endless frozen rivulets. Just above his loincloth, his taut belly swelled slightly forward, as if allowing for some measure of fleshy pleasure beyond all this grave drama, this saving of miserable mankind. He was twisted with love there on the cross. Had his hands and feet not been nailed securely, he would have writhed in pleasure. Only too well did I understand this dangerous place where I found myself—this temple to the joys of martyrdom. Especially did I understand it when sitting next to my mother. I sang to it, and then, at the mysterious transubstantiation, I ate and drank to it.

I am a baby, a child being dressed. It is morning, the early light comes clean and gray through the window. I like this light, and lying on my back as my mother struggles with my diaper, I can see it fall onto the yellow walls. Yellow, because in 1960 parents cannot know the sex of their child before it is born, and if they must be materially prepared for the arrival of their baby, the color of their preparation is yellow. The warm walls recede from my eyes. A mobile turns slowly over the crib to my left, and a lamb hanging on a silken cord floats into view.

It is too easy to do it to me. She cannot resist. I never cry or fuss, at least not while it's happening. A finger to start, or better: the handle of a toothbrush, a pencil (the eraser end). Nothing too big, nothing that won't go in easily, nothing that would break me, really. Whatever it is, it slips inside the pink folds of flesh easily: a little disappearing trick.

I am not a baby who cries much. A look of surprise, though, informs my features. The small dark secrets of my nostrils widen, and my gray eyes, which, when I am two, have a curious odd depthless quality, harden. They become like two marbles pressed into dough: my soul has fled. My small mouth opens as if I may cry, and Mother looks anxious, but I do not. My lips simply remain parted, as when I am expecting some solace in the form of a pacifier or a bottle's rubber teat.

Sometimes, as I lie with my mouth open in surprise, Mother reaches gently forward and, with her thumb on my chin, her fingers just under my nose, she presses my lips closed.

Is this the secret, then, to whom I become? to this terrible passivity which has so often allowed me to go silently into danger and evil? I never cry aloud. Still I feel the faint pressure of those cool fingers on my lips, the almost imperceptibly malign suffocation of that slender, perfumed hand.

For years, as a small child, I had a long red scar running down the length of the front of my right thigh. On occasion my mother might point at it, gesture in its direction and say, "I'm sorry, Isabel. It's just that you slipped, you were so slippery when you were wet."

Apparently, once when she had bathed me, I had squirmed out of her hands and fallen. She had tried to retrieve me, she said, but managed only to claw at me before I hit the floor, and her fingernail left a long scratch on my leg. The mark remained for years before fading away. And after that incident, it was my grandmother who bathed me.

"You were just too small to pick up. You frightened me," my mother said, excusing her negligence, her disinterest. My mother had what was politely referred to as a nervous collapse after she was delivered of her first and only child. She took to her bed weeping. Not the usual case of postpartum depression, this was a puzzling complex of ailments: refusal to leave her room, strange painful rashes, fevers, boils, hyperventilation, an afternoon of hysterical blindness—in all, a rather biblical-sounding scourge. Undoubtedly, she found herself unprepared for her responsibilities. She hadn't really wanted a child. She was young, too young. So, gradually and naturally, the burden of my care shifted to my grandmother, who had always loved babies, who had an almost unhealthy lust for them.

Most high school girls are warned about pregnancy: so was I. But the urgent message from my grandmother, delivered in the linen closet as we folded towels, was that I was never to consider an abortion if I was "in trouble"—Mom-mom would take the child. In this way, she ordained my making a mistake. Possibly, she had extended the same invitation to my mother sixteen years before. Only my mother had taken her at her word.

When my mother returned home from the maternity ward of Cedars of Lebanon Hospital, there was a nurse in her bedroom, waiting. She went to bed, as one did in 1960, and for several weeks she was cared for by Annie, who had nursed my grandmother during her confinement years before. My mother didn't want to have much to do with me, and she didn't have to, since she wasn't feeding me herself. The doctor gave her a pill to suppress lactation, and Annie used the Old World treatment of binding her breasts in yards of muslin. The milk dried up within a week, as it would were her child born dead.

Much later, when she was sick, dying of cancer, she would say that she should never have allowed anyone to convince her not to breast-feed. Obsessed with the idea that the binding had somehow planted the seed of the cancer that was destroying her, she would weep over that particular maternal failure, years past. But in 1960, America still believed that Science was the better parent, that laboratory formulas could outperform mother's milk. And besides, nursing could ruin the shape of one's breasts, and my mother was just eighteen.

Years later, as I administered morphine through the Hickman catheter—a device originally implanted in my mother's chest for the infusion of chemotherapy—I would stare at my mother's right breast, the one which remained intact, finding it beautiful. I couldn't prevent myself from crying sometimes at the sight of it, weeping selfishly for having never shared it with her. My attraction to it was curiously erotic. Even the insidious catheter, a technical advance meant to save what was left of her veins after chemotherapy had killed most of those in her arms and hands, ceased to be repugnant. The clear tube disappeared under her skin just inside her ruined cleavage and required an enormous and detailed regimen of disinfecting each day to prevent germs from entering the unnatural opening in the body. I sat beside the bed conscientiously swabbing ten times with rubbing alcohol, ten times with Betadine, ten times ten. First the pucker in the skin where the tube disappeared, secured with two thick black nylon sutures, then the polyurethane plug at the end of the catheter. Good for twenty-five punctures, the plug was a great convenience, and made giving shots easy. With the needle in place, and while depressing the plunger very slowly, I could watch my mother's eyes glaze, as do the eyes of infants as they nurse, their beings inward-focused, gratified. I was aware of returning to my mother's breast some comfort that I had never found there. Such a crazy process of reverse nursing—of the daughter infusing a chemical, synthetic sense of well-being and euphoria, the freedom from want and care, into the same breast whose natural solace had been forcefully suppressed years before.

Morphine, a magic bullet, and mine to bestow, gratifying in its power to comfort. I swallowed some once—some of the oral suspension, blue and minty and thick, like NyQuil. I took a generous amount for a novice, and retired to the bathroom where I dreamily manicured my nails, dumped a profligate half-bottle of bath salts under the tap, and bathed languorously, forgetting my dying mother downstairs. I ran my hands, gentle and slick with lather, over my own breasts, my ribs, my stomach. I closed my eyes and sank until only my nostrils were above the fragrant water. I wanted to know what it was and where she went when my mother's eyes twitched and rolled up into her head, away from us all. It wasn't long before she had learned to use morphine to avoid conflict, to quell pain that was not physical, to warm herself with its lovely, gentle fire against every cold fear, every bleak thought. And I encouraged her in this, I enjoyed giving her those shots, loved their cheap comfort. And I wanted the excuse to look at her naked chest, the necessity of touching it. This was the closest I ever remember being to my mother's breast, her body.

What strange alchemy is this, the radiation treatment? After the dreadful ride to the hospital—the medieval back brace laced on and the clumsy cane resting on the backseat; after the desperate serpentine course avoiding every pothole, the car as crippled in its movement as my mother in her tortured walk up the wheelchair ramp—it will not be much longer before we have that piece of equipment as well; after the ride and the slow creeping walk, we gain entrance to the big white building and make our way to the treatment wing. There, the waiting room is curiously always empty and we are immediately shown to the dressing rooms.

Behind the translucent curtain, I unzip her sacklike dress, a garment free of any constricting dart or seam, and go to work unhooking the brace which compensates for vertebrae as fragile as eggshells. By now the cancer has spread into her liver, her

27

lungs, everywhere. Bone scans reveal a series of tiny skeletons, printed in two rows of five on one large sheet of film. They look like some Halloween greeting card, each image only three inches high, delicate and elegant, the body seen from ten different angles. The bones are drawn in black with isolated, shining white spots. "So these are the malignancies," I say, pointing to the decorative, silvery-white lesions. "No," answers the radiologist, and he looks at me carefully and gently. "Malignancies show up in black."

Under the ugly brace is a cotton shirt to protect her skin. I pull it up over her head, and on her thin back is revealed a hieroglyph of black lines which resembles, absurdly, the sketch of a complex football play. It is inscribed with indelible ink that wears away only as fast as her skin itself and tells the technician just where to aim the saving rays.

In her white robe, lying flat, with the comfort of just one thin white pillow on the white draped table, Mother looks like some poor sacrifice offered up during a famine season to demonstrate to the gods just how miserably we fare. I am not allowed to accompany her, but can watch the silent magic on a video monitor in the adjoining room.

The polite young acolyte follows all instructions read from her back and her chart. When her spine is finished, irradiated for today, he turns her, gently and reverently, and pulls the gown up over what's left of her chest. The remaining breast has what looks like a bull's-eye drawn on it, a target toward which he aims the barrel of his complicated gun. Below her frumpy new underwear—somehow silk tap pants don't complement her scars or the black ink—her thighs are very thin and white. She had been too proud of her long, pretty legs when I was a little girl. Many times she had pushed me off her lap complaining that my sitting there would cause varicose veins.

The video monitor renders each step of the silent, grainy black and white ritual so apparently distant that it is like a telecast of

28

a NASA experiment, a probe into a distant galaxy. Only the very occasional cry of pain—the contact between her poor bony joints and the cold metal table—would indicate the immediateness of the event.

This is not the regular waiting room for family and friends, but I am here so often that the staff no longer sees me. I am allowed to sit here in this barren antechamber, a room empty but for two hard-backed chairs and a black wrought-iron rack of old issues of the Journal of the American Medical Association. *An article on last year's new treatment for nephritis lies open and unread in my lap, my eyes on the monitor.*

While the treatment takes a half hour, in total, it is a time removed from time. The months of regular twice-weekly, sometimes daily visits all run together, and when we are there, intervening life drops away, and we have been there forever and will remain forever, Mother on her altar cloth, the godlike eye of the machine regarding her from its ceiling mount. And I watching from my safe distance as the angelic rays, the cold invisible fire, penetrate to her heart, her soul. Matter can neither be created nor destroyed, and so I am witness to the transubstantiation of the flesh that bore me.

She pulls a linen dress, white, crisp and fresh, out from under the film of the dry-cleaning bag which, deflated and empty, she crams into the trash can under the vanity table. My mother is dressing to go out. Her youthful arms emerge gracefully from the sleeveless sheath and struggle with the zipper—that one irksome spot just above the clasp of the bra. Her arms are long and not tanned because she always stays under her umbrella, but they smell of the beach, of Coppertone, of Ivory soap and, finally, of perfume, Chanel. Her hair, freshly shampooed and set, dark brown, catches a ray of light from my grandfather's reading lamp in the living room; it is inviting hair, but brushed just so, in place. Talc is spilled on the floor before the dresser; its floury dust records ghostly bare footprints stepping away from the deep drawer that holds the lingerie. A cast-off slip, creamy white, slips from the old chenille spread pulled tight over the bed and crumples on the floor at its foot. I hear the cool click of a discarded ring placed on the glass top of the vanity table, the sibilant whisper of pedicured, powdered feet slipping into high-heeled sandals.

If I could stay out from underfoot, if I could resist the seduction of lipsticks in their smooth shining cases, perfumes in coy winking bottles, hose in tight bright packages, styling gel, Dippity-Do, cool and blue and like Jell-O wobbling in its jar. If I could only not touch all these things, if I could only not touch her at the magic center of all these sweet-smelling ablutions—then I could watch my mother dress.

That summer I was four, and she was twenty-two. For a few days in the bright month of August when the afternoons were still impossibly long, the evenings starting late and maddeningly near to my bedtime, my mother was joined by her best friend, her childhood friend, Amanda, who stayed with us—my mother, my grandparents and me—in our summer cottage on the coast. Amanda came with Thomas, her fat, pale and, to me, repugnant toddler. He was a terrible two, he was unhappy with everything.

When we went to the beach—my mother, Amanda and I—Thomas came as well. He hated it: the sun, the wind, the sand. If even one fragrant white shining grain touched his foot, he screamed, it was terrifying, as if he were being burned. All the other babies who accompanied the other families played contentedly in the sand. They drooled, and sand encrusted the saliva on their chins and necks and chests; sand was in their mouths, along with shells and cast-off candy wrappers: they were self-respecting beach babies and embraced it all; philosophically, they took the good with the bad. When they tried to stand and stray, the weight of sand in their diapers secured them in their places.

Comparing our fretful charge with these reasonable infants,

I found Thomas's presence excruciating. Worse, I was too young to go off and play out of earshot of his piercing, piteous howls.

Amanda seemed utterly immune to her child; she slept in the sun, her limbs leaden with its heavy solace. Her very posture said she could not lift herself, let alone bear the melancholy weight of her little boy. Thomas was left alone under his own umbrella in the dead center of his own blanket. Even there he wasn't safe from irritation. The wind picked up the sand and threw it at his wet cheeks, riffled through his fine dark hair.

For the first hour or so my mother took pity on Thomas; he was, after all, not her baby; she wasn't bored with his despair. But she, too, was finally beaten by his persistent crying—no amount of dandling, not even one of her repertoire of silly faces, had any effect, and so she left him to himself. Exhausted, he fell asleep by mid-afternoon, just as the sun crept under his umbrella and stole his shade. That night, his white cheeks were crimson with sunburn and stinging from the salt of his tears, and he cried himself quite literally sick. But in the heavy, sunny afternoon, we were all happy to be spared his grief, to have the quiet luxury of ignoring him; and, as I built castles which, too dry, crumbled before they were finished, my mother and Amanda lay next to one another, the transistor murmuring between their dark heads, and whispered like girls.

Probably, they had much to talk about. Each had married young and disastrously; each had been left with a child she didn't know how to care for, much less love; each had returned to her parents—to live, to think, to save money, to plot another escape. I wasn't listening then, but I imagine they were comparing notes.

We came back from the beach in time for dinner, my dinner, that is. Amanda and my mother were going out; they had dates. And, as was usual and expected, my grandparents were there to take care of the children. I, of course, was a given—

they had cared, and would continue to care, for me for years. But Thomas was not so graciously accepted; after all, he wasn't family and he certainly wasn't easy. *Easiness* was an important concept in my grandmother's scheme of things. I had been easy: I ate well, slept a lot, cried infrequently; my disposition was good. Thomas cried incessantly, slept sporadically, and spat up nearly everything he ate. When I considered his habits, it amazed me that he was so fat.

Mom-mom did not look forward to an evening with Thomas and his screams, but she accepted her lot; that is, she agreed ungraciously to care for the baby. Her lips stretched into an insincere smile as Amanda hugged her in thanks. But after the girls had left, she complained bitterly to my grandfather. I remember the two of them looking into the crib with distaste, and with sadness; for you cannot hate a baby, and this one was so stridently unhappy, so red-faced with crying, so enraged and despairing, that he did summon up grudging sympathy.

As for myself, I was also displeased with the evening's plans. Watching my mother dress, sitting sandy and sticky in the broken-down cane rocker, I wanted to enter that bright circle that held her and Amanda, their high girlish laughter, eager and expectant. It strained the limits of my self-discipline to remain in that chair, rocking creakily in vicarious excitement, to keep from tumbling forward onto the sandy carpet and into her smooth legs. I knew what a heaven it was to hug those legs like columns and press my face into the dark sweet trough between her thighs, the place where I was magically for one moment in a tight, impenetrable blind, where no one could separate me from the very smell of my mother. She didn't like me to hug her legs. I only had a chance to be there in that dark safety for a moment before she pried me off impatiently. If I gave in and ran to do it, collided with her knees and interrupted the choreography of her preparations, I would be thrust out of the bedroom, I would have to hear her scolding me, I would be humiliated, forced to take refuge with my grandfather, my head in his less glamorous lap.

When they were ready, at last—my mother in her starched, sleeveless linen dress, and Amanda wearing a tight-bodiced print in which her high breasts seemed squeezed to the point of bruising—they stood by the door, for a moment reticent like teenagers. They bid my grandparents good-night, they asked that no one wait up. They were, after all, grown up now.

Spoon in hand, I came around from behind the old table in the breakfast nook. The oilcloth caught against my shoulder and my grandmother reached for my plate before it fell. I looked at my mother, and at Amanda, at the warm light on their faces glowing from the sun, at their height there by the door in their heels. From the table I could smell them, and I rehearsed, to myself, each spot where my mother touched the stopper of the perfume bottle to her flesh: wrists, throat, behind each knee and, finally, one shy, hesitant brush, like an afterthought, between her breasts. I knew I could not touch her: my hair was damp, there was applesauce on my arm. And, in that moment when they stood, asking, almost, for our leave, I couldn't even speak—my throat swelled and ached with my mother's loveliness, and distance.

I was too young, that summer, to be consciously jealous; I didn't imagine that soon some man would put his head just where I wished mine could rest. I knew only that once again she was leaving, escaping, fleeing from us all, and that she looked happy to be doing so; whereas I felt leaden.

They were through the door in an instant; the screen slapped shut, there was the sound of high heels on the path, and then the quick percussive jolt of the car door, once, twice. Laughter, muffled behind glass, then ringing clear as the car windows were rolled down. The gasp and cough of the engine, tires on gravel; they were gone. I would be asleep, nonexistent it seemed to me, when they returned. I put my spoon down on the table.

Mom-mom was leaning into the crib, Opa standing at its head. She was shaking her head. "It isn't right," she said, "leaving a baby when he's sick."

"She's just a girl, Regina, twenty-one."

I pressed my face between the slats of the crib and looked at the sour sheets where Thomas lay, inert, for a moment, in his despair. He had thrown up cottage cheese and it was puddled, clotted, by his angry little red face. I hated him, despised him simply because I was being relegated to his cranky, sodden company when I belonged with my mother, buoyant and fragrant and gliding out into the cool night. His prickling hot cheeks burned with what I imagined must be embarrassment at being such a beastly, bothersome child, and I turned away angrily, butting my damp head into Mom-mom's hip as she reached to lift him.

My fingernails are blue, all of them. Seven I've colored in with a magic marker, but the middle, ring and smallest fingers of my left hand I purposefully smashed with a paperweight, bruising the flesh under each nail.

I split my lip the same way: one carefully aimed blow, and the soft flesh yields. Caught between my teeth and the heavy glass weight, my bottom lip bleeds and puffs up. I cannot resist checking it throughout the day, running my tongue over the swelling. If it goes down, I hit it again. Anything hard and heavy will do the job, but I prefer my mother's paperweight. The Italian glass sphere weighs awkwardly in my small hands, a field of tiny flowers magically caught inside. Mother says it is called "Mille Fiori," and that it came from the island of Murano, a place that sounds enchanted.

At night, under the covers, I pick at the rough, scabbed skin on my knees and elbows; it bleeds. A painless mutilation: darkness and solitude provide the anesthesia.

"What happened, child?" Opa says. Sitting in his armchair, he draws me between his knees and takes my chin in his freckled hand, turning my face into the light cast by his reading lamp. I shrug.

He touches my fat lip with his finger, gently, tracing the swelling, and the pain comes alive with his attention. I hide my face, my shameful purple lip, in his vest.

All the "accidents" are like that. They never hurt. Even the fingers don't throb until they are noticed, until the inked ones come clean in the bath and leave the bruised ones undisguised.

I am very young when I discover that sympathy is a catalyst for pain. The hurt floods in, sublime; each numb lip, finger, toe aches blessedly at the expression of compassion.

"Did you fall?" Mom-mom asks. I am covered in scabs and bumps and bruises, small punishments.

I say nothing, shake my head no, overcome by the relief of tears.

We were not a family who took many photographs. In fact, it was only my grandfather who took any at all, and as he was inclined to compose poor shots, decapitating his subjects or placing them in a corner of the frame while something curiously insignificant filled the rest of the picture, he was never encouraged to catalog the family's birthdays or holiday celebrations. I've looked again and again through the old albums, the consistent displacement of the subject almost leading one to conclude that the photographer flinched from what he saw. There are a number of pictures of me from infancy to the age of twelve or so, and then almost none.

As a child I was cooperative, pleased for the attention; as a teenager I learned, like my mother and grandmother, to protest so vehemently at the sight of a camera that Opa gave up in disgust and put his old Leica away for good. Mom-mom, in particular, set a terrible example. She reacted to the mere sight of the camera like an aborigine, screaming as if Opa meant to steal her soul away. Later she butchered the photographs, chopping herself out of group portraits, so that anyone sifting through the collection might chance upon successive images of family gatherings all with the same curious hole cut out, as if one member had been long ago disinherited, all evidence of his or her presence expunged.

We did have a rather disappointing drawer full of old prints, disappointing because they contained no picture of me or even of people I knew. They were all pictures of my grandmother's family: her parents, her exquisite sister, their cousins and suitors and chaperones, black and white pictures taken in Japan and hand-tinted to a fairy-tale delicacy of pigment, pictures of tobogganing in the Swiss Alps, bathing at Lake Como, picnicking on the French Riviera. Pictures of a tall dark man in a suit and vest and homburg: my grandmother's father, the only person in my entire family capable of making sensible and profitable investments and the man whose wealth I later discovered still supported our family. Now most of these pictures are gone. I have some; others are packed among my grandmother's effects; a great number must have perished. When we sold the old armoire that had housed them for so many years, they were deprived of a resting place, scattered among other, less significant papers, and lost.

Although our home was the kind in which a seemingly endless supply of papers and photographs were casually and forgetfully stuffed in this drawer or that box, there were some documents that were hidden carefully. My grandfather had his safe, a small one made of cast iron with whimsical, decorative clawed feet and a combination lock so old and noisy that it announced with a click which digit was the correct stop on the dial. I learned to pick it on the first try, and inside found a dusty sheaf of investment records. Not a man of my great-grandfather's intuition, Opa lost money on stocks, bought bad bonds and, most notably, passed up an opportunity to buy property on the Las Vegas strip, thinking it too vulgar a place ever to become popular. Buried underneath the yellowed securities were those few bureaucratic issuances that attended the passages of his mother's life: her birth, marriage and death certificates; and a bill, paid, for the services of a musician at his parents' wedding—nineteen shillings paid to a cellist, Egbert Cruikshank. There was an envelope with his parents' two rings inside, his father's plain, his mother's with an oval pigeon-blood ruby set into the band.

Whatever papers were important to Mom-mom were either hidden so well that I never found them, or so poorly that they circulated with all the other detritus and in that way escaped my notice. My mother, however, had her own private niches which I routinely plundered. After she moved out of her parents' house, her bedroom was left intact, the deceptively virginal bed with its dust ruffles and canopy, the dresser, the ballet barre bolted to the wall opposite the bed, the school desk: together all these furnishings made up a shrine, as if she had died rather than left. Lacking storage space in her successive small apartments, my mother filed all her business papers in her girlhood desk and would come home to pay her bills and balance her checkbook, a process that often required the ballast of a few hundred dollars from Mom-mom. More personal records, letters from admirers, tiny leather-bound diaries, she kept in her car. Currently interesting documents were secured in the glove compartment; more historical artifacts she saved in the trunk in a locked metal file box. As my mother lived her life poised for flight and escape, it made sense that all she valued remained locked in her car. Not only did the old blue Pontiac represent her freedom but it was the only place that was completely hers. It wasn't the cramped, chaste apartment she shared with another young woman, and it wasn't the captivity of her parents' home. Tearing along the Southern California freeways at eighty-five miles an hour, a dozen or more dry-cleaned dresses flapping under their plastic bags in the windy backseat, five changes of shoes on the floor, the perennial case of makeup and undergarments and the old bonnet-style hair dryer stored behind the driver's seat, a new life was always a possibility for my mother; and as a child I girded myself for what seemed the eventuality that she would one day simply sail down the long private drive onto Stone Canyon, slip into the heavy traffic on Sunset Boulevard, enter the interstate highway just a few miles from our house, and disappear forever.

For as long as she was around, however, I intended to pursue the evasive details of my mother's private life and was always alert to any chance of breaking into her car or her purse or her glossy, cordovan briefcase, not to steal, but to discover. I searched out all that I could, usually waiting for Mother to get thoroughly embroiled in a fight with Mom-mom, which would guarantee me anywhere up to an hour, sometimes much longer. Examining the papers in the car required time-consuming work. An impossible lock on the trunk that could be opened only with its key demanded the further criminal activity of going through my mother's handbag and borrowing the key ring; then there was the additional lock on the file box. But if the car itself was left open, I could pick the latch on the glove compartment within five minutes. Stacked inside were my mother's most carefully guarded papers: her collection of manila envelopes stuffed with newspaper clippings. These weren't front-page news but the smaller items buried in the middle of the paper—freak accidents, murders noteworthy for their inventiveness rather than for the identity of the victims, crippling and incurable diseases and, of course, kidnappings.

For years, someone sent these packets to our family. They came addressed to all of us: my grandparents, my mother and myself. He sent sometimes one or two clippings, sometimes as many as a dozen, and I refer to the sender as "he" because, although it was never proven, and certainly never even reported to any authority, we always knew that the mysterious person was my father. Or perhaps it was my mother who *knew* it, and the rest of us believed so absolutely. The envelopes didn't bear an Arizona or California postmark, were in fact mailed from Chicago, but it would have been easy enough for him to forward them to an accomplice in that city. After returning to his hometown, my father eventually moved to Needles, California, just on the border of that state and Arizona. He settled in California, but barely—like an uninvited guest lurking on the periphery of a party—and in one of its least attractive towns. A hot, graceless way station along the highway, Needles was trapped between ranges of the sharp Sacramento Mountains, a typically no-place place with only a K mart, a Greyhound bus station and a few other ubiquitous American institutions to distinguish it.

The clippings, selected from various and obscure small-town papers, were intended for me as much as for my mother, according to the address on the envelope, but as I was never allowed to read them when they arrived, I had to wait for the opportunity to slip into her car and work on the lock to the glove box. More challenging than Opa's safe, it required the sensitive manipulation of a small tool I had fashioned from a hairpin and wire. The compartment was deep and contained no maps or flashlights or greasy lint-flocked nickels, like the glove box in Mom-mom's car. Everything had been cleared away to afford more room for the clippings.

After the first few of these peculiar communications, Opa threw the envelopes away unopened, but my mother would dig them out of the trash and read them with the rapt attention usually reserved for love letters, sometimes returning to one passage over and over again. I picked the lock and read each story, too, stumbling over the sentences in my haste, reading quickly so as not to be discovered, not understanding strange words like "coprophiliac," and not finding them later in my children's illustrated dictionary.

It is clear now that these summaries of human disaster and loss were love letters of a sort. They were, anyway, a record of passion, and if the sender did not reveal his identity, he could at least express the intensity of his feelings. The content of the articles was distasteful, but more disturbing to me was the compulsive neatness with which they had been cut from the various papers. The edges of the clippings bore evidence that the sender had gone so far as to draw a line around each piece with a ruler and pencil and then had used a careful hand with a scissor or razor blade to cut them out. The text itself was underscored in places with a ruler and red ink lest the reader miss some detail—"and was discovered with the combine machinery *still running*"—and the cited phrase or sometimes even just one word never made sense to me. They referred not to some essential aspect of the crime or accident, but to something seemingly insignificant, like the color of the victim's shirt—although they might have made sense to my mother: they might have been clues, they might have represented fragments of one long, endless letter which she put together week by week from the unceasing flow of clippings.

Perhaps th' ⁓ns why she lay in wait beside the garage—making sure my ⸗ ɪndparents' bedroom light was finally turned out, and too agitated to ever catch me hiding behind the kitchen door in my pajamas—and then meticulously went through the garbage. I would watch her as she laid newspapers neatly on the cement floor of the carport and turned the dented metal trash can over. Dressed in a narrow skirt and heels, she would kneel down uncomfortably and gingerly pick through the grapefruit rinds, the soiled paper towels, eggshells and other muck until she found what she wanted. If the envelope had gotten dirty, she carefully wiped it off, but never threw it away. She'd smooth out the creases, make sure the mailing label, typed neatly and centered absolutely, remained firmly affixed. Then she'd take a nail file from her purse and slit open the envelope and peruse the contents quickly before righting the garbage can and clearing away all evidence of her trespass. The slower, careful reading she did by the overhead light in her car, sometimes making notes in a little book in her lap before locking the envelope away.

Perhaps they were not love letters, but just some petty reprisal—and not an unusual one, prosaic even, but effectively nerve-racking in that it implied that it was only a matter of time before our own family perished like all the unfortunate victims in the newspapers. Later, after I met my father, it was easy to imagine his indulgence in such fanatical behavior, his long, gloved fingers slicing out the articles, underlining the words. His message was that somehow we would come to no good end. Fair warning, perhaps, as we ultimately were undone as a family, not by some freak event, however, but by the usual means of ruination, the pedestrian agents of lust and revenge that destroy so many.

During the summers in La Jolla we didn't receive mail; Opa paid the household bills in advance and didn't have any letters forwarded from Los Angeles. So, in La Jolla, where we lived each July and August in a rundown cottage on the coast, we were, at least for a while, immune to my father's terrorism. The cottage had no telephone—Mom-mom brought an empty whisky bottle filled with carefully misered dimes and we used the pay phone at the lifeguard station—so no one could bother us. And even our tense family succumbed to that relaxed consciousness peculiar to beach towns, a sense of limitless time and daylight, of health and youth and easy contentment. At the beach we composed pictures that lied about the family, saying we were happy and even-tempered, if a little eccentric: shots of my grandparents in resort wear and panama hats, of me with a stripe of zinc oxide across my face, of the little table and chairs and umbrella, the picnic hamper with real china and silverware. My grandparents didn't believe in going to the shore without dragging half the cottage with them, and they replicated the living room on the sand, complete with magazines, radios, sometimes even the music stand and Opa's accordion. The instrument had belonged to his father and he was slowly teaching himself to play it. For one hour each afternoon he stood before the metal stand stacked with songbooks, pulling and squeezing and producing very idiosyncratic versions of popular songs. On the worst days, he accompanied himself with the lyrics. Like no other beachgoers, my grandparents afforded me a full measure of youthful embarrassment, and I spread my towel as far from their clutter as possible.

It was during the sixties that I spent these early childhood summers in La Jolla, and hippies were everywhere I looked, people who were young and dressed in dashikis from Africa, sarongs from Asia, serapes from Mexico: clothes of all colors. The tiny loincloths on the men were like a sudden angry burn of color against their tanned skin; the women wore even smaller bikinis.

The hippies seemed not to be organized into any expected family groups—a fact which pleased me greatly. Here were people who did not question my not belonging to a mother-father-child set, but traveled together in packs in faded Volkswagen buses, spending the night in places like "The Red Roost," a rundown old boardinghouse on whose peeling, weathered porch were three or four old sofas where people slept at all hours of the day. I couldn't stay away from these people, especially their uncombed children who didn't have to bathe each evening and who accepted me as a friend immediately and without introduction. At the time, I was seven and attended a progressive school for "exceptional" children, whose extended calendar left only six weeks of relative freedom. During the school year my every waking hour was filled with some kind of instruction. If I wasn't doing baby algebra, my grandmother was drilling me on where to put the salad fork and soup spoon when I set the table. Everything about the hippie children's lives seemed preferable to mine, especially after I learned that they spent the whole year in this state of relative undress, not, like me, released for only a short while from the constraints of a school uniform and ballet lessons, monitored homework hours, the regimented clockwork of the school year.

Seduced and unable to understand my grandparents' horror of these people who must have seemed to them to be dangerous American Gypsies, drugged and dirty, I would disappear for hours, ignoring my grandfather's hoarse calls from the street outside our cottage. I would follow these children, whose names I often did not know, into their sandy homes or vans, into their parents' bedrooms and bathrooms, witnessing strangers in all manner of undress. Their homes, like their bodies, were dusty and fragrant. With my cheek to the carpet, I could see the manic fleas jumping from dog to cat to human, and because I didn't wear the plastic collars that all the hippies wore, around wrists or ankles, by the time I came home, late and disheveled, welts would have bloomed on my legs. I was scolded each time by both my grandparents, but as the summer wore on and I continued to disobey, they gradually became less anxious, and their lectures became perfunctory, bored and boring.

Allison was the only child I saw for consecutive summers. She lived with her mother and brother and little sister in an apartment, the whole of which was smaller than my bedroom in Los Angeles. They were amazingly intimate with each other, and with me, and I grew used to the sight of them all walking around nude in their curtainless room, almost feeling that I should strip off my swimsuit when I entered their home. Allison's mother, Jeanette, didn't use a razor and was covered with a fascinating growth of blond body hair, her legs almost furry and her pubic triangle blurring up onto her flat wrinkled belly, the hair reaching up and embracing her navel. She was very tanned and didn't seem to own any clothes beyond her bikini. She walked with her children to the beach, carrying all that they owned of any value in an enormous string bag that hung from her thin shoulders. Their apartment door had no lock.

When my mother came down from Los Angeles, she scoffed at her parents' disgust, saying only, "Oh, Daddy, honestly!" to my grandfather's protests about how La Jolla was overrun with riffraff; at the beach she made friends with the hippies' children. They must have found her fascinating, with her picture hats, her white skin and her beach wraps that coordinated with her modest, flowered swimsuits. She handed out cookies and smoothed Coppertone on burned cheeks, and the little boys especially came and sat under her umbrella.

It was foggy in the mornings in La Jolla, so foggy that it often threatened to be what my grandmother called a "dull" day, referring to the flat, gray sky rather than to my boredom at losing a few sunny hours at the beach. But whether it would be cloudy or fair, the mornings were always overcast, the edges of buildings melting back into the soft mist, the plants dripping with moisture, the green of their leaves bright and intense. On these mornings my grandfather and I would climb the flight of ninety-four stairs to the town, my short legs moving double time to his spry limbs, and walk farther on up Girard, the main street, to the bakery. Opa liked a particular pastry, round and flat and crumbling with sugar and cinnamon, and he liked the walk required to obtain it.

The bakery, past John's Waffle Shop, past the newsstand, past the Rexall and the market and the hardware store, was always hot when we entered, hot like an oven almost and smelling like one, thick with sugar and butter. It was early enough, before seven, that we were always the only customers and were ushered straight into the back, where an enormous man swathed in white with grease and flour up past his elbows was twisting up fat slugs of white dough into croissants and laying them on a great flat metal sheet very quickly—the tray was filled in a minute and he would begin on another. It was all I could do to keep my fingers out of the dough, and I would stand eye level with the great wooden table where the baker worked, watching with my hands in my pockets. I was always rewarded: the girl who worked behind the counter would produce something for me as she added up our purchases—a doughnut, a day-old cookie, a little roll, round and peppered with poppy seeds.

Opa and I would leave the bakery laden with unwise purchases: a coffee cake big enough for a family twice the size of ours, a bag of Danishes sodden with red filling, cookies glazed with unappetizing colors of sugar, green and orange, even blue—those were my choice. On the way back to the cottage, we stopped for a copy of the *Los Angeles Times,* and at the newsstand I would try to wheedle some further indulgence out of my grandfather: a pack of gum, a piece of candy, a comic book. But, already regretting his extravagance in the bakery, and anticipating the protests of my mother who firmly rejected breakfast at the hour of eight or nine but finally ended in succumbing to a pastry by eleven, he would never part with that extra quarter that I begged, and, satisfied with my triumph in the bakery, I never pressed beyond an unconvincing whine or two at the newsstand.

Later, when I was ten and my interests had shifted from sweets to entertainment, or from a more clearly oral gratification to a more subtle one, I would always get that quarter, and more besides. After Opa was eighty, he stopped climbing the long stairs every morning and sent me up to town alone to get the paper. His blood sugar had grown unstable, so he had given up the pastries, and without his company, I had lost heart for the bakery. If I had to go alone, I didn't want a pastry, and my grandmother now bought a frozen coffee cake along with all the other groceries.

Smelling of shaving cream—I remember the exact fragrance of his particular brand, and the striped can, Barbasol—he would sit at the breakfast table stirring his coffee and call me away from my books in the living room. Reading at the table was not allowed, but he wanted to have the newspaper waiting by his chair as soon as the meal was over. He would hand me one quarter and then look away, teasing me and ignoring the hand that was still outstretched, soliciting more change. "For what?" he would ask, and I would answer quickly, making something up, because the fun was in getting as much money as possible and then seeing what it would buy. I never made it out the door with more than a dollar, but it was enough for a Super Ball, or jacks, or an *Archie* comic. With the change in my hand I would run down the cracked sidewalk, my feet drumming past the designs we drew on the cement with juice from the jade plant's fat leaves held tight in our hands like clumsy crayons. Dried, they left tobacco-brown patterns of swirls and lines and pictographs and the occasional silly word or phrase: Scott and Carey up in a tree, K-I-S-S-I-N-G. Up the ninety-four steps at a run, skipping those I could, and around the corner, panting, to the newsstand, already counting the leftover change for the drugstore's toy shelf.

As the month progressed, my room filled with trashy little toys. My favorites were tiny plastic men who came trussed up in threads attached to a little parachute. The summer children congregated on the roof of a neighboring hotel, an old, graceful Spanish building with pink stuccoed walls. The south side of the roof's cracked red tiles gave over to a small sun deck, crowded with broken Adirondack chairs and a snarl of laundry lines upon which the colorful flags of the guests' bathing suits flapped. Around the perimeter of the splintered wooden deck was a fence to which we clung as we hurled the minute figures from the side and which prevented us from falling to the street in our enthusiastic sport. As soon as the tiny plastic men had floated down and their whereabouts were marked, we tore down the stairs, past the hotel laundry, past the kitchen and into the street where we would collect our toys and then climb breathlessly back up the sandy beach-worn stairs to the roof to begin the game again.

Sadly, these little men who cost a dime each were not sturdy. Their parachutes came off within a few flights, and sometimes they never made it to the ground, blown off course into a tree or under the wheels of a car. A morning's entertainment depended upon at least fifty cents' worth of forces, stored in my pockets until each soldier was launched and lost. By the end of the month, with the loyal fascination of four or five children playing at this game each morning, the street and the neglected hotel lawn were littered with tiny men of all colors, trailing ragged parachutes, as if a Lilliputian army had invaded this alien land and perished in the hostile climate. We walked back to our cottages kicking their gaily-colored plastic bodies.

*One summer, Mother doesn't accompany us to La Jolla. In-
stead she goes to Jamaica with a man named Rubin. She is gone
for two months, nearly, and when she comes home, I no longer
recognize her. She arrives in a taxi, and when she steps out, I
hide behind Mom-mom. No longer white-skinned and a bru-
nette, now she is brown and her hair has bleached to a streaky
red. She brings me a hat with a fringe of long palm fronds that
stick straight up from the brim. And a claw from one of the big
white land crabs. She says that every day, when it rains at noon,
the crabs come out of their holes and pinch whomever is in their
path. Once they pinch you, the claw never lets go and you have
to break the crab off and go to a doctor to have the claw removed.*

*There are a lot of little donkeys on the island, she tells me,
all wearing little crosses on their backs. They are marked that
way in memory of Mary sitting on a donkey just before she lay*

down in a manger and had Jesus. I would have liked them, she says.

I give her the sewing case I made for her in art class. The stitches are uneven, in yellow thread on blue felt, and I can see she notices. Her teeth look very white, like a dog's.

Later that night, before she dresses for a date, she lies on the bed in her underwear, facedown. I sit on the firm cushion of her bottom, knees straddling her hips, and carefully, carefully, I pull the dead tan skin off in big strips. Where it has started to bubble between her shoulder blades, I pull gently, my fingers trying not to tear. It's very hot this evening, and her sweat gathers in tiny blisters that lift the dead skin away from the fresh layers underneath.

When I'm finished peeling, her back is all smooth and coppery and I save the one biggest piece in my sock drawer. I hide it because I know she wouldn't want me to have it. The skin dries flat, and when I hold it up to the light, I can see a pattern of tiny holes where little hairs were growing.

A couple of months later, after she moves out, I go to retrieve the piece of skin and admire it, but it has fallen to pieces, leaving only dust under the socks.

It was the first time I had ever been aware that my grandfather could cry. Tears were squandered by the women in my family, myself included, but Opa never wept. However, when the figure of a man, bundled in his space suit to the point of shapelessness, as if battling some terrible cold, stepped onto the screen, through a blur of snow and static, each of his footsteps deliberate and chilling in its slowness; when this fragile soul, his head obscured by the white halo of his helmet, looked briefly, blankly toward us, seemingly blind as well as speechless, my grandfather cried.

For days we had followed the progress of the rocket as it moved through space, through nothing, bound for that orb that existed for me in whimsical rhyme: the moon was a disk for the cow to jump over. The moon was a picture of Jack and Jill. The moon was a silver bowl whose contents spilled away each month and then were magically replenished. The moon was the Earth's cold suitor who forever circled her, caught by her magnetic charm.

I was nine, and Apollo XI was only another fact among the many that I learned each day. At nine you are not much surprised to find that two men travel to the moon; it is no more peculiar than many other events.

But for my grandfather, born in 1890, who as a child in London watched the gas man go by each night to light the streetlamps, who never rode in a car until the year he owned one in 1925, an automobile that reached the dangerous speed of thirty miles per hour; for my grandfather, the moon landing was a miracle.

In his excitement, he pulled me toward him roughly. We were the only ones in front of the television, my mother and grandmother involved in some desperate flight and emotional landing of their own—I could hear their voices, angry but muffled behind the kitchen door. I squirmed, fighting against Opa's hand on my arm, hurting me. His voice quavered with emotion over the static.

"I would have said they were mad. *Mad.* If anyone had told me such a thing." He shook me a little and I was frightened by his vehemence, the tears on his cheeks shining in the light from the television.

A voice distant, so very distant, and crackling with static came over the air. My grandfather dropped my arm and then took it up again. He turned my face away from his and directed my gaze to the screen before us: and we watched, his one hand clamped on my arm, the other a terrible weight on my head, as Neil Armstrong slowly and deliberately placed our nation's bright flag on the dead blue surface of the moon.

I didn't watch much television as a child, not by choice but because too often I was grounded and the groundings extended far into the future, weeks, sometimes months ahead of my memory of whatever misdeeds had inspired them. Even during the brief interludes when I was not grounded, I saw only snatches of programs. The school that I attended embraced a philosophy that spared no room for television, and parents were admonished to limit its entertainment to one hour per week. Mom-mom and I quarreled tirelessly over this issue. I wanted to be like other children, like the boys next door: to get up early on Saturday morning, take my box of Froot Loops into the living room and watch endless rounds of cartoons while spooning up the sweet, pink milk and lying on the rug in my pajamas, to stare at the set, inert and sated, until noon. That was impossible, and the compromise that we came to, the decision made by Opa who was sick of the argument, was that I would be restricted from television programs I might choose to watch, but allowed to remain in the living room if the set had been turned on by someone else.

There was an expansive, shabby Oriental rug in our living room, a carpet that had traveled originally from Baghdad with my grandmother's father to Shanghai, and on finally to the United States via London and the south of France. Thus, it had been underfoot for much of the drama of my grandmother's life, and while I knew little about her rich and complicated past then, I was intimately aware of the rug, its pattern, and in which spots time and human action—the pacing of anxious feet? the passion of lovers sunk to their knees?—had worn it thin.

The living room was large and inadequately furnished, not tastefully spare, but verging on empty, and lacking a comfortable seat. The couch was huge and understuffed with feathers. Guests sat down and despaired of ever rising. Of course, my grandfather did have the armchair; complete with ottoman, it was pleasant to sit in, and, like the carpet, had belonged to my grandmother's father and had come to this country from the

Orient; but it was not a seat for company. As a small child, I swam in the capacity of its generous cracked leather seat; and when my grandfather died, I lay in that chair, my face pressed down into its weary cushion, and breathed in the smell of the first man I had ever loved. But when Opa was alive and well, that chair was his and his alone. Up until I was a sulky thirteen or so, I sprang out of it at the sound of his footfall. Later, in the throes of adolescent moodiness, I would wait until he stood patiently by its arm, and then would slink resentfully out of its warm depths where I had been painting my toenails or reading some complex, tragic romance. It was the only seat worth occupying and was placed comfortably close to the fireplace which usually had a generous heap of ashes spilling forth onto the slate hearth. Long before I was a teenager, at night, while I slept, Opa sometimes borrowed a pair of my own small shoes and dipped them in the ashes. With them he would make little footprints leading out from the fireplace onto the carpet in a crazy pattern of steps. From the living room, they would continue down the hall to my bedroom door where they would vanish. The next day, Opa would tell me that goblins had slipped down the chimney, had cast spells and danced a farandole in the living room—he hopped and spun to demonstrate the steps, and it looked very similar to the pot-and-pan jig he sometimes did in the kitchen—and then had come to my room to take me away. But he had stopped them, had chased them off. "They were just about your size," he'd say, and as I measured my foot against the sooty marks, I could see he was right, for my foot fit the prints exactly, and gooseflesh came up on my arms. Each time I believed him, even when I had outgrown such inventions as the tooth fairy. I wanted to believe, and, always an accomplice to my feverish imagination, my grandfather cleaned the ashes from my shoes very carefully.

Far from the heat of the fireplace, which we used on all but truly warm evenings, were a cluster of crotchety old mahogany straight-backed chairs with scratchy brocade seats. These gathered uneasily around a nest of unsturdy little tables which were wrested from their communal embrace when company came for tea. Then they threatened to dump cups, saucers and shortbread onto the faded, rosy rug. There was the television, circa 1964; its speaker, to the right of the screen, had gold threads woven into the fabric which covered it. And there was the once elegant, scarred mahogany coffee table, stacked with back issues of *Life* and *National Geographic* which I never tired of perusing. I had paper dolls dressed in the smart suits and pillbox hats cut from *Life* magazine photographs of Jacqueline Kennedy.

One solitary standing lamp stood to the right of the armchair. Through its red glass shade—a shade which was replaced four times as I grew taller but not more graceful and knocked it to the floor in play—its bulb cast a ruby, faintly illicit light over my grandfather's newspaper, and over me, lying near him on the Oriental rug, its crimson and blue geometry blooming around my fair, childish head.

On Sunday evenings, I would creep into the living room and lie on my back on that rug and watch, surreptitiously, with my grandfather, one of his favorite programs on television—*The Jackie Gleason Show*, "Live from Miami Beach!" and with the June Taylor Dancers. For an instant—a month? a year?—in my childhood, I found all the mystery of grace and femininity, of ridiculous womanhood, embodied in those improbable dancers. The June Taylor troupe was a company of professional women who danced lying flat on their backs on the stage. I was sure that I could do that. All my struggles with ballet, every arabesque miserably half-accomplished, each tour jêté disgracefully failed, disappeared in the face of the indomitable practicality of women who had the good sense to lie on the floor to dance.

Arranged in a circle and clad in vulgar, sequined leotards, the June Taylor Dancers put their heads together and kicked their long, chorus-girl legs. They scissored their thighs together and apart, together and apart; an overhead camera recorded the smooth shiftings of their shins, the waving of their arms, the patterns their bodies made against the floor. In retrospect, what a foolish and even degrading way to make a living. But when I was seven, I believed that if I must dance—and my mother thought it mandatory—this was the sort of dancing for me. So, prostrate on the old, fading rug whose pattern had witnessed and absorbed the collective sighs and laughter and conversations of my ancestors, I moved my own chubby, pale legs to the beat of the June Taylor Dancers. Their slender limbs parted, their fingers and toes touched those of their neighbors and formed patterns on the floor of flowers, stars, fireworks; the lights reflected from the sequins on their breasts. And I panted along with them, my head straining up to see the screen so I could follow, just exactly, their movements. My plump shins parted, my toes reached for the toes of my invisible neighbors, and I was sure that somehow I too was learning to be a woman, to be graceful, but the easy way, the sensible way, while keeping company with my grandfather's familiar size-eleven feet.

We bought that old television set with Blue Chip stamps, at the redemption center where you turned in your sticker books for appliances and sundry household items: dishes, towels. Mom-mom saved thousands of those stamps which the grocery store doled out with each purchase. She also saved dimes in the big dimpled bottles that Scotch whisky came in, and quarters she hid in tiny thirty-five-millimeter film cans, each of which held a five-dollar stack of twenty coins.

My grandmother grew up in circumstances of extraordinary wealth and has always shopped as only a woman of old money can, avoiding extravagance but instinctively appreciating quality. But when she came to live in America in the thirties, she was seduced by certain products that were new, improved, *modern*. She disapproved of the United States in almost every way, except when it came to the accelerated technology of the new world, a force that could supply such a creation as Naugahyde. When the leather upholstery of her father's armchair and ottoman finally cracked completely and fell to pieces, she had the chair recovered in peanut butter–colored, slippery, ungrained vinyl. Since it was developed by American technology, she had faith that Naugahyde was better. For as long as I have noticed such things, she has carried a vinyl handbag. I bought her a leather one when I was fifteen and was embarrassed by unnatural textiles; she exchanged it for a better, plastic one. Alligator Baggies. Saran Wrap. Mom-mom always went first to the "paper goods" aisle, where she could stock up on sandwich bags, freezer bags, garbage bags, plastic wraps and containers. She stored extra cartons of them in the garage.

For all her profligacy with respect to packaging, my grandmother was a thrifty woman, and the Blue Chip Stamp Redemption Center was one of those few American institutions that she loved. And when I was seven or eight, I loved to "stick stamps." On a Saturday, every two months or so, Mom-mom would put an old plastic cloth over the round oak table in the breakfast nook. On its rough surface of a molded pattern of plastic lace, she placed a bowl of water, a plate upon which was a cellulose sponge lying sodden in a puddle of water, and a shoe box full of Blue Chip stamps. She would hand me a new empty book—it had a drawing of a chipmunk on the cover, grinning maniacally—and she would sit opposite me with her own. We would begin with the big stamps, valued at ten times the smaller ones. Then the large sheets of regular ones. And last, the odd single ones. Each page required a value of fifty, satisfied by either five large or fifty small stamps. Mom-mom liked working only with the big ones or the little ones that had been dispensed in perforated sheets. She had no patience with the strays which were crumpled and whose gummed backs had dried to the point that they frequently no longer stuck and had to be glued. It was my job to collect those from the tabletop, the floor, the bottom of the shoe box, and jigsaw them together onto a page. I liked my job for its tidy quality; I knew that if I did not salvage and paste the stray stamps of little value—the twos and threes and even single stamps—Mom-mom would lose patience with them and throw them away. Sometimes at the market, after she had paid, the checker would count out her stamps, handing her the big ten-value ones and then making change with the smaller ones, and she would let the strip of three or four fall to the floor or into the depths of her handbag. Unless I was diligent and saved them, they would be lost.

Whatever we bought at the redemption center with our filled books Mom-mom valued above those things purchased with money. There was a thrifty pleasure associated with the toaster, the television, the set of Pyrex that had been paid for with redeemed stamps. Of course, my mother hated it, the saving of stamps or dimes, or any other financial watchfulness. She used to dump a handful of dimes out of the Pinch bottle to fill her car's ashtray with meter money, but not when my grandmother was watching.

My mother spent Mom-mom's money with a vengeance, an intent to repay herself for past injuries. She held her mother accountable for myriad injustices, including ruining her marriage to my father and frustrating every other romantic opportunity that presented itself. If Mother was unhappy, it was Mom-mom's fault.

A folding plastic insert in my mother's wallet was crammed with credit cards—all connected to Mom-mom's accounts—and with them she intended to settle the score. Each month there was a tearful reckoning when the bills arrived: hundreds of dollars owed to the pharmacy, the fish and poulterer, the liquor store, the dry cleaner, all these only a prelude to the department-store totals.

Mom-mom could not bear to demand that Mother return the cards, not when she responded by accusing a withdrawal of love. But, finally, my grandmother began canceling her accounts, calling up Saks and I. Magnin's, the butcher, the dry cleaner. She returned the cut-up credit cards with a final check.

I was with my mother in Saks when she tried to buy a pair of sandals and her card was refused. Her slender white hand was resting proprietarily on the shoe box when the saleslady tried to pull it out from under her grasp, saying "I'm sorry, that account has been canceled."

A look of puzzlement wrinkled my mother's smooth white forehead. "Perhaps you wouldn't mind checking again?" she said. "Perhaps you missed one of the numbers."

The woman shrugged and picked up a black phone receiver from under the counter. She read the numbers from the card into the mouthpiece. "Yes," she said, and then, after a moment, "Thank you." She replaced the receiver. "Closed," she said, and handed Mother the card.

I backed two feet away from where I had been standing by Mother's side. She wasn't speaking, but she didn't look as if she were preparing to leave, either. The card remained in her hand, and she and the saleslady stared fixedly at one another, each with one hand resting on the pink shoe box. I was just tall enough that I could rest my arms on the heavy glass case under the cash register and look at its contents from above. Inside, under the glass which was warm from the display lights, was a pair of sandals like those my mother had chosen. They were black silk evening sandals, high-heeled with a tiny gold buckle, and they were displayed next to a beaded jet bag and a pair of black suede opera-length gloves. The accessories—black and seductive—reminded me of Cat Woman, of the secret life my mother apparently lived.

Suddenly, she withdrew her hand from the shoes and grabbed my arm. We left the store immediately, our pace picking up to a sprint through the cloyingly sweet perfume department. In the parking lot, I had to run to keep up with her. She slammed the car door, gunned the engine, and we said nothing on the drive back to my grandparents' house. She stopped in the driveway, reached across my chest and opened the passenger door. I got out and she slammed the door shut behind me.

Then she sat in the car without turning the engine back on, her arms crossed. I stood for a minute beside the car door, but she remained behind the wheel, staring fixedly at the windshield, and so I left her there and went into the house.

Mom-mom was sitting at the breakfast-nook table, writing a letter. "Hello Isabel," she said, and she looked at my empty arms. "Didn't you buy a party dress?" she asked.

I had forgotten that Mother and I had set out to buy a dress for my tenth birthday party the next weekend. Earlier that day, Mom-mom had offered to give Mother cash for the purchase, but she had refused it.

"No," I said. "We couldn't find one."

"Not one!" Mom-mom exclaimed teasingly, but then she looked at me quizzically and raised her black eyebrows. I shrugged and gestured toward the window.

Mother's blue Pontiac was parked under the carport; she was still sitting in it with her arms crossed. As Mom-mom got up from the table, I started toward my bedroom, expecting an explosive fight.

I watched from inside the cocoon of my bedroom curtains, invisible to anyone who might look up from the driveway. But nothing was said. Mom-mom went outside and stood by the car, probably waiting for Mother to roll down her window, but she never did. She just stared straight ahead, for nine minutes—I timed her by the clock near my bed—and then she turned on the car engine and drove slowly out from under the carport and down the long driveway onto Stone Canyon.

She didn't come back for almost two weeks. I think Mommom would have called her—perhaps even apologized and offered to reinstate the Saks account—on the morning of my birthday, but of course we didn't have her number.

This child will punish herself. I am this child.

I am like a freed animal who returns to the familiarity of its cage, the comfort of the intimacy of the smell of urine on newspaper, stale water in a dirty dish, dry food and its terrible proximity to feces.

I am the animal who understands only this cage. I am the child who, missing her captor, reinvents her. When my mother, the one who violates me, is not here, I will invoke her presence by hurting myself. In this way I am comforted.

A child is first practical. I know that if my mother strikes me or pushes the handle of her hairbrush inside me, she also feeds me, hugs me, and puts me to bed.

Beat me, or pinch me. Introduce to my genitals which have been so many times deflowered objects of ordinary household function—why do I scream when I see a wooden spoon? No one understands it. Put inside me some hard cold thing, your letter knife, dull and frigid, for a period of time not long enough to break me, but of sufficient duration that I understand who you are, Mother. And then leave me.

I will punish myself in order to feel your presence. Because there is no one I love so much as you.

One summer, my grandparents enrolled me in an urban day camp. Fifty or so children, all culled from Los Angeles prep schools, were gathered into vans on Mondays, Wednesdays and Fridays, at nine in the morning, and taken to edifying places. The tar pits, the art museum. Children's theater in MacArthur Park, the Griffith Park Observatory. I didn't want to go to camp, but this was a compromise of sorts between a sleep-away and nothing at all, so I went. I liked the tar pits, the sorrowing old bones of the dinosaurs buried in the flat oily lake, the acrid smell of the tar in the summer heat of the city. There was a fence around the pits, to keep children from that same wallowing, slow death, I imagined, and the grass grew yellow and sickly at the black edge of the ancient lake.

We visited a few industrial amusement parks as well: Wonder bread, and Busch Gardens, where we took a monorail through the brewery and watched bottles being filled, my head swimming with the thick smell of the hops.

One Friday, we drove miles to get to the Mattel toy factory, which was far away from the Los Angeles I knew. Deep in the industrial south of the city, it had a huge red sign turning slowly over the freeway that said, for the girls, HOME OF BARBIE on one side and, for the boys, HOME OF HOT WHEELS on the other.

In my own bedroom I had an immense distance, about fifteen yards, of orange track laid down, and ten little cars that I sped over it and wrecked dramatically—especially on the steep descent from the top of the bureau. I was hoping we would get a free tiny Corvette or dune buggy when we finished the tour. After all, Wonder bread had given us each a miniature loaf of doughy white bread which I found too cunning to unwrap and eat; it was now on the patio, green with mold.

I liked the inside of factories, I loved conveyor belts and the shining competent machines, the workers all in the same uniforms. I wanted to see how Mattel made the little cars. But when we got inside, the boys were separated into their own group and led away, the girls forced to follow a large blond woman to the doll injection molds.

I never liked dolls, but even if I had, that afternoon's entertainment would have put me off them forever. A huge vent blew hundreds of disembodied, bald heads, fashioned from fleshy plastic, onto a conveyor belt from which droves of big black women snatched each one up and ran it under the needle of a monstrous sewing machine and stitched a mop of colored plastic hair onto its head. They threw them, about a hundred a minute, back onto the rolling endless belt from which other workers grabbed them and quickly painted eyes and a pink smile onto their little molded features. Thus enlivened, all the heads tumbled along the belt and joined the flow of necks and torsos, the two tributaries forming a giant pink river of body parts.

I stared, horror-struck, as heads were jammed onto necks, given a twist by a large hand so that they faced forward, and then pitched into a great rolling hamper that took the little quadriplegic figures on to the arms-and-legs section, where limbs were forced into appropriate holes.

The workers, most of them huge women weighing at least two hundred pounds, their hair tied back in regulation pink nets, their bulk swathed in immense pink aprons, never looked up from the carnage that flowed before them. Their hands were a blur of productivity, articulating tiny joints. Every once in a while a doll would come out wrong, legless, perhaps, or otherwise handicapped, and she would be dismembered, her parts thrown by the doll-undoer into various separate bins.

Once assembled, the river of naked Barbies flowed on to be clothed, their huge breasts and minuscule arched feet and wasp waists all jumbling together. First, a pair of tiny, flimsy underpants, and a frothy blue party dress and matching plastic pumps. Hair was combed back into demure flips, secured with clear polyurethane bands, and then each doll was ready to be laid in a little paper and plastic casket with her name on it, and sealed into a package for the stores.

I fainted with fear at the end of the excursion. Or at least, I sat down suddenly on the floor, unable to speak, and my eyes closed briefly. The woman who led the tour seemed very upset, and she gave me two extra souvenirs, so that I had three different little dolls, each locked in its own plastic brooch, that I could wear on my shirt. They had different color hair, pink, green and purple, and were scented like flowers, each no taller than my thumb.

The gift didn't have the desired effect; I thrust the little dolls away and had what was later described as hysterics. My grandmother's payment for the last three weeks of camp was refunded, and she was asked that I not return. Mother, for her part, was quite disgusted with me, and the nicest thing she said was that at least the camp had kept me longer than the swimming school.

I love Francesca because she is the only child who does not demand explanations of the circumstances of my family, who does not question my father's absence or the fact that I live with my grandparents. This is not because she is more polite or philosophical than other little girls, but because she too lives with her grandparents, and does not know her father. Even worse, she rarely sees her mother, but perhaps this is a blessing.

I am present for one of Angela's homecomings—an Italian textile designer, she lives in Rome for most of the year, wears frightening muumuus and turbans, and reeks of perfume. She embraces me at once with Francesca—a waif who doesn't even merit a private hug—and we disappear into the red cave of her gown, emerging with our hair on end with static electricity. Angela—her daughter is not to call her "Mother"—embar-

rasses both Francesca and me, and my friend never speaks of her.

> *En route to an amusement park, in the back of a station wagon filled with a party of little girls celebrating a birthday, Francesca and I touch tongues. We lean into one another, her long red hair and my brown flowing together and hiding our faces from the others. Quickly, urgently, we dart our tongues together. They touch for only a moment and then, frightened, we each withdraw quickly, suddenly aware that we have crossed some border. We look about us to see if any of the others had noticed, and I run my tongue over my gums, the taste of her mouth, slightly metallic and stale, mingling with my saliva.*

> *We cannot look at one another. My face burns and I lean my hot cheek against the window.*

> *One Saturday when I am supposed to come over and play, Francesca's grandparents call Opa and tell him that I cannot visit that day. On Monday, at school, after I ask many times, Francesca tells me this:*

> *Grandmother and Grandfather, as she so formally calls them, make her pack an overnight bag. They have her put all her underwear and a nightgown in it. She doesn't need any play clothes, they say, because she'll be wearing a uniform all the time that she isn't asleep.*

> *Her grandfather calls a cab, and when the cab comes, he says to the driver, "This little girl is too naughty to live here anymore. Take her away." They make her get in the back of the cab with her bag, and the old yellow car pulls away from the big colonial house with the white columns and the lamp hanging over the front door on a long chain. The cab goes down the block and out of her neighborhood; it drives around Beverly Hills for about an hour, it feels like to Francesca, before it comes back and lets*

her out. The whole time the driver tells about his brother's dog and how it had to be put to sleep.

Francesca says she wasn't scared because she knows most of the streets he drove on and she could tell they were going in circles.

In the dark end of the garage, where the light from the dirty windows did not reach, and keeping company with the four or five cartons of Christmas decorations that summered there, behind the old Cadillac, I found a box made of corrugated paper that was old enough that it had split into three layers, the two flat outer sheets revealing a rumpled inner tongue of paper. I was so interested in this decay of the cardboard that I didn't at first examine the contents of the box, but carried it out onto the driveway so that I might play with the paper in better light. But as I placed the box on the warm asphalt, it burst, and out spilled a heap of small seashells, all of one species. I was mystified, because they had clearly been collected from Shell Beach in La Jolla, but they were the one kind I had always left behind, thinking them too plentiful to be of any value. Too, they had no luster, but were a quiet functional little house, with no intent to beguile with a whimsical twist of calcium, not even a pink rim or any variation of their modest beige pigment. These were the very shells I threw back into the water. But someone had loved and collected them, counted them of value. Who?

I had spread them into a layer one shell deep and was rolling them under my palm when Opa walked out from under the carport, pushing a sack of dried manure in his wheelbarrow. I looked up from the shells and smelled the sharp sweetness from the sack with the laughing bull's head.

"I see you've found your mother's shells," he said, and he moved on toward the back garden where he was working over the vegetable bed, folding the manure into the soil.

I threw away the box and collected the shells and took them to my bedroom, spilling them onto the bed where I lay next to them and smelled the salt fishiness of them, still fresh after twenty years. I piled them up and then dumped my own collection next to them, making sure not to let them mingle and be lost among each other.

What a peculiar child my mother had been. I knew that already, had seen pictures of her and how tidy she was, always in a dress, never rumpled, prissy. It seemed mysterious to me that she had chosen to collect only one shell from a beach that was so rich in possibilities, another proof that we were not at all the same person. And yet, the shells, their existence, the evidence that she had, like me, gone down to the beach very early, before others had picked over the offerings, and gathered these up, was comforting.

It had been three years since my mother had moved out. There was relief in her absence—the cessation of daily fighting between her and Mom-mom—and sadness. I missed her, the after-school visits insufficient, and I had begun to have nightmares. I sat up in bed at night and was unable to breathe. Now I was taking asthma medication, an inhalant that made my scalp prickle unpleasantly. It all seemed puzzlingly connected, and at night, when I couldn't breathe and my mother was not there to know that I couldn't, I was overcome by grief and anger and buried my head in my grandmother's long-boned, uncomfortable lap and cried and said things that I hoped were not true. I said that if Mother loved me she would not have left home, and my grandmother replied with words that were meant to console but did not. When I woke, and it was daylight, I didn't really remember what had happened during the night, my fears seemed childish and silly, and I took comfort in the familiar. It was true that the romantic center of my life—the person whom I loved unreasonably, immoderately, desperately—was absent, but my grandparents were steady and present, and the love that I had for them did not choke me.

Still, any tangible evidence of my mother, the possessions she had left behind in her bedroom down the hall from mine, the clothes, the china shepherdess on the bookcase, the old satin toe shoes, those cosmetics that were not vital and were left in the cupboard under the bathroom sink—all these things had an ineffable and weighty presence for me. I handled them in her absence, trying to navigate, by touch and with my unagile, unpracticed young soul, into some understanding of my mother. I always ran aground, foundered upon their muteness, their basic impenetrability. The best I did was with the old abandoned dresses in the closet; those smelled of her, of her perfume and of *her*, a musky young animal smell which spoke to me through the cloth. I tried on the old pink toe shoes and, destined never to graduate from my flat ballet slippers, fell immediately into the closet and smacked my head on the back wall.

The shells were another thin line upon which I might reel in some elusive truth about my mysterious parent. I knelt by the bed, rolling her shells in my left hand, mine in my right. They had come from the same little beach, albeit eighteen or twenty years prior: they were collected during the same month of the year, August, gathered at dawn (the only time to collect them) when my grandparents were just waking in the cottage up the road. They implied some connection between the child that my mother had been and the child I yet was. We might have played at the same game together, gone for a walk, shared a secret. This was something that had never been imaginable from any picture or story of my mother as a little girl. I liked the idea and ended in dumping the shells together into a box, the shell that I had previously rejected now well represented among the collection.

A few days later, when Mother had come to the house and was looking about my bedroom, she came upon the box of shells. "Isabel, I didn't know you had so many," she said, "and these, these are my favorites." She held up one of the ones she had herself picked up from the beach perhaps twenty years before.

The following August, in La Jolla, I even collected a few more of the little periwinkles. But there were other developments that summer, two events affecting all beachcombers, that distracted me from the plain little beige shells.

The first concerned sea urchins. I arrived on the beach very early the first morning I awoke in La Jolla, and it was a perfect morning because the sun, for once, was out early and the tide was so low that it was possible to walk all the way out to the big rock that the sea lions rested on. And I had beaten the fat girl to the shore—essential because she had a giant sieve which she dragged over the sand, collecting everything larger than a dime and wrecking the pickings for everyone else. The first time I had seen her, two years earlier, I had been unable to say anything beyond "Where did you get that?" to which she had responded, disdainfully, "My father made it." That said, she had marched resolutely forward along the beach, her fat white thighs chafing together and her plaid shorts riding up in an ugly way from the back.

I sat in the sand and watched her greedy progress down the shore, watched as she bent to discard the kelp and stray driftwood, the occasional picnic cup, before she dumped her haul into a huge garbage bag, folded her contraption and presumably went home to sort out her loot. I felt amazed and disgusted by her lack of understanding of the whole aesthetic of collecting, the careful search of the sand, the practiced glide of trained eyes over minute terrain, the joy of a good find glinting wet in the early light. She was ruining everyone's sport for something she wasn't properly enjoying herself. I would never speak to her again, or try to be her friend.

But this morning she was not in sight and the sand was clean of footprints, untouched by the long raking scars left by her sieve. And something very odd had occurred since last August. The beach was littered, utterly buried, in the shells of sea urchins. The whole shell of a sea urchin is, usually, a rare prize. They come in shades of green and purple, very beautiful, and very fragile. One is lucky to come upon a recognizable fragment; the waves break them upon the rocks. After hours and hours of collecting for the past five summers, I had but one or two. And now there were thousands. I sank to my knees in the sand.

At six o'clock, on a clear bright morning, I ran up and down the beach, fevered, scooping handfuls into my Baggies. I ran up the hill to the cottage for more bags, filled them, again, again, and finally sat down on a rock. This somehow was not as it should be.

I found myself thinking of Ferdinand and Isabella and saw them walking up the aisle of the A & P and noticing that there were boxes and boxes of salt to be had for pennies. My precious shells, the two of them on my bookcase in Los Angeles, were worthless now. The initial sense of having wandered into an Aladdin's cave evaporated, and I stood up and began pushing aside the sea urchin shells and looking underneath for the other old favorites.

A man appeared on the beach and I asked him what it meant, the plague of urchins. He told me that the kelp farmers had poisoned the urchins. They were attracting too many sea otters whose fishing for them had disturbed their crop. It made a sort of grim sense, and seemed to fit in with the ecology of the fat girl who by this time was trudging up and down and gathering heaps of the round green and purple shells, grinding others to crumbs with her sieve. In my mind the poisoning kelp farmer became her father, manipulating the ocean now so that she could bring home more and more of the best shells.

And another thing had gone wrong. I looked down at my feet and they were plastered with an almost impenetrable layer of tar and sand. For this was the summer, also, that an oil spill had occurred off the coast of California, leaking from one of the wells off the coast of Ojai. The crude tar settled all along the shore, sticking to everything. Mom-mom bought a can of Energine and every time I returned from the beach I went up the back porch steps and sat with a rag and an old, dull knife and the pungent solvent, first scraping with the knife, the tar curling off in sticky licorice-looking strips, then soaking the remaining stain with Energine and rubbing rubbing with the rag, until my flesh was red and hot and clean.

Mother says *"Damnation"* very loudly when she is angry, and I hear her say *"Damn Nation,"* and imagine the solemn ranks of people stretching from sea to shining sea all standing meekly under her terrible wrath. To me her anger is easily large enough to apply to a whole country full of people.

The power of her temper is the stuff of legend. When she says if I don't watch out, she will smack me into the middle of next week, I believe her and see myself flying out of time like a crumb being shaken from off the calendar, landing in the future.

Once I'm out, I might not fall back in the right way. I could land somewhere else with the wrong people, in an entirely wrong place.

When I was twelve, my grandmother bought a cat and had it flown from a huge London cattery to Los Angeles. Mommom was a cat fancier and raised purebred Persians—not for profit, but as an avocation of sorts. For a time, she felt more of a calling to cats than to any other cause.

We went to the international airport at night and picked up the animal from the customs hold; it was in a little crate and its nose was grazed from having pressed it for so long to the air holes. The cat was eighteen months old, ready to bear kittens, and Mom-mom soon had it mated with a champion stud for a fee of $250. All the thought and planning that this had entailed—the finer points of breeding, the selection of bloodlines and type—meant little to me, but I looked forward to the kittens. I had never had any pets, and while Mom-mom's show cats weren't playmates, the kittens seemed like they would be, for a while anyway, just kittens, and fun to play with.

They were born while I was at school, five of them, each healthy and perfect, nursing at their mother's clean white belly by the time I came home at four. I was surprised that their eyes were not yet open, and as I was then a solitary child, shy and resistant to the company of other children, I was impatient for the kittens' transformation into real playmates.

They were a beautiful litter; each little body was white and gracefully formed. Their ears were closed against sound and their eyes tightly sealed and blind, protected by pale mauve, lightly furred lids. Separating each set of lids was a line, like a faint perforation along a page of paper, drawn where they had yet to part beneath the delicate fringe of white lashes. I cupped one kitten like water in my hands and brought its warm body to my lips. It smelled sweet like butter, uncorrupted, and I felt the slight quickening of its heart under my mouth. The mother watched me anxiously.

Each day after school I hurried home and threw books aside, and before I was out of my uniform, my hot prickling navy wool blazer still scratching at my neck, I was with the kittens, looking at each tiny enigmatic face to see if its eyes had opened yet. But they remained shut, their faces blind puzzles infuriatingly slow to engage with the world. Each kitten that I shook from slumber—just to be sure that its eyes were not closed in sleep—moved its head vaguely in cognizance, eyes absolutely sealed.

On the ninth afternoon, I had exhausted my childish reserve of patience. While the kittens remained blind, each was like an unopened present, a box with contents unknown, and so I undid them. A tiny head between my hands, its weightless body supported on my stomach as I curled my back in concentration, I applied pressure with the sides of each thumb, that place against which the boys next door would stretch a blade of grass to make a whistle. One thumb against the upper lid, the other on the lower, gently, slowly, I pulled one tiny, delicate membrane of flesh from its mate until the skin tore apart neatly, like that of a perforated coupon carefully saved. Underneath was a bleary, pale, ice-blue eye.

Methodically, and with almost surgical attention, I opened each of the five kittens' eyelids. Still, they were not ready to play. Their eyes remained squinted nearly shut, and they teared a little, darkening the fur on their faces and making them look strangely tired. The kittens buried their heads in their mother's warm belly and slept, and I went away disappointed.

The following afternoon when I came home from school I was stricken with fear and guilt. Within only a day, their eyes were swollen completely shut, infected. Each little eye had been tightly resealed beneath lids now angry and faintly red, a yellow crust in the corners matting the little hairs. I pressed gingerly against one of the tightly shut lids with my index finger and, horribly, a thin worm of pus shot out. The kitten made no sound but struggled briefly in my hands and I dropped it in fright.

I tried to reason in my panic. Mom-mom would never suspect that I had caused such a plague upon her new kittens, but she would worry and grieve over them. I imagined them all permanently blinded by my foolishness and wondered what I could do. The right thing was to get them to a veterinarian, but I was too frightened to confess, and how could I get them there myself, without Mom-mom's help? Paralyzed by my guilt, I only hoped that she would notice herself before it was too late to save them.

But my grandmother's own eyesight was not good, and the little crusted eyes escaped her. This was the first litter she had bred, and perhaps she didn't think it peculiar that the mother washed her kittens' faces so furiously and desperately.

Each morning and each afternoon I crept miserably into the little sewing room where Mom-mom had set up the breeding pen, and having, too late, washed my hands with pHisoHex, scrubbed each little face with that harsh soap on a clean wash-cloth. The kittens sneezed and struggled, but I carefully cleaned their blind wobbling heads.

My guilt was tremendous. I hid in my closet and prayed for the kittens, the front of my gray uniform jumper wet with tears. I fasted, skipping breakfast and lunch and taking my dinner to my room, allegedly to eat while studying, but, in truth, letting the food slip off my plate into the camellia bush outside my window. Reeling with hunger, I selected sharp stones from the garden to keep in my shoes. But none of the self-flagellation worked for me as it had for the saints in my four-volume set of their exemplary lives. This, I knew, was because I was un-clean and had not confessed. But I wasn't brave enough to tell Mom-mom. It took less courage to starve myself.

It was three weeks almost and the little eyes were still tightly shut. The kittens had more energy and coordination now, and they gamboled about, playing with one another and knocking their heads together or against the side of the wooden pen, their tiny whiskers too short to save them from clumsiness. I soaked a cotton ball in warm water and laid it over one little face, trying to melt the crust away from the fur. The kitten had strong miniature claws now, and it dug them in and escaped, scratching my wrist. I sat back on my bruised heels and watched in despair. Five valuable kittens, ruined. The one with the wet face was miserably rubbing its little head against the towel in the pen. Clearly I would have to tell my grandmother something.

"When are their eyes going to open?" I asked her in the kitchen, feigning interest in the contents of the cupboard. I'd had no after-school snacks in the past week, and there were two boxes of cookies, untouched. My eyes watered at the sight of them.

"Soon, I hope. They were supposed to be open last week, but they never did, so I took them to the vet. They have an infection."

"What did the vet say?"

"Oh, he gave them shots and cleaned their eyes with some solution. He said he'd never seen anything quite like it."

I didn't say anything, trying to determine if she was implying any mystery, or worse, some culpability on my part.

"Are they blind?" I finally asked.

"I hope not. I just don't understand how something like this could happen. I've taken such good care, they're so clean, I change the towels in the pen every day." Mom-mom paused and looked at me pointedly. "I felt very embarrassed," she said. "The vet seemed to think it was caused by dirt."

My poor grandmother, so scrupulous in her care of the cats. I wanted to confess but was too frightened of her anger and disappointment. Maybe she would be so angry she'd never let me touch them again. I went upstairs to work on my math assignment, but was soon back by the pen with the kittens, driven, like a thief, to reinspect the scene of my trespass. I brought with me the cotton balls and some disinfectant but found myself unable to touch them; their plight had become repellent.

In the fifth week after their birth, three weeks late, their eyes opened. The kittens were not blind, but their tear ducts were permanently scarred, and their eyes wept and ruined them as show animals. Four of the kittens we were able to sell at a modest price as pets. The last we kept, its baleful wet face forever a reminder to me of what I had done, and of the price of a confession withheld.

Mabby—her real name is Mabel—is seventy-five years old and just my size. When Mom-mom and Opa are away, I stay with her in the trundle bed that pulls out from under her very high mattress upon which I am never allowed to sit. We play endless rounds of war, a card game which neither of us likes very much, but it passes the time, and she lets me cheat: I hide cards on my lap under the folding table and produce the high ones when I need them. The game is over sooner if one player cheats.

On her wall are two pictures, one of Martin Luther King and the other of Jesus with a dove coming out of his forehead and his robe open to show us his red, beaming heart. There are a lot of little folded white papers with blue writing in the tiny apartment and they say Jews for Jesus on them with a blue star in the middle.

Mabby used to take care of my mother and she lived in the

house with my family long ago. She tells me things about my father, where he lives and what he is like. He still writes her letters sometimes and she takes the letters out of their neatly slit envelopes and shows me the lines where he has asked how I am.

It is Mabby, years later in a rest home, who tells me how my parents met and separated, who tells me that it was to her that my mother came when she learned she was pregnant, not to Mom-mom but to her. Mabby has a little picture of my father and my mother in her drawer, and she takes it out and shows it to me every time so I'll remember what he looks like.

The letters and the picture scare me, and one day when Mom-mom tries to drop me off, I complain to her in front of Mabby that I don't want to be left with a baby-sitter, that I can take care of myself and that I want to stay home alone. After Mom-mom leaves, Mabby picks up a whole sack of lemons—a gift from Opa's garden—and throws them at the wall behind me. The pictures of Martin Luther King and Jesus shake on their nails and the lemons fall out of the bag and roll around my feet. Her outburst makes us both cry, and after we pick up the lemons I lie and tell her that I'm sorry and that I love her and would prefer, actually, to live with her than with Mom-mom and Opa.

I am eighteen when Mabby dies. She has been in a rest home for years and I haven't visited very often. I have forgotten her, nearly. But after she is gone, I dream of her and the picture in her drawer. She holds out the little snapshot and says, "Here are your mother and father." But when I look, I see myself in his arms.

Years have passed since my mother's death, and I find myself mystified by this passage of time. The fact of her death is no longer shocking—although on the deepest level it will never cease to be so—and is part of the now irretrievable past. Her life is like something dropped in the tide: its trajectory observed, it has now passed the point where one could reach into the waves and pull it back up. The water is beginning to distort now as it sinks slowly; everything is a little unclear. How peculiar to be gaining hindsight, the perspective of years, while losing the clarity of presence. I understand that which was obscure and confusing while she lived by piecing together information, extrapolating—I read her letters, the ones she saved; I have discovered the tape-recorded sessions of her consultations with her psychic, Edna. But, at the same time that I learn of my mother in theory, I have lost her in application.

No longer can I remember her smell without pressing my face into one of her old sweaters.

Certain oft-repeated stories have acquired that burnish that comes from handling, a smooth familiar quality of a favorite object in one's hands. Other facts have grown rough from disuse; spoken aloud, they have a terribly ambivalent feel: are they true? It is no longer quite clear.

To myself, aloud, I might say, "My mother was an unfulfilled person and unhappy." Or, "Mother always regretted that she didn't pursue her ballet." Or the more dangerous, "Mother loved me, she just wasn't ready to have a child. It wasn't that she didn't love me, she was just young and selfish. It was because I reminded her of my father that she was sometimes unkind. . . ." I am rarely able to evaluate the truth of my words, or their importance. She loved me, she loved me not: the age-old image of the suffering lover. After a certain excess of scrutiny, I was blinded with looking. Still I return, inevitably, compulsively, to such statements, speaking them aloud, turning them over in my mind, listening, waiting for them to betray themselves as truth or falsehood.

And it is all so tangled with the presence, the memory, of my father, first the mystery of who he was, then the fear of what he became, and of what he made me. I have no interest in who he is; I no longer see or speak with him; our lives do not intersect. But for two years—those years when I was eighteen and nineteen, the years which circumscribed my mother's illness and death—he was a pivotal presence.

To the question of a stranger, or at least stranger enough to not know this essential fact of my history, I always answer that I met my father when I was eighteen. This is not strictly true, although neither is it a lie.

After their divorce, my parents remained in contact, but the relationship they maintained involved me in only the most tangential way. I am told that my father came from Needles to visit me when I was three, but I have no memory of the occasion.

I do remember seeing him when I was ten: he spent two days at our home, and we went to the Los Angeles County Museum of Art where he reprimanded me for touching the toes of a monumental woman carved from irresistibly cool white marble. It was very hot in the gallery. He reprimanded me often in those two long days—it was clear that he totally disapproved of the way I was being raised—and I was greatly relieved when he left. He seemed to me to be a very uncomfortable sort of person, the kind with whom it was not possible to get along, or even to have a reasonable conversation. He had asked what I liked to do and my response, "Read," seemed acceptable, but, after we pursued the topic, it seemed I was reading the wrong things.

He stood by the front door of our house as I played in the garden, not joining but observing. I had a badminton net which Opa had stretched between the two tallest lemon trees, and as I played—hitting the slow shuttlecock high into the air and then running under the net to return it from the other side—he stood, arms crossed, with his blond head inclined appraisingly to one side and watched my strange, solitary sport. I felt my face grow hot with running, and with a sudden awareness of my foolishness as I played by myself at a game meant for two. He seemed hateful to me, watching and making me understand my loneliness.

Two years later, when I was twelve, he reappeared, this time interrupting our summer in La Jolla. His visit transformed my mother from her more relaxed summer self into a woman alternately elated and cross, one liable to take me at a moment's notice to the bookstore and buy the entire set of Laura Ingalls Wilder's *Little House* books, and at the next to scream about a pair of socks left on the chair by my bed. After two years, I had almost forgotten who my father was, he existed merely as the memory of some irritant, just as I might have recalled the week I had caught ringworm from the cat, or had sprained my wrist falling from my bicycle. He had been a short-lived presence that hindered the usual and comfortable progress of my days, my childish pursuits. Now, here he was again, spoiling the very best month of the year.

This time, I dismissed my father more quickly and definitely as an eccentric and undesirable person. The first outstandingly weird thing about him was that he wore his shoes and a long-sleeved shirt, unbuttoned, into the water. We waded into the surf together, my hand crushed by his large perspiring paw, and my humiliation was boundless when I was under the care of this huge and embarrassing stranger. I felt that every eye on the beach must certainly be trained upon my father's enormous feet covered in their glaring, beaconlike sheath of white canvas. The fact that the sneakers were new and undoubtedly purchased for this very peculiar purpose added to my extreme self-consciousness and I was relieved when finally we were out in the water and the tide had covered the horrible shoes. "Why are you wearing those?" I hissed at him under the louder strident conversation of the waves. He responded that he was a "tenderfoot," that the rocks hurt his feet too much for him to be able to stand on them. At that point, he utterly lost my respect.

Of course, I wasn't trying much to like the man. I was angry that his birthday had the unfortunate poor timing to fall during that very week and that some sense of propriety had forced me to spend my savings on a bottle of cheap after-shave, the value of which was equal to at least twenty little plastic paratroopers. Even the fact that he didn't smoke cigars like my grandfather I held against him. For Father's Day or for his birthday I always bought Opa as many Cuban cigars as I could afford. Twenty-five cents apiece, and I hand-selected them from the fragrant box with the beautiful Spanish señorita on the lid, her eyes sparkling under her mantilla, her slender white arm raised over her head. With the thick, slightly nauseating smell of the tobacco filling my small head, I could hear her castanets snapping and see the young matador click his heels at her side and bow. No, it was clear to me that my father was not only judgmental and difficult, reprimanding and disagreeing with me at every turn, but worse, his inability to walk into the water and his preference for English Leather over cigars meant that he wasn't even a Man.

He had rented the cheapest room in the old pink hotel, the same hotel whose creaking staircase the summer children climbed a hundred times a day to reach the roof and launch their little plastic paratroopers. Not only did this room have no view of the ocean, or of anything beyond the lawn and its litter of torn parachutes, but it was representative of those poorer accommodations that are filled only during the tourist season and was in the basement with one solitary window high up over the twin bed. From the outside of the building, the two long, squat panes of glass were just at ground level and nearly obscured by a scraggly hibiscus shrub. Inside the room, to which I accompanied my father one afternoon when he left the beach to reapply tanning lotion, the light was swimmy and green and uneven. The soft summer wind blew through the hibiscus leaves and shadows dappled across my father's chest as he smeared the white cream over his skin. For some reason I couldn't have articulated, I didn't like to see this, and I left the room, its meager furnishings and damp smell, and waited in the dimly lit hall.

But later that evening, I returned to the window of his room and sat outside, in the dirt under the hibiscus. I hid myself in the plant and nervously stripped the long pink furled buds from the lower branches as I waited there. I had told my grandparents that I was invited to play at Allison's until the sun set, at nine, and so I had almost an hour before I needed to be home, but it was only a few minutes before someone knocked at the door to my father's tiny room. From where I sat, I heard the rapping distantly, as though in a dream. My father got up from the bed where he had been lying on its thin plaid coverlet, his arms crossed behind his blond head.

It was my mother at the door, as I knew it would be, as I was waiting for, and she was wearing my favorite dress, a rose-colored strapless sundress with a snug bodice and full skirt that made her waist look so small, so girlish and vulnerable, as though it might take very little simply to snap her in two. She shut the door softly behind her and put her naked arms around my tall father's neck. Even as she greeted him with this strangely childlike gesture, his hands were busy in her dark hair, stroking and tugging thick fistfuls of it so that her head bobbed as he pulled. When the embrace was over and they moved apart from one another his hands remained, one over each ear, and as he spoke to her he moved her head so that she appeared to nod in answer to his words.

I had expected that they would make love and had secreted myself in the hibiscus to see just that, I suppose, but now I was afraid, and having rehearsed all that might happen—I knew the basics of sex—I was completely unprepared for what did. Before they moved away from the door, before anything further transpired, I considered leaving and I looked away briefly, testing my willingness to go. When I looked back, they were still standing at the entrance to the little room, and my father had pushed my mother up against the door. He continued to talk to her and to move her head in reply, but I could hear no words, just a low murmur of voices. In response to one of his utterances she struggled against his hands, shaking her head *no* in defiance of his forcing her, like a puppeteer, to nod in affirmation, and he laughed in a way that was unpleasant, two short barks of amusement. He led her out of my sight, to the bed I imagined, and my toes curled in the dirt in apprehension. But when I moved into a better viewing posture, my cheek pressed against the rough pink stucco of the wall, I saw that he had sat my mother in the little folding chair before the vanity table. He was cutting her hair.

It fell away in long, thick, shining curls. It dropped into her lap, onto her breasts, her thighs. Each lustrous, dark lock glistened as it fell from her head. Dizzy with the hugeness of his crime, I closed my eyes and leaned back against the hibiscus's slender trunk, feeling the small tree bend as it accepted my weight.

When he was done, she looked awful, her hair shorter on the left than on the right and choppy in back. My mother turned her head from one side to another, looking at her reflection as if considering the job, as if it were a normal haircut received under normal circumstances. My father, however, didn't pause to appraise his handiwork, but was on his knees on the floor, picking up the hair, sweeping it into a pile. He collected it from her lap, brushed it from her white shoulders, and when he had it all together in one shining soft heap, he took a plastic container—Tupperware, the same that Mom-mom used for leftovers—from his suitcase and put it all inside. He snapped the lid shut. I watched him slip the container into a small paper bag and put it, with his shiny, new-looking scissors, into the battered brown leather suitcase. Obviously he had come prepared, had arrived in La Jolla with the intention of stealing my mother's hair.

I hugged myself as she stood up from the vanity table and shook the last strands from her rose-colored skirt. He had loved it, he must have, the generous flow of it washing down her narrow back. It was unchanged in style and in its rich, radiant health from that of the girl he had married. My mother had a slight widow's peak, and her hair sprang up with frank energy and life from her pale forehead. It was like a promise, the abundance of it. We had all loved my mother's hair.

I crept out from under the hibiscus. The sun had set and I was surely in trouble, especially if Opa had come to collect me from Allison's and found that I was not there. But when I cautiously entered the back door of the cottage, using the doorknob to ease the tongue of the lock silently into place, for once I eluded punishment and found myself feeling disappointed, even neglected. I had counted on the distraction of an argument, the comfortable ritual of my grandparents' scolding, my protesting. But Mom-mom was absorbed in a television program and Opa was reading *Gardeners' Digest*. He pulled a leaf from my collar and pushed me gently in the direction of my room.

When I saw my mother the next morning she had just returned from the little beauty salon uptown, a three-chair establishment at which she had always turned up her long nose, and there was nothing left of her hair but a short cap of dark curls. Bared, the back of her neck looked very long and white.

She asked Mom-mom if the new style didn't look chic, and Mom-mom said no, it didn't.

I felt sorry for my mother and stood up from my cereal at the breakfast table. I looked to make sure that my fingers were quite clean and then I touched the back of her head, that tender spot where the skull curves in.

"I think it's nice," I whispered. But she didn't answer, was looking off at the ocean which was very flat and glassy that morning, no boats in sight.

What I did not understand then, and which I learned many years later, was that my father's visit to La Jolla was just one of a series of such meetings. Probably my parents saw one another twenty or more times as I was growing up. They spoke on the phone, not regularly, but sometimes, after two or more years of silence, there would be a rekindling and new hope and one month's phone bill would be many hundreds of dollars, the price—the material price and not to be compared with the cost to one's soul—exacted for passion, for those fevered conversations in which suddenly it seemed possible: yes, they would remarry. Never mind his new wife, unwitting, at home with her small children in the hot, dry town of Needles, California. Never mind the town itself, for that matter, despite his recent appointment to its city council, his ambition to be, one day perhaps, its mayor. He could leave everything and come back to my mother.

I was to learn, later, that my father's one undeniable talent lay in impassioned speeches. He was, constitutionally if not morally, well suited to his vocation as a politician. He lived to convince, to bend people under the weight of his words, or by the force of his passion. He was very clever; he was obsessed; he had all the answers. And both my mother and, later, I were women searching for conviction.

My mother is serially monotheistic, trading gods with more frequency than lovers. For the first years which I remember, it is Mary Baker Eddy's Science and Health with Key to the Scriptures, and we see a practitioner. I miss most of my childhood shots, and my childish nonbelief in germs being insufficient to convince them—the germs, I mean—I catch every mump and pox and measle and see the fevers out with the cool hand of the practitioner on my forehead as she prays.

After Mrs. Eddy, we turn together to our catechism, but before it takes, there is a brief flirtation with transcendental meditation.

For some reason, she cannot practice TM in her own apartment, so on her way home from work, Mother stops at our house, which we enjoy, but she doesn't come to be with us, but to lock me out of my bedroom while she meditates. It is all very confus-

ing and I spend countless hours with my cheek to the carpet outside the closed bedroom door, trying to hear the secret mantra which she murmurs over and over to herself.

It sounds like "chicken," an unlikely word, but it is always so close to dinner when she meditates, and I am forbidden snacks because she says I am fat, so perhaps I am hungry and hear chickens where there are none. She says that when she is finished she is very peaceful and fulfilled and that is why she doesn't have dinner with us; it would wreck her spiritual satiation, all this earthly gobbling.

Sometimes she comes quietly down from my bedroom while we are eating and we all look up guiltily. "Pull up a chair," Opa says halfheartedly, not because he doesn't want his daughter but because the most she will do is take a slice of meat and eat a sandwich standing at the sink. Her fugitive stance, on the edge of our small gathering, makes me ravenous and I clean my plate and nervously contemplate asking for seconds. If her gaze is focused out the window, I take some food and bolt away from the table, to my bedroom. Where she has sat meditating, murmuring, is a small hollow in my soft bed, nothing more. I sit there in its vanished warmth to finish the food I have taken.

When I was lost to girlhood and became a woman, that is, when I moved in with a man and Mom-mom was forced to perceive me as a woman, my grandmother gave up her parental pretenses and grew much more candid about matters she considered private and vulgar—which is to say, female. She told me all the stories I had heard previously from my mother who loved to reveal the indiscretions of those near to her. Anything which I had suspected my mother might have embellished (or *embroidered*—the family word for lying) and made juicier, I have now heard from the heroine herself of these romantic and, yes, often indiscreet adventures. I know that Mom-mom did have an affair with a White Russian. And that, as with all the other men my grandmother loved, her father found him dangerous and boorish, and obviously after her money. It is hard to protect a daughter with a fortune.

"God in heaven," he yelled, a tall man with a deep voice, "the man is a Mohammedan! He could have another wife!"

I have now heard from both my mother and my grand-mother about how the chauffeur tried to blackmail my young bold grandmother, and how she tricked him. She had affairs when it was not fashionable to do so; she could not force herself to marry any of the men who were chosen for her—one she jilted on the wedding day and spent months returning outland-ishly extravagant gifts. Her wedding gown and trousseau, made to order by Lanvin, were of course not returnable. Donated to charity, together they fetched the highest bid for the Shanghai Smallpox Hospital. After her father died and she realized that she hadn't the courage, quite, to bear children out of wedlock, Mom-mom married my grandfather.

"He was no wiz," she told me once, and from that I was supposed to understand that he was not very skilled as a lover. Briefly, sharply, I was humiliated for Opa, my only gentle parent, and at the red light on the corner of Wilshire and Santa Monica boulevards, I blushed deeply.

My grandmother was far more likely to make such revela-tions in the car; like me, she was lulled by the movement and the fact that she was in transit: not anywhere for a moment and freed from responsibilities implied by place. Urged toward con-templation, perhaps by the illusion of forward progress, the neat equation of getting from there to here, she thought and spoke her thoughts aloud.

Well, in truth I can't imagine that Opa was a "wiz." About matters of sex he remained a true Victorian well into the 1970s, his nineties. While Mom-mom feigned the delicacy she had been taught to display, my grandfather really was a prude, incapable, for instance, of fathoming Mom-mom's pleasure in ribald jokes. Any report that Opa had been a great lover would not have rung true, but still I felt acutely the shame he would have suffered if he knew that his most private and, as he would have considered them, low or animal, urges had ever been the topic of discussion with anyone, let alone with me.

My grandmother had not always been so forthcoming about sex. For many years, she assumed a false mantle of modesty and seemliness. As for my mother, when I was a teenager she undressed and bathed in the dark so that not even she could witness her nudity. As I grew older, the woman with whom I showered as a child of four or five became pathologically modest.

She had been lovely nude, when I was little more than an infant. Having concluded, in her fastidiousness, that it was a tidier operation simply to bathe with me than to lean over a churning tub of child and water and soap and toys, my mother would strip with me and wash us together in my grandparents' big stall shower. Today I can tip my head back, eyes closed, and still see her as I did then, a great tall expanse of fair flesh, the dark surprises of pubic hair and nipples—hers always so much redder than mine, livid even—the shower boiling like a cauldron. My mother taught me to like showers so hot that I have never been able to bathe with anyone else without ultimately feeling damp and chilled; no one can bear the bath to be as hot as I want it to be.

My mother would stand like a Madonna, lather and shampoo rolling down her shoulders. I could hardly see her face for the steam, her strong fingers moving over my scalp, our skins turning pink then red in the spray. I hated to get out. A few years later, when I was bathing by myself, and after she had moved out of my grandparents' home for the last time, I remember bath time differently. When I showered, I did so alone, and the water was simply wet, not pleasurable or seductive. Our household frowned upon my tears, and as the tiled shower stall was one place where I could cry undetected, a red wet face being natural after a good washing, I fell into the practice of crying in the shower. Since I hardly ever cried at any other time, I saved all my sorrow for the shower and would begin weeping as I took my clothes off, not for any particular reason I could identify, but out of habit. Even today, when I bend to fill the tub or to adjust the water temperature before turning on the shower, I feel the ache in my throat. I am probably one of very few people who shed Pavlovian tears when the water pours forth from the tap over my hands and feet.

After Mother had left home, and before I was trusted to wash competently by myself, Mom-mom took charge of my baths. They occurred at six o'clock, just before dinner, and they were not particularly recreational. Occasionally, in a rare mood, my grandmother would sit on the side of the tub and tell me a story while I slowly soaked clean. But usually she would instruct me as I learned how to wield a washcloth properly.

The dirtiest place, the spot that had to be washed not once but twice at least, was *down there,* which I immediately understood to mean my genitals. I scrubbed myself; frightened, I washed there four or five times, my fingers never touching the soft folds of flesh, a washcloth doing the job; I scrubbed myself raw. And I never looked to see what I was washing. I didn't want to know what was so mysteriously dirty, what clearly got dirty by itself, of itself. My knees, gray with grime from play, required only one cursory soaping.

Only when I was almost eighteen and considering the curious fact that I had allowed a man to see what I never had did I stand naked in a dorm bathroom one night, behind a locked stall door, and put a mirror between my thighs to look, to find with my eyes the place that I had learned, like the blind, by touch. It was in college that I spent several tearful consultations with a patient doctor who asked me, please, to take only one shower a day, to give up scrubbing *down there,* to stop using feminine hygiene spray. I was so clean, so squeaky clean, that it hurt to walk; intercourse was impossible, nearly, and I had concluded that I had some horrible social disease. Between that fear and my chronic requests for pregnancy tests if my period was even a day late, I visited Student Health often enough that one concerned nurse redirected me to Student Mental Health.

Both things are true: I have never wanted not to be a woman; I have always believed that being a woman was dirty, inherently and unavoidably dirty. Once, many years after the happy hours we spent showering together, my mother told me that there were only two things that smelled like fish, and one of them was fish. I hear those words over and over, the refrain to my period, but not only then; I check during the rest of the month, too. At the end of the day I pull down my underpants and cannot drop them into the hamper without smelling the crotch, trying to decide if I should take the extra, second shower. It has been years since I have purchased or used a feminine hygiene spray, but I remember once going home from high school after my third class, because I had forgotten to use that pink aerosol can, the sweet, flowery blast of powder, cold and frosting my pubic hair like a winter beard, dusting the cotton crotch of my underwear. I went through a can every two weeks, wouldn't buy it myself, afraid that a checker might think I was a peculiarly smelly sort of girl.

My grandmother and I had some bitter, if absurd, quarrels in the supermarket. When I was fourteen or so and at the insane height of my self-consciousness, I would not buy certain products. I had the money, could get to a drugstore, but couldn't make myself gather and pay for what I needed: Kotex, Midol, feminine hygiene spray. Anything that indicated that I menstruated or smelled was too humiliating to handle in public. And the size of the Kotex box—too horrible to imagine. I wished I could use tampons, but I was too frightened, and Mom-mom was of the opinion that only fast girls, those who had been penetrated by something other than a sterile plug of cotton, used tampons.

When I finally developed the courage to push that little white applicator inside, to feel my way between my thighs, my grandmother didn't speak to me for days, assuming I had also had the nerve to leap out of virginity, and not only out of the humiliation of wearing a heavy, bloodied napkin strung between my legs by an absurd elastic belt whose clasps pinched my bottom in the back and plucked out hairs from the front. So, at the market, in the aisle marked "Health Care Products," my grandmother and I waged a desperate war. It was my habit to drop what I wanted into the cart surreptitiously—if one can sneak a two-foot box of Kotex past a spry old woman of substantial stature—and then disappear when it was time to go through the checkout, leaving my grandmother to face the indignity alone.

"Don't you see that it is much more embarrassing for a woman of my age to buy these?" she would say in a loud angry whisper. "I want you in line with me." In response I could only shake my head, tears of embarrassment smarting already in my eyes.

Ironically, the only place in the market where Mom-mom wouldn't pursue me was to the magazine stand where I would publicly page through a copy of *Playgirl,* rendering my grandmother mute with rage—she would not speak to me with that magazine before my face. I was unabashed about looking at pictures of men's penises in public—I had followed Opa to the garden toilet once when I was five, to the pool house where the floors were covered in hemp mats that smelled of chlorine. Frustrated by the gray light through the keyhole, seeing nothing more than a dark mass, ancient and larger than anticipated, I had been looking ever since at men's genitals wherever I could, trying to penetrate some mystery. I could look at *Playgirl*—relishing my grandmother's fury—but could not stand in line and pay for any product that told other people that I was a girl: that I bled and smelled. Later we would meet, Mom-mom and I, at the car as the bagger was lifting our purchases into the trunk, she too livid to speak, and I silent in my triumph.

I was apprehended late one summer night by the store detective at Barrington's supermarket. It was very hot, still in the nineties at ten o'clock; I was wearing a short tennis dress and sneakers, a cotton cardigan—not an outfit that afforded much place to secret stolen goods. The detective who took me by the elbow in the parking lot, the Santa Ana wind scattering trash between the cars, was a sober balding sweaty man with yellow teeth. He smiled as he asked me to follow him, and I started to cry, both with fear at the prospect of what I imagined would be a police record, and with humiliation because I had been caught with a box of ten tampons stuffed up my sleeve. When the time had come to pay for them, all the checkers had been men. I had developed the ability to purchase tampons from women—after all, they, too, secretly bled and smelled—but I could not let a man ring up my Tampax. And so I stole them: it seemed reasonable, I wasn't frightened walking out. After all, I'd been shoplifting for years, nothing expensive and not from good stores, but I was practiced in the art.

Upstairs in a room over the supermarket, the noise of shoppers and cash registers rising distant and dull through the floor, the kindly exasperated manager explained that the store's policy was to involve the police only after a second violation. But, since I was not yet eighteen, whoever was responsible for me would have to come pick me up from the market, they would have to be informed of my transgression. I settled into a sullen miserable heap in a yellow vinyl chair as the manager called my home. I could imagine my grandparents sitting in the living room, watching television, the phone call startling them. I had always been such a very good girl.

No amount of pleading could induce the manager to let me

go home alone. I promised that I would never return. I promised that he could arrest me if I so much as stepped through the automatic doors and into the chill wind of air-conditioning. But he was unmoved, and my grandparents soon arrived, in their overcoats, with sleepwear showing underneath. I was sure that I had finished crying until I saw the limp striped flannel legs flopping over my grandfather's gardening shoes, and noticed the frayed lace nightgown collar under Mom-mom's coat. I had sunk into an insulted silence and was glaring blackly at the door, waiting for their arrival; but that pathetic glimpse of their pajamas, the implication of crisis, of their struggling hurriedly into winter coats on a hot summer night, stepping out of slippers and into garden shoes, driving too fast to the store, only blocks from the house: this was too much. And my grandfather's shocked insistence that the store had made a mistake, that I was *incapable of stealing,* foolishly clothed in striped flannel, his red-faced choleric indignation that was sufficient to rupture my hard-won self-containment and unstick my insulted glare from the window.

Fifteen minutes later we were driving home. Mom-mom had not said one word after "What has she done?"; she was always ready to believe the worst of those she loved. So very unlike my grandfather, whose love did not allow for another's frailties. It was for him that I tried never to cry in public, always to uphold the code of stoic dignity. He was shaking his head as Mom-mom drove, apparently unable to fathom such bull-headedness on the part of the store detective who had not ultimately backed down and admitted he had been wrong, had made a mistake, had seen some other girl walk out with a box of tampons.

The lasting fear of that night was not from the sting of humiliation. As I had promised the manager, I never returned to the market, and a blush of shame rose every time I passed the store or even saw a billboard advertising one of their specials. But that was incidental, not so very troubling. What mattered most was that my grandfather refused to know me, refused to know the part of me that was wrong, that would be weak, criminal even. And because I had been caught stealing tampons, a product which was intimately connected to the Undiscussable, I could never go to him and explain my transgression. I was never allowed to have his honest love of my weakness, but only that which disallowed imperfection in his love-object. For I understood that night that my grandfather fully subscribed to the chivalric code; he could have only a reproachless princess.

When we returned to the house—the television still speaking softly into the empty living room, Mom-mom having turned down the sound as she always did when answering the phone—my mother was standing in the hall looking perplexed. She was dressed formally, in a black dress and impossibly high heels, her makeup flawless even after a long evening. She watched as Mom-mom and Opa hung up their overcoats and walked back to the living room in their pajamas. "What happened, where were you? I was frightened," she kept saying. But no one answered her.

The gynecologist has fat fingers. He presses them together and asks me questions.

"Have you ever had sexual intercourse?"

"No."

"Has a boy's penis ever been close to your genitals, during sexual play or while necking?"

"No."

The doctor is trying to discover why I have not menstruated for several months. It is the third time my mother has taken me to this doctor. He is the same man who delivered me.

Each time he asks me these same questions and he asks them twice, once while my mother is in the consultation room with me, and again after he asks her to please leave the two of us alone together for a moment to talk. My answers are the same whether she is in the room or not, and I can see that the doctor is disappointed that I do not keep girlish secrets from my mother.

Next, and in a different room, I am examined on an uphol-stered table covered with white sterile paper. There is nothing wrong with my uterus. It is small and slightly tipped forward, he tells me, but that is fine, there is no reason for it not to function. I am thin. Do I eat enough, he wants to know, and I tell him I think I do.

I should bleed, but I do not. The doctor prescribes a series of small white pills that contain synthetic estrogen and for two months my underpants are stained with a black sullen substance like mud. It is not a hopeful color, and I stop taking the pills so it will go away.

I think of fifteen as my unhappiest year. There were others, but the sadness I felt at fifteen was wild and desperate and confused, the betrayal of adolescence. I didn't yet know who I was, and there seemed no solace in who I might turn out to be. It was the year that I began decidedly to look beyond my family for love, and to try to ignore my unrequited passion for my increasingly cold and distant mother. When I was fifteen it was Corrine whom I loved.

Corrine was my best friend; she was everything I wanted to be. She was tall and thin and blond and graceful; she was a poor student and she didn't care. All those hours that I spent studying, obsessively recopying each page of homework in my tiny perfect penmanship until it was free of every possible mistake—not one smudge or blot—all the weekday evenings I earned my A's, Corrine spent watching television, waxing her legs, experimenting with eyeliner and trimming split ends one by one from her beautiful mane of hair with manicure scissors. She was flat-chested, as I longed to be. Her fingernails were more than an inch long; she had a hundred bottles of nail polish, even black, scented like licorice. Her parents were wonderful in their eccentricity: they believed they communicated with spirits. Possibly they took drugs.

There were framed photographs of Paramahansa Yogananda in each room of their house, and tattered copies of his *Autobiography of a Yogi* were constantly emerging from under newspapers, piles of clothing, tumbled in with the greasy silverware in the kitchen drawer. On Sunday afternoons, the Martins went to a beautiful park in the Pacific Palisades where they participated in Buddhist meditation gatherings. It was called the Self-Realization Fellowship Center, and I accompanied them there some summer days; I would sit in a wooden temple, on a dusty floor, and self-consciously murmur with other swaying, chanting Californians. After we chanted, we walked, not speaking, through the park. The days were bright but I was usually cold in the wind from the sea, and I remember my long hair snapping with static electricity.

Naturally Corrine was far less interested in the spiritual progress of her parents than I was; she despised their affected bohemianism and complained about the way her mother walked through the house naked. I remember playing in the pool at Corrine's house when we were thirteen or so, and seeing Ingrid—I was not to call her Mrs. Martin—in their living room reading a magazine. The spring light reflected off the glass of the French doors, but still I could see that she was wearing no clothes and her breasts were sad and pendulous, heavy with—at least this is how it seemed to me at the time—sorrow. Corrine had a secret stash of photographs of her mother as a young model in Copenhagen, and she had so changed that I felt sad whenever I saw her after that afternoon, sorry at the sudden recognition of human frailty and mortality.

Later she came out onto the patio to bring us towels and, although she had put on a long T-shirt, when she bent over to set the towels on a chaise, I could see a blond smudge of pubic hair, and I, too, felt Corrine's embarrassment. But, for the most part, I found relief in the Martins' liberalism, certainly in the escape from discipline that going to Corrine's house represented. When I grew up, and grew sufficiently apart from Corrine to be able to see who she really was, I understood that even as I had loved her parents for their lack of stability, so she had loved Mom-mom and Opa for their apparent normalcy, for the security they conveyed, for their age and their constancy. She had needed some sense that life proceeded according to rules and expectations: she needed people who had tea each day at four. I needed something else.

Even so, we spent most of our time at Corrine's house instead of at mine, and there was a time when I spent every Friday night at Corrine's. I took an overnight bag to school and after our last class together (biology, which Corrine was failing despite my tutoring her each Wednesday, a useless exercise that devolved after a few tries into hourly sessions of giggling and gossiping) we rode the bus to the Martins' home in the canyon, the wood house almost obscured by tall, fragrant eucalyptus trees, the walkways clogged with their long graceful leaves.

As soon as our uniforms were off and we had ravaged the kitchen—never a satisfying foray since the Martins, dietary Californians before it was popular to be so, had only things like lumpy whole-grain bread and cold lentils in their refrigerator, a few dried fruits in the cupboard on a good Friday afternoon— we would lie on the floor in our shorts and tank tops and make prank phone calls. Like a lot of the parents of children who went to our prep school, Corrine's father worked in television. A producer, he had a separate phone line in an office that was set up in the Martins' den, and once, when Mr. Martin wasn't home and Mrs. Martin was on a sleep cure in their bedroom, we spent nearly ten hours—from five until almost three in the morning—making calls.

In the beginning we dialed randomly, and asked the standard "Is your refrigerator running?" sort of questions. But, soon bored with that, we developed elaborate ruses, often scripted on paper—they were too complex to memorize—the object being to keep the chosen victim on the line for as long as possible. We made up a company, the Handy Dandy Plastic Bathroom Products Company, and offered ten items, soap dishes, towel racks, wastebaskets and more, in decorator shades—Avocado Green, Harvest Gold, Parrot Pink—and took countless fake COD orders from housewives. After midnight we called night attendants at mortuaries. Bored and lonely, they were our best bet and would stay on the phone for hours sometimes, until a body came in.

On Saturday morning we would get up very late. We were unrepentant vandals and shoplifters in those days. Four blocks from Corrine's house was a half-constructed apartment complex, ten units at that stage of construction whereby they were skeletons half hung with Sheetrock, exposed wires and plumbing, windows in phantom walls. One Saturday we climbed the building like monkeys and came upon a sealed plastic sack of a white caulking material. We squeezed the toothpastelike substance into pipes that were not yet connected to toilets; we finger-painted with it in wild ghostly scribbles on the gray Sheetrock. We snarled up the wires and broke the windows and then slipped out the empty door frames onto Cardboard Hill, a steep grass slope right next to the building site, and a favorite place among the local hooligans, who used great broken pieces of packing boxes as rough toboggans and slid down the ripe dry summer grass into a gulch filled with trash. Once we found a switchblade in the rubble at the bottom. Not far from it was a yellowed excerpt from a snuff magazine; the article was called "Cold Glass and Hot Ass," and I remember that we read it, fascinated, and later put the two—the knife and the pornography—together into an imagined portrait of a crazed sex fiend who roamed the hills behind Corrine's home. At the very idea, the hair on my arms rose and my heart beat fast.

Pic 'n' Save was ten blocks from Corrine's; we robbed it every Saturday. A discount store that sold closeout items that other stores couldn't unload, it was crammed with trash, especially cheap, vulgar clothing and clunky costume jewelry. We wore big bulky army surplus coats and filled the linings with necklaces and earrings, bracelets, scarves, sleazy tank tops, hats even. In the naïve supposition that we would never be caught if we left the store with a purchase, paying for one item, we squeezed past the checkout with our clothes heavy, sometimes rattling with contraband, and gave the clerk a handful of change for some plastic ring. We were never caught, but I was deathly afraid each time—even more so after being apprehended for stealing the tampons—and saw stars as I handed the ignorant or totally uncaring checker my money.

In a short while Corrine's closet was filled with trash: clothing we wouldn't normally be caught dead wearing, gaudy costume jewelry, hideous scarves and accessories. Suddenly one weekend, inspired by all the loot which had piled into great drifts, no hangers left, every box overfilled, we created two characters or alter egos, creatures of our imagination but fully formed. Corrine idly put on a red hat and earrings, a slutty lace shirt, and began to talk. Her voice came out different, high and nasal, and Cornelia Schnook was born. In a green miniskirt, white vinyl boots and blue glass tiara, I found myself transformed into Edwynna Goulashe. A vista of unsupervised Saturdays took on a whole new character.

Hours of preparation preceded each appearance of the "dreadful tarts," as my mother and grandmother called the characters when they saw them, only once, on the day of our school's Halloween parade. Cornelia wore a red wig, Edwynna was a peroxide blonde; each wig required washing, setting and a vast amount of carefully applied hair spray in order to remain intact for one of our escapades. We spent the night before an outing sorting through clothes, picking out coordinating jewelry, setting the wigs, doing our nails, and, of course, planning the next day in detail. After a few months, Cornelia and Edwynna had every prop imaginable—Corrine and I had spent hours, days, in the creation of fake driver's licenses, fake credit cards, pictures of boyfriends and family members, all drawn and inked meticulously on scraps of paper and laminated with layers of cellophane tape.

We were delighted to discover that, dressed as Cornelia and Edwynna, we could pass as adults, we could drink in bars, we could explore the creepy shops on Sunset and Hollywood boulevards, the ones whose windows were painted over and that showed movies for a quarter. It wasn't that anyone accepted our obviously forged identification, but that all the makeup and the wigs, the layers of bizarre clothing, masked our real age as much as it lent cover to our usual shyness.

Neither of us had a car, so we enlisted our friend Robert as a chauffeur, one whose name became Rocco Zim de Boco. With Rocco we visited every cheap tourist attraction, trailing dyed and shedding feather boas. We went to Grauman's Chinese, the sculpture garden at Forest Lawn, homes of the stars located with "movie maps" which we bought from a man in an old white station wagon parked at the intersection of Sunset and Rodeo. The maps included the homes of !One Hundred Stars! marked by little asterisks on a poor-quality Xeroxed road map of Beverly Hills. Many were out of date or simply wrong, but enough were correct to hold our interest for weeks.

Once we had positively identified a few bona fide movie-star residences, Corrine decided that we should return in the middle of the night and steal movie-star garbage. Robert would pick us up at one in the morning, after Corrine's parents were asleep. He'd cut the car engine and coast down the hill to her driveway, where we would be waiting in the shadows of the eucalyptus, our footfalls muffled by the thick carpet of leaves. Once we were in the car, he'd release the brake and we'd slide slowly down past a few more houses before he'd turn the key and gun the engine back to life.

We took the big black bags from the Dumpster behind Cher's house, from Lucille Ball's six shining new metal trash cans, from the end of Charo's private road. We ran, crouching, down the little service alleys behind the big Beverly Hills homes, throwing the bagged garbage into Robert's open trunk as he drove slowly before us, lights off.

Collections emerged from the refuse. Having long watched *The Sonny and Cher Show,* we were both half in love with the tall beautiful singer, her raven hair, her bare midriff and spike heels. We could live without Sonny—were pleased that Cher had dumped him for a rock star—but every clue that could be gleaned from Cher's garbage we pursued zealously. We found empty packages that had enclosed a particular soap or cosmetic and combed pharmacies and department stores until we found the same products. We switched underarm deodorants and used Secret, which came in the same little pink flowered box that we had found in Cher's garbage. And we salvaged the little mats of black hair we assumed were combed out of her hairbrush and soaked them in diluted shampoo and then conditioned them and combed out the snarls into long shining strands. After twenty or so trips, we each had a sparse ponytail, a charm almost, or a fetish, which we kept in our lockers at school.

*W*hen I can't sleep I slip down the stairs from my room, stepping carefully on only the outer margins of each carpeted step in order to avoid a creaking floorboard. I stop in the kitchen to make a cup of instant coffee, very black, and then I slip into the living room and close the door behind me. Mom-mom doesn't let me drink coffee, but I have discovered its seductions on my own and keep a jar of instant hidden behind the canisters of tea. Ever since the beginning of the eighth grade I've been drinking it at night after they go to sleep.

In the living room, I get the remote control from the depths of Opa's armchair and flip the channels past the late movies and prerecorded news recaps—it is after midnight—and I land on 52, the prayer hotline. Sometimes I have to call twenty or thirty times, but I always get through.

"Jesus does love you, what is your need?" One of the fat, earnest operators takes the call.

"I'm an amputee. I have no arms or legs," I say. Ever since Brother Andrew asked all the crippled viewers to put their *"afflicted limbs"* on their television sets so he could cure them over the airwaves, I've said I didn't have any limbs. I don't want to be dismissed by some hocus pocus panacea.

"I had the operator connect me from my special speaker phone. I lack for nothing material, but I am so unhappy. Please help me. Every day I'm in torment. My husband left me after the accident—he sends money but never visits. I have no children. I want Jesus to send me a friend."

I watch as my call is taken on the air. Not broadcast, but the fattest woman, the ringmaster of the ten or so operators standing by, paraphrases my wish. She asks all the viewers to keep me in their prayers, to start to pray for me right this instant.

"What is your name, honey?" she says into the receiver.

"Saraphina," I say—this is currently my favorite name. I do not hesitate; I'm a pro at this, having rehearsed the answers to all possible questions many times, and having talked to so many of the hotline volunteers. This is the first time, though, that my call is chosen for the show.

"I'm talking to Saraphina," announces the woman, and she sways slightly with emotion. *"Saraphina, sweetheart,"* she says, *"You always have a friend in Jesus and you've got to hold on to that promise. Jesus understands your loneliness. Remember the Garden of Gethsemane. He knows that you need mortal companionship and we're all going to ask it of the Lord."*

It's over then and I thank her.

Oddly, and despite my healthy adolescent cynicism, when I turn off the television, I feel ashamed. The living room is very dark and quiet and I lie curled in Opa's chair. I cannot muster the glee I had anticipated, and I fall asleep and dream that I am *forced to wear a placard with the word "Afflicted" written on it with big black letters. I am a sort of ambulatory prop for Brother Andrew's prayer hour, and every time there is the sound of a chime, a high sweet bell like the one used during the Eucharist at mass, I must come onstage and stand in the spotlight with my placard.*

One August, Corrine came to stay with us at our cottage in La Jolla. No other friend would do to assuage my loneliness, to relieve the midsummer confinement. All through junior high, there had been no other best friend, no one who could penetrate the secret blind of our complex, endless practical jokes and coded conversation and vast enacted fantasies.

This was the summer that our blood ran suddenly hotter, that our families complained we were "out of hand." Everything was by turns funny or tragic; we were constantly convulsed with chaotic emotion, doubled over chairs in laughter, or weeping limply in our bedrooms. A month before, I had broken my toe, having kicked the dresser in an attack of mute rage against my grandmother—I no longer remember the cause, merely my huge and apoplectic tantrum, my incapacitating anger with all things adult and stodgy and insensitive.

When Corrine arrived I stopped speaking in the usual native tongue, my vocabulary suddenly constricted to a hundred or so favorite coded words, those dozen phrases we could apply to every situation before falling into spasms of helpless laughter.

Each morning Corrine and I woke late and went immediately to the beach for a full day of tanning. We pulled on our bikinis and gathered our towels and baby oil and novels and radio and Tab. Corrine wore a T-shirt over her flat chest—she was so thin that her top never fit and she did not always remember not to raise her arms over her head. When she did, it rode up over her ribs and exposed her nipples, their pale pink almost invisible against her white skin. My own bathing suit was scant—three scraps of cloth and a complex arrangement of strings (I had long ago learned to gauge the success of my swimwear by the vehemence of my grandmother's protests)—and I spent a few minutes before the mirror, settling it over my flesh and aligning the pieces of fabric with my tan lines. I pulled on shorts to walk down the hill to Shell Beach, but left my chest bare, nearly.

On the beach at last, we left no exposable flesh unburned, careful even to tilt our heads back to bare the length of the throat, like the figure of the choked victim in the poster that described mouth-to-mouth resuscitation, the poster hanging in the forgotten high school's science building. In this uncomfortable posture, we avoided the dreaded white crescent that appeared under careless tanners' chins. We would lie first on our backs listening to the radio, then on our stomachs reading, then on our sides, talking. Whenever we were too hot we walked self-consciously to the water and then swam out to the big seal rock, climbing up its side, laughing, the water slipping in thick streams down our oiled legs, our fastidious fingers avoiding the birdlime as we climbed onto the top.

Back on the beach we shook the sand from the towels, and

realigned them with the sun's angle. Spreading oil between each other's shoulder blades—that one unreachable spot. We remained at the beach until the sun went nearly down and the chill breeze came in off the ocean and made our long wet hair feel cold and brackish and heavy on our backs, the flesh of our arms and thighs rising in goose bumps. Then we would stand finally and fold the towels, silently gather our gear and walk back to the cottage.

We ate dinner later than my grandparents and then joined them for television in the front room. But my grandfather was sole controller of the programming, and we rarely wanted to watch the shows he liked—*Meet the Press, Washington Week in Review, 60 Minutes.* Soon we would return to the bedroom we shared and lie on the big mushy queen-sized bed to talk. The old chenille spread was sandy and scrofulous, testimony to years of carelessly discarded suits and towels, and we picked at its threads with our long, manicured nails. Or we might go uptown for an ice cream. Or walk to the beach where we had lain and see its difference under the moon. Around midnight, when my grandparents had gone to their room with its two chaste twin beds, we seized control of the television. The master bedroom was ours—we shared the huge soft bed and rolled unconsciously into its depressed doughy center each night as we slept, waking with limbs tangled; the smell of sleep and youth and the sea washed over us with the bedclothes, the limp sheets, twisted and heavy with salt air. As Mom-mom and Opa slept, unwaking in their deafness, we watched old movies, lay with our heads together on the old sandy rug as faded images of Clark Gable and Claudette Colbert, Bette Davis, played over our lazy long legs, shaved and oiled and fragrant, the barest cutoffs trailing white threads on our thighs. Soon the effects of hours in the sun, of swimming and playing and talking, acted on us and we fell asleep under the muted drama.

We woke to a test pattern and went to bed just before dawn.

But one night we turned off the television after my grandparents were in bed and, we hoped, asleep. We weren't tired, not a bit, and we wanted to get out of the cottage. Silently, we dressed in the bedroom. Slipped into our sundresses, sandals. Brushed our hair and put it up on our heads. Lip oil, scented like musk and applied with a wand. We shared an old eye pencil I had filched from my mother's makeup drawer, and quickly collected our money.

Uptown, breathlessly crossing the street after the ninety-four stairs, taken two at a jump, we knocked on the door of the corner liquor store which had closed at midnight. A young man of twenty-five or so, his face livid with acne, called out "Closed!" but we stood until he relented and unlocked the bolt. Corrine slipped in before me and waited at the counter. Alcohol was clearly out of reach, despite the expertly wielded eye pencil. We would try for cigarettes.

"Register's closed," said the man. Corrine's hand was on a package of eight slender cigars.

"They're for my father—he sent me. You don't think I'd smoke cigars, do you?" The man said nothing. "He asked for these, too." She selected a tiny flat box of ten aspirin from a display on the counter and slid it toward him, as if the medication would lend an air of legitimacy to the purchase. He looked at us, then shrugged and took our money.

"No change," he said, "register's closed for the night."

He unlocked the door and we fled with our cigars.

When we unwrapped them in the half-light by the billiard hall, they smelled sweet, terribly sweet, and we examined the package and discovered they were cherry-flavored. Corrine produced the lighter that she always carried and we lit the long brown "cigarillos" and inhaled the thick smoke deeply until we could hardly stand. When we were dizzy enough to feel drunk, we ground them out and went into a local bar, The Round

House Pool Hall. Out of place in the affluent resort town, it catered almost exclusively to sailors from the nearby naval base and was up a dark flight of dirty, carpeted stairs, over the delicatessen on the corner.

The long, sticky-looking bar was deserted and the pool hall was empty, nearly. Two sailors, their thin necks thrust forward in concentration, watched as an older officer broke the racked set of balls. The billiards rolled smoothly over the stained felt; under the light, they provided the only color in the drab room. As we walked toward the table, the sailors looked up. Young, barely eighteen, their faces sunburned and earnest and sweet. Their voices and the shy ducking of their heads said they were from Kansas or Nebraska or Michigan—not California, but a state less brash. Landlocked, they must have sought the end of the land and the soil that had perhaps indentured their weary fathers. They wanted the sea. San Diego. Now they had a weekend pass.

We stood shyly just inside the circle of light from the ersatz Tiffany lamp over the table. We lit new cigars and scuffed our sandals along the filthy indoor-outdoor carpeting. Corrine launched into a hushed complex story of an imaginary friend—staged gossip—and I laughed unnaturally.

Another man appeared, gray-haired and in civilian's clothes: he joined the officer in a game of eight ball. They seemed not to notice us, or the sailors. When they were through, they returned to the bar and one of the sailors collected the balls from the net pockets and arranged them, as gently as if they were eggs, and neatly, each number displayed on top, in the plastic triangle. "D'you play?" he said when he was finished.

Corrine shrugged, put out her cigar and took a cue from the rack. With the little blue square of chalk, she coated the end of the cue, screwing the morsel so hard that a fine blue film settled on the polished wood frame of the table. I wiped it away as she took aim and bounced the cue ball toward the regiment of colored balls. One rolled slowly, slowly toward a side pocket and then finally dropped in after an agonizing pause. "Yo're stripes," the sailor said.

Their game progressed slowly, and the other sailor moved ever closer to me where I stood by the rack of cues. Had the game not been so boring I might not have noticed his approach. "D'you play?" he asked.

I shook my head no.

He said nothing but watched the game for a moment. Just as Corrine's green ball cracked into her opponent's blue and knocked it into the pocket, he put his hand, hot and rough, in mine. I said nothing and he left it there—I felt a callus, long and ridged just at the top of his palm where it met his fingers—until the game was over.

When his buddy asked then if I played, I said yes, and took Corrine's cue, handing her my still burning cigar as she stood in my place by the cues. As we played—I, too, became stripes out of clumsiness—I watched and saw the sailor's hand creep into Corrine's as well. Shy, she turned her head toward the opposite wall, but left her hand with his. I tried to divide my attention between the game and Corrine, but after I once glanced up from an impossible arrangement of billiards—not a shot to be had—and saw the sailor's rough hand slip into Corrine's sundress to explore her chest, I lost all concentration and the game was quickly over.

The sailor took my cue stick, pulled it from my loose grasp as I stood awkward and silent at the end of the table, and replaced it gently in the hanging rack on the wall. He looked at me and at Corrine carefully, as though trying to estimate our ages, and then asked if he could buy us a beer. I might have stayed out of a sense of adventure, but Corrine said, "No thank you," refusing his offer so quickly and in a voice so low that it was almost a whisper. She took my hand and pulled me toward the exit. The vision of his face, confused by the swiftness of the rejection, imprinted on my consciousness and lingered, surfacing unbidden over the next few days.

At the cottage we smoked the last two cigars, their smoke rising thick and blue and sickening around our heads. The moon was high and hard and bright and in its light I saw where a blemish was coming to the surface on Corrine's chin. I wanted to ask about the sailor, why she had let him touch her and then fled so quickly, and I wondered if she had seen his dumb look as she turned abruptly away. The bodice of her sundress, its pink ribbons, still looked rumpled. We had run from the pool hall quickly and awkwardly, my sandals catching in the dirty torn carpeting as we chased each other down the staircase and onto the corner. The liquor store was closed, dark, and we walked silently down the long flight of cement steps from the town.

It was almost three o'clock and very quiet, no cars on the street. I wanted to walk all the way down, past the houses and the park and down onto the beach, to feel the clean surf before we went to sleep, but was too tired suddenly and felt the smoke in my throat and lungs. I thought of how we would wake in the morning, her long warm thighs bare against mine, our nightgowns having ridden up around our waists as we slept. Sometimes we kicked one another: a mistake, a dream. Her blond hair would smell of the cigars, stale and rank. I could still feel where the sailor's callus had rested against my palm, and I imagined the feel of his hands, dry and hot, on Corrine's small smooth breast.

I dream of Mother and she is beautiful. Wearing black, her hair so dark and her skin so white, her beauty is like a fairy tale unfolding, luminous. I am in bed in a dormitory, and this apparition of my mother approaches my bed. On her breast, pinned to her black gown, is an orchid breathing: I am strangely aware of the flower's respiration. Suddenly, a wind picks up, and the sweet breath of the orchid is torn from the petals. I am afraid, remembering that plants must be taken from the bedroom at night because they steal oxygen from the air, and as she comes closer I think with a sudden clarity, this is the angel of death and she is beautiful, so beautiful, but I must not let her touch me. And so, when Mother reaches toward me, I strike her. I hit her breast and she begins to cry and wail and she asks me why I want to hurt her. I am ashamed and cry too, and I tell her that she was so unearthly that I believed she was an angel come to

126

take me away. But she will not stop weeping, she cries and shakes her head. "Isabel," she says, "Isabel. You were always a lunatic." And I take her words literally and try to remember what phase of the moon we are in.

Waking, I remember that the dress she wears in my dream is the one she and I bought together.

We look for that dress for days, as I remember.

We go to I. Magnin's, to Bonwit's, to Bullock's, and finally to Saks where she finds the perfect dress.

My father, whom she has not seen for some months—not since before the mastectomy—is coming to Los Angeles, and they are going to have dinner together. She has not eaten very much for a few weeks, and the cut of the dress reveals sharp collarbones. The tight black bodice smoothly sculpts the remaining breast and its false twin into one lovely youthful line. It seems impossible that she look so beautiful, so vulnerable: like a girl before a prom.

The date is as disappointing, as clumsily botched, as irrevocably wounding as a terrible prom, a first dance upon which too many hopes were laid.

I stay too long at my mother's apartment, and he arrives too early. I open the door wearing my mother's new dress. Like Cinderella, I had slipped it on, just to see if it would fit, while she was in the bath.

My father invites me to come with them: he takes us both to dinner. At the old-fashioned Italian restaurant, he pays for a violin serenade, and for a man dressed like a magician in a cape to take a Polaroid photograph of me.

He says three times to my mother that he cannot believe how beautiful I have grown, and there is something predatory in his comment. His eyes are very blue and very bloodshot and the redness of their rims intensifies the gaze of his one good eye; the other drifts as if it has found a more compelling subject at another table. He reaches past the cutlery, the wine bottle, and takes my hand in his, and his skin is dry and very smooth. When he releases my hand, he picks up the photograph from the table and tucks it into his breast pocket.

I am still wearing my mother's dress: a switch, after the initial mistake, useless. I can see two things in my mother's face. She is silent but her eyes convey, in equal measure, anger and fear. The anger I understand: I have once again appeared somewhere that I am not wanted. Her relationship with my father is one that, starting with my birth, has always been compromised by my arrival. The fear I do not understand, but I catch it and find myself sitting on my hands, as I was forced to do in grade school, a means of punishment and of preventing further offense. Whether from embarrassment or wool, I am very hot in her dress.

Two years later, I wear that same dress to her funeral. It is the only formal black dress I have.

I know my great-grandmother because Mom-mom has told me of her mother. She was the woman who stepped out of her bathtub in Shanghai and into the great white linen bath sheet that her servant held up, high over her dark head, eyes closed, and face turned away even behind the sheet. My grandmother's mother was modest; no one ever saw her nude. In 1930 she died of breast cancer, the terrible kind that ulcerates the skin. Her doctor had seen only a small area of flesh, out of context.

They say it skips generations, breast cancer. So, were I to have a daughter, she too might die. Mom-mom tells me this, speaking with sad, hostile conviction.

"I shouldn't have chanced it," she said. "It was a mistake to have a child." She never offered her breast to my mother, believing it was a means of transferring the disease.

"Don't worry," I answer tartly. "I wouldn't think of having children."

My great-grandmother's doctor insisted that she eat ham—he believed in it for strength. Orthodox about matters of diet, she refused, and later died, as she would have anyway, ham or no ham. Many years before, in 1901, when her only son was to be circumcised, she had not been so concerned with the laws of her faith: she refused to allow the only rabbi in Shanghai to touch her son's genitals because she saw that his fingers were unclean, dark lines of grime under each long, yellowed nail. Her son died uncircumcised, and for that, and because she had again disobeyed and had a stone cherub put on his headstone, the Pharisees of Shanghai came in the night and desecrated the little monument. They tore the angel down and broke the imported Italian marble that blanketed his short grave.

On the morning that her little brother died, of meningitis following an infection and high fever brought on by teething, my grandmother saw her father weep for the first and only time. He was kneeling by his bed—not *their* bed, for his wife slept alone in the big bed he visited, but his own narrow bed—and his head was in his hands, and his arms were resting on the counterpane; and he was sobbing, quite aloud, so that a small girl of five could understand, even from the hall, that her father was crying. My grandmother remembers the scene very well, and has told me of it often enough so that I too remember it, as if it were a record of my own sorrow and loss.

I know my grandmother's mother, because I can see her before me. Her name, affectionately, was Dolly; she had five sisters: Vera, Maisy, Daisy, Violet and Rose. They all were born and lived in New South Wales, in Australia. Dolly married my grandmother's father when she was quite young, twenty. His first wife had died, with his newborn son, of the sort of disease that a delicate aristocrat might contract in Asia;

130

that is, she died of a tropical fever, raving. Dolly, Mom-mom's mother, met her husband through the family of the dead bride, who had been a childhood friend. Dolly was not quite so aristocratic, and hardier. Still, her pictures show a woman who is reserved and pale; even as she looks directly at the lens of the camera, her vision is inward and away from those who might want to know something of her. Mom-mom said that her aunts, especially Maisy and Rose, were quite different and complained of Dolly's shyness. All of the sisters except Dolly played poker. Dolly, though, when traveling uphill—she was a slender woman, not burdensome—would always get out of the rickshaw and walk. She walked before the coolie, not beside him, but she did walk when her sisters would have ridden.

I know my great-grandmother because I can feel her in my heart and blood and bones. She is the woman and womb that started me, the first one that I know, for all Mom-mom can tell me of my great-great-grandmother is that she was "sweet and refined and thin as a stick," and I do not know her. But Mom-mom's mother, Dolly, I feel. The weight of her long curling hair on her neck as she took it down each night: I feel that. The gentle pull of the boar bristles as her servant, perhaps the same one who held the linen towel aloft—perhaps not, they had a staff of forty coolies—the young Chinese girl, dispensed with the tangles, her touch very light so as not to disturb Missee Dolly who often had headaches. I feel those too, the sick headaches in the terrible humidity of Shanghai, the fear of typhoid and cholera. I know that she worried that the carbolic soap on the vegetables from their own gardens was not enough to protect them, that the rabbits would become rabid, that the cows would again die, mysteriously, and that new ones would once more have to be brought, thin and sick with the lolling of the ship, from England. That the chickens, buff Orpingtons, white Orpingtons, shining black Orpingtons, all too beautiful for chickens, would again start to lay the eggs that were not right, membraneless yolks that bled into the whites and ended in one viscid mucoid dollop slipping from the shell into the mixing bowl. That yet another cook would leave, and again she would have to begin the laborious process of training a frightened, slavish and nervous coolie; that it would take a month perhaps before the woman would even approach the towering enameled gas stove.

My grandmother had nightmares in Shanghai. The country frightened her so that years later, safe in an American city, she would cross the street to avoid walking under the awning of a Chinese restaurant. "I don't care if the Communists have cleaned it up," she'd say. "If you'd seen the filth I have, you'd never set foot in such a place." Just the words *chop suey* brought on a tirade. Once I made her a cup of ginseng tea. After she drank it, complaining between sips about my allegiance to unpalatable health foods, I told her that I'd bought the root in a Chinese apothecary downtown. She stood up from the table, went straight to her comprehensively stocked medicine chest—a real chest with brass hardware— dosed herself with a cathartic and didn't speak to me for two days.

There was a creek on the perimeter of her parents' estate in Shanghai's British concession, and she told me that the smell that rose from the creek was fetid, thick with pestilence and danger. It crept under the doors and over the sills of any windows left open for a breath of air; it slipped like a foul ghost through the mosquito netting. It lay on my grandmother's chest like a putrefying corpse, and she sat up and screamed in her bed. For I am not the only woman in my family to be afflicted with nightmares.

Agie, her nurse, stirred in the next room. Drunk, she had been drinking heavily ever since the death of the baby. Not her fault, of course, but still her insupportable sorrow. Mom-mom's father, a very proper wog in his stiff collar and waistcoat, his watch fobs, coming in each morning to pick up William, his son, to take the baby, freshly bathed and dressed, down to the breakfast room. The sight of that man disheveled and on his knees in his bedroom, praying, bargaining with the unseen, unknown, as the fever rose. This was the second son he lost. Weeping when the little boy died. Agie, who liked brandy well enough when things were fine, embraced the bottle after the death of the child, gave it to the little girls sometimes.

My grandmother's cries and screams could not penetrate Agie's stupor. She thought it must be another child, dead for months now, who was crying, begging at the windows. Finally Agie was sent back to Scotland in disgrace, her career as a nanny over.

I look so like these women who are now gone, the echo of my mother's flesh in my own; each finger wears her nail. More startling are the similarities when I see myself nude. Though you are dead, Mother, we talk through this sameness of flesh, each bone, each rib, dust unto dust.

The full-length mirror reveals your knees, not a feature I would have chosen to preserve, but never mind, our breasts the same fullness, the identical droop, nipples winking in collusion, cheating death and time and all that would separate us.

It frightens me, this terrible sameness, for we are not one woman, are we, and yet there is this unassailable truth of being hers and theirs. Even my great-grandmother can call to me and claim her ears and jaw. Were all the features returned to their rightful owners I should be unclothed, without any flesh with which to breath and eat and speak. My lips, even, yours.

In summer, the hills of Los Angeles, the dry canyons, the highways—everything was burned to a ripe yellow, the oak trees were black against the gold hills. California is beautiful in the dry summer when forest fires are raging, the skies smudged with smog and smoke. The pleasure I take in driving a car will always be associated with such a landscape—of arid, dusty desert-ocean air, the wind and the heat and the dryness making inanimates—clothing, hair—alive with static electricity; the deceptively carefree radio and its songs of summer and of love, of teenage loss quelled within a week by a new love. The car windows down, the screams of boys cutting through hearts filled to bursting with youth, my own heart climbing the ladder of my ribs with the crazy joy of being sixteen and driving by myself on the old gray highway through the dry gold California hills, on the way to the beach. The songs on the radio said all that I wanted to feel, pushed all that I didn't from my young dark head; for a moment I could imagine myself as who the radio, the television, the billboards all said I should be.

My grandmother's car was long and smooth; I could not feel the road beneath the wheels and sometimes as I drove I also could not feel the distance traveled by my heart, the emotional road.

In college I started taking amphetamines, at first because they provided a means by which I could stay up all night and study. But soon, on a trip for cigarettes, perhaps, I discovered the pleasures of driving while on speed, and then for years I never made a long road trip without drugs. The euphoria of physical motion forward coupled with the illusory chemical freedom and strength was intoxicating. The road spun out from under my car, I shifted gears with angelic grace and power: my head absolutely spun with the sense that I had escaped the snares of daily chores and worries. My brain leaped ahead of the spinning tires. For a moment I had transcended humanity and felt that anything was possible, achievable. My head flamed with love for everyone I knew. Each time I took speed I would plan reconciliations, mentally reunite myself with people I had lost. Often, when I returned from a long drive, I would write letters, and if I went so far as to mail them, they became letters I very much regretted for their fevered devotion. I had composed them in the car, but once the drug wore off and the enchantment passed, they seemed foolish, and my hopes for communion foolish as well.

When my mother was in the hospital, I ran errands to escape her deathbed. There was one month that I spent almost every night with her, sleeping fitfully in the unoccupied bed next to hers, because Mother was in a crisis: a sever bladder and kidney infection, high fevers. Her life was threatened in an immediate way, death suddenly closer, and we didn't want it to happen when she was alone. Mom-mom or Albert came on those mornings or afternoons when I was in class, and so we spelled one another in the attempt not to leave her. I was lonely. I almost never saw my grandmother or Albert, just passed them in hallways, exchanging a word or a brief wave, and I didn't really interact with my mother who, much of the time, was too ill to talk. And, of course, I had little time for friends or school.

I felt claustrophobic in the hospital. I slept badly if at all, since out of cowardice—not wanting the silence—we both chose to leave the television on all night, its light playing wanly over the walls and bedclothes. When I did manage to stay the entire night—sometimes I'd go to Mom-mom's at around four after Mother had fallen asleep—I would spend much of the following day in the car, if I didn't have a class I absolutely had to attend. My temporary absence was all right with Mother who, despite her delirium, usually had a little list of errands for me to run, things she didn't really need but felt comforted by: novels she wouldn't open, lip balm and pink Kleenex and hand cream, socks, bed jackets, a bacon-cheese deluxe from the Fatburger on Melrose which she never even unwrapped.

While most of the errands were simple to accomplish, trying to find a wig became a major trauma. Everywhere I went I carried a scrap of paper with measurements of my mother's head written on it: crown to ear, nape to forehead, circumference of her skull at just one inch above the ears. You'd think there would be a hundred wig stores in Los Angeles. What about all those failed B-movie stars? Surely they didn't all wear their own hair. But they must at least have been able to afford a custom wig maker, a custom wig maker with an unlisted phone number.

I could find only two "Wigmarts," each about twenty-five miles from the hospital, and I went back and forth through the late September smog, bearing unacceptable purchases. The

ladies behind the counter soon lost all their effusive sympathy
for the brave generous young woman I had at first appeared to
be: they began to examine each return with deliberate care, as
if I were a person with some shady purpose, rather than a
daughter with a rapidly balding, impossible-to-please mother
who had always preferred to shop for herself, but was now
incapable of doing so.

Each style of wig had an embarrassing name, such as "Fancifree," and the salesladies insisted upon referring to the hair-
pieces by these names, demanding clarification when I
mumbled a description. "The short, sort of curly brown one"
would not do; the errand must be as humiliating as possible.
"Fancifree, do you mean, or Glorious?" they would ask sourly.

Each Breezette, or Lindabella, or whatever, was rejected in
turn by my mother, raised up to full stature in her electric bed.
The slender IV tube—dripping antibiotics instead of chemo—
got snaggled around her arm when she pulled one wig off her
poor threadbare head, and we actually contrived to pull the
needle out as Breezette went askew and summarily fell down
behind the bed. The hank of false hair draped itself limply over
the tangle of wires and oxygen tubing that projected from a
panel on the wall. I snatched it up and stuffed it back into the
shopping bag just as an irritable nurse appeared in answer to
the electronic IV monitor's desperate paging. So near, apparently, to death was my mother that her open vein didn't even
bleed when the needle fell out. The nurse, one of several who
were new on the wing, examined the vein with desultory care
and glowered at me in suspicion. The night before, on a walk
down the hall to the linen supply closet for a fresh towel, I had
been mistaken for a patient on the lam. One of the other new
nurses had made me sit in the waiting room in my flannel
nightgown and knee socks while she got the supervisor, who,
having seen me for so many weeks, dismissed my captor's

concern with merely a flick of her hand before turning back down the hall to the front desk. That had been at three A.M. Now the afternoon nurse said nothing as she went to work finding a new vein and puncturing it with a fresh shunt. The wound responded with a reassuring spurt of blood.

I started to leave, bound for another return and temporary purchase, as the nurse swabbed up the smear of life. Mother was too snowed by the morphine, too dazed by the fever, to take much notice of her wrist's being manipulated, her slack arm tied off with a rubber tourniquet. After the frenzied trying on of this last wig—a process requiring so much of her attention and energy that she didn't even speak, merely pulled it off and thrust it back in my direction just before it fell behind the bed—Mother was so exhausted that she seemed to fall asleep while the nurse was taping the clear tubing to her wrist. She muttered in an aggrieved way, saying "No, No, No," and pulled her arm away, but her eyes remained quite closed.

She moved her free hand vaguely toward me and turned her head so that, were her eyes open, she would be looking at me.

"Isabel," she said, slowly, as if dreaming, "Isabel, you took my dress, my black dress that I bought for your father's visit." She paused as though waiting for a response, and when I made none, she sighed deeply, so deeply that her eyelids trembled.

The nurse, finished with her chore, stood by the bed without moving, as though she didn't want to interrupt.

"Isabel?" Mother said. Her voice was low, faint even, but clear.

"Yes," I answered.

"Where is your father?" It was not a casual question.

"I don't know," I lied. In fact, I was obsessed with him and always knew where he was. "I haven't seen him since that weekend." Two lies. I had seen him seven times since that weekend, months ago.

She didn't answer. She was and was not asleep; she was dreaming perhaps, but she knew I was in the room. I didn't dare leave.

"The dress is in your closet," I finally said. "I'm sorry about what happened. I'm sorry I ever put it on."

A look, undefinable, passed across her face. Her eyebrows arched slightly, as if she were assessing the truth of my words. It was the first time we had spoken about that evening, if this could be called a conversation, she half-dreaming and I so fearful and reluctant to speak.

"Don't do it again," Mother said finally.

I cringed, then said, "I won't," and slipped out the door, leaving the nurse still and silent by the bed.

In the end, after no less than fifteen trips, we agreed that Angelic, a capless model, "much lighter for the summer," was the best wig we could find. After one experimental appearance in it, Mother put it back into its box and left it in the drawer of the bedside table. For the duration of chemotherapy, she wore scarves.

After the purchase of the wig, I found myself with extra hours each week at my disposal, and some afternoons, if my grandmother were with Mother—Mom-mom would usually fall asleep in the vinyl chair under the window, the two of them breathing lightly with their mouths open—I would go out. I would drive from the hospital to the shops at the Beverly Center and try on clothes, hundreds of garments, pulling them on, evaluating them, tearing them off, all within an instant. They were clothes I had no intention of buying. At first the process of selecting and appraising them in the double mirrors, solitary as it was, assuaged my loneliness and conjured the memory of those hundreds of Saturdays spent shopping with my mother: the smooth transit of department-store escalators, the cloying smell of too many perfumes, the implicit promises of beauty and desirability. But soon, by myself on those stolen afternoons, I seemed to vanish in the clothes I tried on. It was as if I saw the skirts and trousers and dresses reflected back empty, as if neither of us, Mother or I, were there. And it wasn't long before I stopped going to the Beverly Center, or any other mall, for good. Even today I buy many of my clothes, sometimes even shoes and underwear, from the catalogs, which arrive in our mailbox each week, some from the very stores my mother and I used to frequent: Saks, Nieman-Marcus, I. Magnin's. I am a true size six—I've never had to return a purchase because it didn't fit correctly—and it is less painful to leaf through the slick pages of catalogs, easier to see a photograph of a dress on an anonymous woman, than to face my solitary reflection in dressing-room mirrors. I can't bear to see myself walking alone through the vast, shining corridors of cosmetic counters, moving silently through the endless racks of clothing, always lost without the assistance of her quick discerning hands as they thrust undesirable garments aside, held a sweater to my shoulders. "Ugh, you just cannot wear red, Isabel. You are absolutely sallow." Her fingers as they brushed my cheek lightly. "Are you wearing that rouge we bought? You're so pale, you must always wear rouge." Her hands buried again in the chaos of the sweaters, selecting a blue one, "Much, much better," moving on, small demons of efficiency.

Without the destination of the Beverly Center then, I found myself driving around Los Angeles with no purpose other than to soothe my agitation with the dulling motion of the car. I would slip out the door while my mother was lulled by the potent combination of television and morphine, take my grandmother's long, powerful Cadillac, its eight cylinders misfiring and the muffler rattling and belching, and head for the freeway. I would drive hard and fast in my grandmother's old car, the radio playing very loudly to muffle my screams.

Later, when my mother was dead, that car was the only place

where I could go to cry for her, and cry the way I wanted, my throat thick, choked, the noises I made startling even to myself. No words came out, just rough, animal syllables, low and hollow with despair, noises no one else should hear, noises I did not make of my own volition but which were dredged up out of the empty cage of my ribs by the highway, the freedom and speed it represented, and the narcotic of its endless yellow line.

I have a dream. In it, I am a cancer research scientist, part of a team of technicians looking for a cure. My job is to test blood samples for leukemia.

I sit at an immaculate white enameled table with a stainless steel rack of test tubes. Each is so clean and shining under the strong laboratory lights; the blood is a beautiful color, rich and true, promising life amid the sterility of technology. On my left is a large dissecting tray filled with flowers, and each is huge and vibrant, the size of a cabbage with brilliant petals and thick firm stems wet with juice and dew.

I take one flower and cut into the plant's flesh with a knife of unusual sharpness; I cut through the calyx just above the stem, revealing the heart of the flower, a pale pale green that blushes with health. Carefully, I open one of the blood samples and with a tiny brush I paint the open incision with the dark rich red

143

liquid, careful to apply it evenly and meticulously, covering the wound. Then I reseal the incision with tiny sutures and place the flower in a cylindrical glass container which I store in a developing cabinet.

I do this with one flower after another, and I mark each bloom with the number recorded on the vial from which I took the blood.

Later, I return and open the wounds, cutting the sutures with my sharp knife. The healthy samples have disappeared, leaving the incision clean and whole and healthy. It is as if the blood has been absorbed into the flower. But those samples which I must conclude are malignant have acted on the flesh of the flowers, changing it and leaving suppurating ulcers. The red and the green erupt together in brown sores which smell sweet with corruption.

Each one I open, each one that bears witness to the disease, fills me with sadness. Wholly invested in my work, I can hardly sustain the anguish of the discovery of cancers. I place my head in my arms on the dissecting tray and weep, the bright knives around my head.

Once, when I stepped without a warning knock into my mother's room at Cedars Sinai, I saw her in the arms of her oncologist. More correctly, he seemed to have washed up on her chest, his legs tangled clumsily in the sheets which were slipping from her bed to the floor. I was alone; Mom-mom visited less frequently than I. She was quite old—in her eighties now—and had developed a tendency toward nosebleeds, of which she was preternaturally afraid. She believed that it was a nosebleed that would kill her, and curiously, she had them more often while visiting Mother in the hospital than at any other time, spending hours lying on the plastic sofa in the oncology wing's lounge, her long feet hanging off over the arm, while nurses brought ice wrapped in towels.

At my entrance, Dr. Weinstein stood quickly, and pulled his white lab coat back into place. He left without speaking to me or even looking at me, but not without squeezing my mother's hand and promising to visit her the next morning.

My mother sat more fully upright in her bed and pulled her peignoir tightly around her. The gown was a peach color and she looked very pretty to me, her hair in disarray, her usually pale face flushed. I said nothing of the incident, and she also pretended that we had greeted each other under normal circumstances.

But it was an almost deliciously compromising attitude in which to have caught her. Or was it merely sad? Dr. Weinstein was not a compelling or even an attractive man. Overweight and a chain-smoker, he always looked tired, unkempt, ill-shaven —his haggard cheeks smooth in one spot, shadowed and bristling in another. How could this man have inspired my mother's fastidious passion? It was not the last embrace I was to find them in. I arrived one hot afternoon around three, sweating and eager to collapse in the air-conditioned room, looking forward to pulling the vinyl easy chair from its place by the window and angling it by the bed where I could rest my bare feet—sandals kicked off—on the cool silvery bars of the bed rail. But when I pushed open the door and entered, the beige privacy curtain was pulled around the bed. I'd never seen this before—my mother had a room to herself, the other single bed empty unless I spent the night—there was no other patient's presence to compromise her shy "recovery." I stopped and watched quietly. A complicated dance around the periphery of the bed: only the doctor's loafers and the cuffs of his overly long pants were visible. The blanket was heaped on the carpet by the IV stand. At one point Dr. Weinstein's legs and feet disappeared entirely—clearly he was on the mattress with her—and I backed out of the door. Perhaps the pleasure of such attentions made the physical pain of contact bearable. She never allowed me to sit on her bed, winced if I so much as inadvertently knocked against it.

This crush on her oncologist, wholly reciprocated, out of pity perhaps, was not the only puzzling attachment that my mother was to develop during her illness and her attendant search for a savior.

Once, while looking through her wallet for her social security card—this being the first step in a fruitless endeavor to convince the State of California, to which my mother had dishonestly not paid taxes for perhaps ten years, to help subsidize the amazing cost of her cancer—I found a small square of photographic paper, heavily laminated. It was gray, with an ectoplasmic blob in the center; it reminded me of a textbook illustration of the Crab Nebula, a relic from ninth-grade science. When I questioned my mother, she seemed embarrassed and brushed the thing aside with a vague motion of her hand. But I couldn't leave it at that and so I asked her about it again that evening. I waited until after the nurse had checked her vital signs and monitored the drip, until I could depend on our being uninterrupted for a moment. From her wallet I took the little card and reexamined it, using my shirttail to polish the slight blur of my fingerprints from its smooth surface.

I held it out to her. "What *is* this?" I asked.

My mother did not answer.

I turned on the strong fluorescent lamp in the panel over her bed. It was a light that was used only by technicians who needed extreme clarity of vision when changing a dressing, examining tissue, trying to find an elusive artery with their needles. The light was overly bright, a cold blue wash of unflattering revelations, and since I knew that my mother hated it and felt ugly in its glare, it was an unkind approach to the issue. But I held the tiny portrait in the clear light and looked at it closely, my nose only a foot from her face. While I examined it, Mother feigned interest in the hallway beyond her door.

We tried, in general, not to pay much attention to what went on outside her room. Patients were not admitted to beds randomly, but grouped into buildings and wings according to disease. It made sense for those who cared for them, and it made a different kind of sense to the patients and their families. In an oncology ward almost all the patients are dying; if not now, then in a year or two. In the halls were clusters of miserable relatives; from their faces and manner, we could begin to see what it would be like for us in a month, a season, a year. I would walk toward my mother's room unable to avert my eyes politely from the grief of other daughters. I searched their faces, their postures, I watched them wring their hands. I wanted to know what to expect of myself in this imminent crisis of losing a young mother.

People were usually more reserved than I expected. Rarely did they fall to their knees weeping. They generally did not cry aloud. They never screamed but rather they clumped together and whispered. They drank far too much coffee and tea and soda. They smoked and ate candy and laughed rather too loudly. And when the patient—their mother or father or brother or child—died, they didn't know where to go and had to be herded toward the front desk where they were given further instructions.

When someone died, and the family was finished visiting with the body, the nurses went down the hall and closed all the doors. In this way, the corpse could be removed without those who yet lived being forced to witness its disposal.

On that night, as my mother looked past my scrutiny of the tiny picture and into the hall, nothing transpired within our limited range of vision from her bed. There was only the flat expanse of rust-colored, indoor-outdoor, eminently scrubbable carpet. A nurse's plump white-stockinged legs marched by officiously.

"It's a photograph of the soul of Maharishi Paramahansa Yogananda," my mother said. Her voice was flat and matter-of-fact, refusing any admission of embarrassment.

I said nothing. Under a thick flexible layer of polyurethane laminate was a one-and-a-half-inch square of Kodak paper bearing an emulsion in which was supposedly recorded, in a ghostly blur of light, the psychic essence, the inner being, of a religious quack.

"Oh," I said, and then, "How did they take it, the picture, I mean?" I held the gray square closer to the light, closer to my eyes. It resolved into a mass of tiny black dots on a white background, like a photograph of a crowd of people standing in a snowy field, taken from the window of a plane. I handed it to my mother and sat heavily in the chair beside her bed.

My mother didn't answer.

"Where did you get it?" I said. "Where do you get something like that? I'd like to know."

I thought of various possibilities, but my mother never answered. She took the little picture from my hand and slipped it into the pocket of her robe. A health-food store, possibly, or she might have ordered it from a cable-television station. A friend might have given it to her. Since she had been ill, she had received some unexpected, if not peculiar, gifts. A few nights before, Edna, the psychic, had slipped in and pinned a scrap of paper to her pillow. On it were the words *NAM MYOTO RENGE KYO*, a guaranteed chant, she explained the next day. Say it enough times and you get your heartfelt desires. Edna was broke and chanting for money. Considering what portion of her livelihood my mother was responsible for, it seemed to me that chanting for my mother's life would amount to the same result and that Edna, in her canniness, was probably repeating the magic words enough times for all of us.

Anything was possible, evidently. If in her pink velour pocket, while she lay on her bed, as toxic chemicals were slowly fed into her veins in the admittedly hopeless attempt to save her life, my mother could have a wallet-sized photograph of the soul of an alleged sage, someone who levitated and produced rubies out of the air other mortals breathed; if my mother, a woman who never kept a school picture of me in her purse, carried such a thing on her dying person, wasn't then, anything possible?

A week or so later, my mother and I were watching an educational program on public television. It was a documentary about experimental botany, narrated by the calming steady voice of a grizzled academic. Back in the laboratory, after a tour of his greenhouse, the scientist showed his viewers some black and white pictures taken by means of a sort of infrared photography. First a human hand, outlined in a bright, almost saintly light. Then the same hand, but wounded, the light dimmed at the sight of the gash. Then some pictures of plants that had astonishingly vibrant auras, their leaves and stems throwing off double halos. The scientist spoke reverently, but without fervor.

In the dimly lit room, with the soothing white noise of life support all around us, I was falling asleep.

"That's how they do it," said my mother.

"Do what?"

"You asked how it was done. That's how."

I looked over at her, still puzzled. In her hand she was holding up the little picture, and, as she had sunk low under the blankets while we watched television, that was all I could see from my chair: her pale arm growing up out of the white bedclothes like a stem, the little flat image of a man's soul its unexpected blossom.

Christian Science. Macrobiotic food. Buddhist chants. Image therapy. Megavitamin shots. Before we turned to waiting, and to morphine, we took up odd and disparate faiths seeking a cure for my mother. Not that she was unambivalent about her disease; at times my mother embraced cancer like a lover. She never told me so, but I am sure she fantasized, idealized her illness. She would be Camille, wan and beautiful and tragic, the center of our attentions as the errant cells of her selfish breast recapitulated themselves all over her body, moving in on bone and lung and liver, denying them life.

In between hospitalizations and the satisfaction of a larger audience, Mother returned to her own home, and my grandmother and Albert and I broke camp in the waiting rooms and cafeteria and halls where we ate little and smoked ourselves sick and followed her back to her apartment. The once spare living room was forced to accommodate a collection of rented, ugly and frightening equipment, and its stylish paired sofas and lacquer coffee table were crammed into one corner out of Mother's sight, where Albert and Mom-mom and I would sit sometimes, our feet up on the cushions and dirty dishes accumulating among the magazines and art books in a clutter she would never have tolerated. From the center of all the appliances and convalescence-inducing tools—a bed which took all manner of positions at the touch of a button, a walker, an oxygen machine, extra tanks of oxygen in the event of a power failure—my mother communicated her desires, received her visitors, lay inert under our careful ministrations, and prepared herself to take leave of us all. When she at last died, she left behind eleven pieces of rented machinery, one hundred and twenty-three tubercular syringes (they had the thinnest needles), an equal number of doses of morphine, five crates of bandages, swabs and disposable sterile bedding, four sheets of synthetic skin with which to clothe her bed sores (an expensive new product: at nineteen dollars a square inch, we had about six hundred dollars' worth), and the imported ampoules necessary for two weeks of "bio-kinesis" injections, sent to us from a famous German herb doctor and consisting of elements culled from sources as disparate as horse urine and dandelions.

I have one dream so often, like the dream of the yellow house when I was a child, the place to which I returned so many nights.

But now it's you that I see, Mother, and you are silent, waiting for me to speak. I know I have to explain everything, try to assuage your great sadness. Your muteness is so unspeakably sad.

I tell you that I never see him anymore, that as always and by necessity we live in the same house, but that he goes out by day and returns by night, whereas I stay housebound when he is afield and prowl the dark hours. I say I am sorry. Yes, I apologize as I never did before you died, and I tell you I don't see him, though we live in the same dark house.

Of course it is my father about whom we have quarreled. Sometimes you are satisfied and leave me. Other times you wait and wait, silent and reproachful, and are still waiting when I awake, a shadow over my bed.

There was a photograph, one that I can only remember now, rather than see, because I threw it away in a moment of vanity, of me standing in my grandfather's garden holding a big green squash in my arms. I am wearing my green Girl Scout uniform, which I hated, and I look rather plump, which I also hated and which undoubtedly was the reason for my disposing of the photograph; and I have an ill-tempered scowl on my face. The zucchini, arguably my grandfather's favorite vegetable, or at least the one which he overplanted each season and which appeared almost nightly on our dinner table from July until October, is a large one, six or eight pounds at least. Large, but not nearly as gargantuan as some he grew. Opa had a trick for creating monstrous squash and pumpkins. When the chosen vegetable had attained a normal size, he would make a careful slit with a razor blade in its stem. Into this opening he would insert a cotton string which he dangled into a bowl filled with his magic vegetable-growth tonic. This foul decoction of milk and barley water laced with vitamins and blood meal was wicked up into the stem by the little string and the vegetables indeed grew huge, but no one would eat them for fear of what he'd fed them. One year he won the prize for biggest pumpkin at the Half Moon Bay Halloween fair. It had taken four men— Opa and three interested neighbors—to get the pumpkin onto a little trailer hitched to the back of Mom-mom's old Cadillac.

The squash in the picture, though, had reached its size without supplemental feedings. Bound for the dinner table, it weighed in my arms like an ungainly green baby, matching my uniform and looking, therefore, as if it were somehow my progeny. In the background are the fruit trees, lemons dragging down the branches of their parent. The old lemon tree, its limbs twisted and gray, bore its fruit relentlessly, perhaps sucking something essential from the soil because, of the other trees, only the plum managed to produce, and even it had a limited season. The lemon turned out hundreds of what my grandmother called "footballs," they were such large and sturdy specimens. The plum tree, however, each year produced from its hundreds of blossoms only one solitary plum, beautiful; its skin, when polished on the hem of my skirt, glowed. The other trees didn't even blossom. And the rose garden to my left had not one bloom. Then, perhaps still, deer lived in the hills of Bel Air, and they walked silently through Opa's garden each night, eating the rose trees. Flowers first, then stripping the leaves and the tender green branches away. Opa didn't have the heart to chase them off: they seemed not real in the midst of the city, enchanted visitors to the garden; no matter that the buds never had a chance to open.

Beyond the frame of the old color print is the victory garden, Opa's vegetables, a tradition begun in 1940 and carried forth each year after that. From the patch, as it was alternately known, came tomatoes, carrots, beets, beans, lettuce, leeks, chives and the inevitable zucchini, which Mom-mom started to call "sick-ini" after that one afternoon when she discovered Opa on his knees in the soil, threading a string into the squash's green stem, a bowl of foul-smelling vegetable potion at his side. He called the magic liquid "Poudrex" after a similar substance that his father had tried, unsuccessfully, to sell to farmers in England at the turn of the century. Opa's father was a German, from the Black Forest, a self-taught veterinarian, plant doctor and accordion player (it was his instrument that Opa was trying to teach himself to play) whose recipes and cures seemed often to involve a length of string or twine. My grandfather himself always had little balls of string in his pockets, pieces of all lengths, and whenever I had a loose tooth that stubbornly refused to come out, he would chase me with one of these filthy little pieces of twine, around and around the garden, threatening to tie one end to the tooth, the other to the door of the tool shed and then *slam!* out it would come.

"Ah ha ha," he'd laugh theatrically. "Never procrastinate," he'd yell, and he'd brandish the string as I screamed in delighted fear, slowing down for his old legs so that I could only just elude his arms. Finally, I'd let myself be caught and Opa would pretend to set about tying the string to my tooth as I lay kicking in the grass, or with my head in the fragrant dust of the vegetable garden.

All of my earliest, happiest memories centered in that one small plowed square, the even rows of tomatoes, beans, carrots. The mounds of earth like soft black swelling bellies that produced the summer squash. The beets which somehow always escaped the conformity of the line and broke into a chaotic tangle of crimson-stemmed green leaves.

From the time I was an infant, my grandfather kept me in the garden with him as he worked. Aged seventy-one the same year that I was not yet one, my grandfather's days were divided between his pursuit of the news—two newspapers and perhaps four broadcasts that were never sampled but attended to from beginning to end—and the cultivation of his garden. Like Candide, it was in his garden that he found the order of the world.

Because Mom-mom was often not in—she went to the supermarket recreationally, so even on the rare days when she saw no friends or didn't stop in at the Red Cross office where she volunteered, she still went out in the big old battered Cadillac—it was up to my grandfather to care for me. In order to do so and to leave his arms free for his work, he built a rolling playpen which he pulled on its little rubber tires, alongside the rows of vegetables, as he moved from one area of the garden to another. Our garden was large, half an acre in total, and the terrain fairly even, so he was able to drag me along behind him as he watered and fertilized, pruned and hoed and planted.

By the time I was three, too large for the big wooden pen whose sides had grown taller as I did, more bars added as I became adept at climbing, I was following Opa at every opportunity. He moved arthritically through his plants, often singing "Me and My Shadow" to his small and inevitable companion, as I trundled after.

When I was six, I asked Opa why it was that the peach tree only flowered and bore no fruit. He explained that it had no partner, that some trees needed a husband or wife to have fruit, the children of the trees. Suddenly, that day, I was overcome by the awareness of the mating of all things, and I walked in my grandfather's garden with a new sense of its mystery and life. It seemed wonderful to me that each thing must have its partner, and I forgave my mother a little if she went away so often seeking male company.

Many years later, I myself came to live with a gardener, not a man whose job it was to garden, but a man found in his garden whenever he was not called to some other duty. The garden was his pleasure, and it gave me great comfort to see him there among the cucumbers. At the kitchen table, on a Saturday, to look up from the paper and see him with his hands in the earth, I would put my coffee cup down, transported for a moment. I would feel that I knew where I was, and whom I was with.

*I have another dream. In it, I am the victim of a car accident,
on a distant highway. Riding in the passenger seat of a tiny
convertible roadster, I have my eyes closed tightly to avoid the
wind, when we crash. My face is broken up like a jigsaw puzzle.
Pieces fall out and are lost, but I have no time to look for them;
and there is no time for corrective surgery because Mother dies
in the middle of it all, and I have to go to Los Angeles and
arrange the funeral.*

*After the funeral I return to the scene of the accident, a place
with no landmarks, a place I can identify only by blood on the
road. My face has healed without noticeable scars, and I tell my
doctor, who accompanies me to the crash site, that I don't want
the surgery anymore: it's too late and I am healed. But everyone
insists; suddenly there are many many people, people I don't
know, who testify that I must have this operation. They tell me*

158

that if my face is not put back together as it was before the accident then later when I am older it will collapse like a ruined soufflé, caving in. But I am afraid and I cover my face with my hands and say No No No.

The doctor, whose mad blue eyes—one piercing, the other wandering—above the surgeon's mask I recognize suddenly as my father's, holds a dissecting tray; on it are all the little bits of my flesh he's collected from the scene of the accident. He wants to put them back in. I ask if it will scar, and he says yes. Then I don't want it unless I can have plastic surgery too, I tell him and all the others assembled. But everyone agrees that I must have the surgery and keep the scars on my face. Finally, I collapse under the pressure of all the voices coming at me, and I acquiesce.

My father the doctor leads me to an altarlike table raised above the crowd like a stage, and he ties me to it. At first it looks to be made of baled hay, but suddenly I realize that it is packed dung, and I become fearful of germs and infection. I start to struggle, but then I see my mother standing in the crowd, and I want so much to get to her, I forget to resist. Remembering that she is dead, I give up calling her name. I know that now I can see her only from a distance and cannot ever go and be with her again, and I begin to weep, and I worry that this will impede the progress of my surgery and cause disfiguring scars.

No matter how much I plead with him, my father will not give me even a local anesthetic; he explains that he is performing both physical and psychic surgery and that I must be alert to pain. He begins to work with his scalpel, to jimmy the tiny dried-up bits of my face back into the spots where they once belonged.

The floating slums of Shanghai, the narrow marshy river congested by the clots of junks, algae growing up their rotted wooden hulls, everything damp and pungent. At nine o'clock in the morning, my great-grandfather, in his office cart pulled by the little white nag his daughters called the Red-mouthed Pony, made his way through the terrible claustrophobic traffic outside the German and French concessions and on the way to the bund. Already, the peasant women were cooking on the little open braziers. They smiled and their teeth, black with opium, were invisible, their mouths dark holes.

Sometimes, only on those mornings that his partner, Mr. Bailey, traveled separately, he would stop in a side street, an alley really, the pony boy pulling at the tender mouth of the little mare and making it redder than ever in an effort to turn the animal off the habitual path. Ever since little William died

160

and he began to leave the house early—no reason now to linger over breakfast—my great-grandfather made this occasional detour on his way to the trading house. It was quite common, really, even in the British concession where the Chinese went as foreigners among their Roman laws. So many people smoked opium. His niece's teeth were gray and she was ever so much more languid this summer than last, when she came home in disgrace, that awful affair over the ship officer who shot himself, unable to bear her insincere flirtation. Poor Daphne, it was difficult to grow up in Shanghai where the British were more British than they were at home, clinging to their Jackson's of Piccadilly tea, their stiff upper lips and woolen knickers as if these all could protect them from the rudeness and dirty disorder of Shanghai. Daphne, who had lived with them since his brother's death, drifted through the house leaving a clutter of unread novels, fingernail buffers, untouched cups of tea in her wake. A stillness in the girl now that was deeper than the boredom that preceded the scandal. An unhealthy environment, women shut into their opulent homes all week, except for Thursday, visiting day, when they traveled from one mansion to another within the concession, pulled in rickshaws by tubercular coolies.

He didn't smoke so much of the drug, just late at night sometimes, in his lonely bedroom where the silence was unbearable, sleep impossible.

"Wanchee, Wanchee? How many piecee?" The tiny, wizened woman would hold out the packet in one hand, the other open and upturned for money.

Each time he bought as much as she had. Better not to make the trip too often. No telling what contagion could burst from the grimy paper. He felt guilty as he thought of poor Dolly, all the vegetables soaking in potassium permanganate, candles always burning to combat the smell of open drains and of human waste fertilizing the native crops. The concession was such a frail stand against all this—smallpox, bandits, cholera, typhoid fever, opium. Now that they were older, his daughters begged to go to Peking, but that was ridiculous, absolutely unsafe.

"What the matter, you belong fooloo man!" The Chinese amah, the woman who replaced that drunken Scot nurse, had banished him and his gift of a little tamed squirrel from his daughters' schoolroom. Her shrieks so frightened the animal that it bit him, and Dolly, upon hearing the story, took to her bed for a week. Rabies everywhere.

A dinner party last month and the Sikh policemen—six of them, three on duty at all times, ridiculous in their turbans and yet no more strange than anything else in this country of strangers, immigrants, opportunists—the private police had been unable to prevent the usual disaster or embarrassment. This time an old coolie had defecated under the dining-room window in plain sight of the guests in the parlor. Had anyone looked up and out of the French doors, they would surely have seen him squatting there. The people were animals, really. Of course no one acted as if he had noticed; perhaps no one did—such events were commonplace. A native chef in the only bakery in Shanghai frequented by Europeans was seen through the back alley door patting flat a great slab of dough, a pie crust no doubt, against his bare sweating chest. Never bathed, the Chinese, only at New Year, frightened of the water. That old man clenched with dysentery or god-knew-what under the leaded glass window, his withered naked legs, scrawny buttocks. What could one do? The same evening the houseboy, after the butler's head count, was overheard reporting to the cook's boy, "seven adults, ten adultresses."

Every day back and forth to the brokerage. Rice and rubber futures. At least he wasn't trading the stuff. Opium was ruining China, her people, her economy. At least his own dealings with it were minimal, too small to matter much. He'd be surprised if most of their friends weren't smoking it, too. Such a place to make one's living, Shanghai. When he had first arrived from Bombay, he stayed in one of the best hotels, one that Europeans considered safe. Each room came with a man who lay on the floor all night outside the door, blocking the crack underneath and preventing the entrance of snakes.

Born in Baghdad, become a British subject in Bombay, now his homburg, his starched collar and silk waistcoat proclaimed him an Englishman like all the other wogs that the great empire had collected underneath her skirts. He spoke five languages—Iraqi, Hebrew, Hindustani, English and pidgin Chinese—and still he couldn't say to his wife what it was that made him so sad. The loss of their son, of course, but something else as well, perhaps just the sense that he hadn't any home. The tintype taken in Bombay, commemorating his receipt of a British passport, showed an earnest dark young man in a fez. The hat still rested on a shelf in his dressing room, with a small box of pictures of his first wife, god rest her. "God is an Englishman," his partner often said. All evidence pointed to the truth of this. And it was staunchly, willfully English that he had become, filling his home with a British wife and British goods, reading the London *Times* every day, even if it came two weeks late.

He lost his sense of humor in the Orient, my great-grandfather who made enough money trading rice and rubber to send me to college almost a century later. When he received a bill "for the hire of sixty virgins," old crones with grandchildren who weeded the vegetable garden and picked bugs off the spinach leaves, it no longer made him laugh.

His little girls, my grandmother and her sister, were his only pleasure, and such a worry they were. Childhood diseases, smallpox and scarlatina, joined ranks with every tropical scourge and tried to take them from him. Each night they slept in their "cholera belts," long itching scarves of wool flannel wrapped tightly around their middles by Dolly. Their stomachs were crimson with prickly heat. Soon, only a few years more, and they would have to go to finishing school in England or Switzerland, and then where would he be, his only joy exported, his wife ever more quiet and solemn.

From her father and his life as an expatriate, my grandmother learned that a home was something created *against* its surroundings. The house in which my mother and I grew up was a bastion of European culture and products erected against the crass influence of American life. Mom-mom, who never liked that New World term of endearment, whose every dress was a Liberty print cotton or scratchy tweed and whose daughter called her Mummy for as long as she lived, Mom-mom married an Englishman. They built an outsized Tudor cottage in Bel Air, on Stone Canyon just off Sunset Boulevard, that street beloved by that most American of phenomena, the movie business: one more totally inappropriate style of house in the crazy quilt of a Southern Californian neighborhood. And they filled their ungainly cottage with English antiques and Oriental rugs.

There was no choice of American jam at the breakfast table, only bitter tawny orange marmalade or lemon curd. Twinings tea brewed in a pot, no tea bags, and the milk had to be poured into the cup first, never after the tea. The cupboards were filled with Bird's custard, Wilkin and Sons preserves, dry goods imported from Fortnum and Mason, Walker's shortbread. Tea every afternoon at four. I was sent to school with lunches as odd as leftover steak and kidney pie, cold Yorkshire pudding, smoked tongue sandwiches. It wasn't long before I was leaving them on the bus. Every childhood vice—cheekiness being cardinal among them—was ascribed to American upbringing and I, as had been my mother, was encouraged to form myself in opposition to American children.

164

It was against this expatriate's desperate adherence to a chosen culture that my mother rebelled. And who better—who more of an affront than my Irish-immigrant-stock, American-born Arizona dirt-town father—to explode the practiced gentility of afternoon tea, the absurdity of refusing, on principle, to buy Smucker's jam?

He must have been irresistible, my father, the compounded insult of his being both Irish and American, his legacy of crazed Catholic missionaries clothed in cowboy boots and a twang. The wrong boyfriend was the one wild card that Mom-mom was unprepared, foolishly, to defeat. She got him out of her house, finally, but too late, not before the contagion of the New World had set everything absolutely awry.

How she would have hated this cemetery, its Mexican Catholic childishness, its innocent, primitive piety.

For Valentine's Day, the grass is strewn with red and silver tinsel, and graves are dressed in hearts and cupids. No holiday goes uncelebrated by these dead. Families from the barrio, from nearby Pacoima and Calabasas, picnic on the graves, conversing with dead aunts. They balance Styrofoam cups on the head-stones. They set places for the deceased, complete with paper plates and plastic forks, festive pink napkins.

Mother's neighbor, Carmen Lopez, has a paper doily at her feet, piled with conversation hearts. TRUE LOVE. FOOL FOR YOU. OH BOY. Some have scattered onto the damp grass, their messages melting away.

Mother couldn't have anticipated such company—the result of having belonged to a parish bordering on a Mexican neigh-

borhood of the city. Several parishes, Anglo and Hispanic alike, share the one cemetery, the graves all mingled: first come, first served.

My father and I are the last to leave the cemetery after the interment. Without a single Valentine, Mother's new grave looks neglected, and I feel as if we have forgotten some essential part of the service.

I look around at the bright, empty field of hearts. It is four-thirty, and most of the picnickers have left. My father bends and selects a pink sugar candy from Carmen's doily. He presses it into my palm.

BE MINE, it says.

Things my grandmother told me:

A cold key on the back of your neck will stop a nosebleed.

If you step on a needle, it will find its way into a vein and travel through your bloodstream until it pierces your heart.

You can get a slow wasting disease from touching garden snails and it's called Snail Fever.

Dreams about water presage a death in the family.

When shingles form a girdle of blisters around your waist, you'll die of them.

Those red birthmarks, the ones called port-wine stains, are caused when a baby is conceived during its mother's menstrual flow.

I have one of those red birthmarks on my thigh, high up near my groin, like a smear of blood. And after that evening when I stayed too long at Mother's, when I opened the door wearing her black dress, I found myself often thinking of the night I was conceived.

Years before, my mother had told me of that night. It was nearly dawn when my father drove his car to my grandparents' house. He'd waited until he was sure he wouldn't be caught by the dorm prefect, and then he'd driven furiously through the canyon, his bald tires squealing on the steep curves. When he got to the house, he went around the back and slipped through the French doors to my mother's bedroom. She had left her door unlocked for weeks, had oiled it so it opened without a sound. My father paused for a moment, searching for the opening between the heavy drapes, and then felt his way through the dark to her bed.

What happened then? Did he fall on her with kisses? Did his lips burn on her face, her throat, her thigh? Did she remove her tampon to let him inside her? Did she even wear such a thing? Was she freshly washed, did she smell of blood, was there blood matted in her pubic hair? When he was finished, was his penis slick and shining with her blood?

I tried never to believe those things my grandmother told me—Opa used to complain that she filled my head with nonsense, superstitions—but what she said made me think of things I'd rather not. I've never knowingly touched a snail, and the sight of a needle on the carpet frightens me to the point that I am never barefoot.

The doctor told me it was absolutely untrue about the shingles. I had them on my neck and right arm, over one side of my chest and on one shoulder: every branch of the brachial and cervical nerves on my right side. My neck began to hurt, quite suddenly and dramatically—I couldn't move it—just one month after I met my father. I had stopped going to class.

After that one evening—that peculiar date I shared with my

parents—I fell into a state of apathy. I registered for courses which I never attended. I neglected to buy any of the required books. School seemed without purpose. What could it teach me? I had yet to penetrate the basic truths of my existence, didn't know from where, or whom, I came.

When I was called into the office of the dean—a sympathetic man with a thin neck that was lost in his starched collar—we decided that I would take a temporary leave, sacrificing the second semester of my sophomore year rather than failing or dropping out entirely. Tuition, minus three weeks, prorated, was refunded and I was asked to move out of the dorm.

Instead of going home to Mom-mom's, I used the refunded money to rent an awful basement apartment. I went outside only at night. A friend would come to my door, ducking under the pipes that ran under the ceiling of the dwarfishly short hall, and knock; I would slip into the closet and hide my face in the clothes hanging there until he or she went away. I spent only one night away, with my boyfriend, and I wet his bed. And then I got shingles and had nightmares about the painful blisters girdling my waist and killing me.

My father came for another visit, this time to see only me: He didn't even tell Mother that he'd be in town. I borrowed a sleeping bag from my old dorm roommate and zipped myself in the first night he stayed with me.

"Come here," he said. It was too dark in the windowless room to see once the light was turned off; his voice came from the bed.

I loved him so much back then. Ever since that night, just a month previous, I had thought of nothing else but the discovery of this father I hadn't known. By chance, it seemed, we met one another. He had been in Los Angeles before, and I had stayed out of his path. If I knew he was coming, I left; if I didn't, that was by design: he and my mother were sharing a secret rendezvous. But, a month before, I had stayed in town, shopped with my mother for her dress. I'd lingered, suddenly and inexplicably curious about who it was that I'd avoided for so many years. When the weekend was over, it was I who dropped him off at the airport.

"Come here," he said. And I came and sat in my flannel pajamas on the edge of the old twin bed.

"Stay here with me," he said, and he hugged me. "I only want to hug you," he said, "to make up for lost time. So many hugs you've missed."

I lay next to him on the narrow bed. It was very cramped, and he held me tight against him. I was stiff, not used to being held, but it felt good to have arms around me, and finally I fell asleep. When I woke in the morning, I was in the bed and he had moved to the sleeping bag on the floor. It was too small for him, and, one of those old slumber-party bags—flowered and thin—it stretched over his big body absurdly, like a tight Hawaiian shirt.

He convinced me to play hooky from school for a week, to leave town without telling my family—after all, he was family too, wasn't he?—and we drove east to meet his mother, my other grandmother who had never seen me. On the way to Douglas, we stopped at the Grand Canyon where we had a terrible fight. Several times, on the long drive, he had put his hand on my thigh, and I had pushed it off. He accused me of being cold; he said it like there was something wrong with me; he used the words "emotionally frigid."

"Oh, fuck you," I said, in exasperation. I was looking down into the canyon. We had parked on the north rim where the wind was strong and blew red dust up out of the bleak crack in the earth.

"I keep hoping," he said quietly. I looked up, thinking that

I'd misunderstood, that the wind had played tricks with his words.

When we pulled back onto the highway, the brown signs for the national park receding in the old car's vibrating mirrors, he started driving fast. He seemed angry, and, familiar with volatile company, I leaned against the passenger door and stared passively out the window at the dusty pines, the occasional tourist stop promising INDIAN CRAFTS! POTTERY! and LIVE RATTLESNAKES! We hardly spoke on this last leg of the trip between the Grand Canyon and his mother's house in Douglas. The scenery changed dramatically from forest to plains to desert as we drove south, and I continued to watch it abstractedly from my window. I asked to stop at one tourist trap, and my father turned off the highway. He stayed in the car while inside I lingered over trash I didn't want to buy, little dry scorpions caught inside bubbles of Lucite, bookends made of petrified wood, tiny cacti in pots the size of salt shakers with *Arizona* painted on the side.

We reached his mother's house at dusk and I gave her the little present I'd bought her at the Navaho Trading Post, a paperweight of polished agate and one of the less objectionable items.

"But I guess you see things like this all the time," I said as I handed her the gift, shrugging in self-consciousness.

She smiled tightly as she accepted the offering, and then returned to her silent preparations in the kitchen. Dinner was painfully quiet. The only conversation was that initiated by my father as he prompted his mother to reveal things about the town, his childhood. But she was not forthcoming. Short and plump and almost monosyllabic, my father's mother was not what I had come to expect from grandmothers. She looked the part, with grey hair caught up in an appealing bun; but, rendered architecturally solid by a substantive foundation gar-

ment, her generous breast was not inviting. It was a challenge
to imagine her as the mother of seven children; and there was
little evidence of them in her house: no portraits, no childish
drawings, no snapshots of her many grandchildren. In fact, her
home had that quality of a summer rental; it lacked any idiosyncratic touches. The prints on the walls were copies of sentimen-
tal favorites—Norman Rockwell, Frederick Remington; and
even the few books seemed to have been chosen for their tried
and true popularity. Between the well-read Bible, its spine
broken and cracked, and twenty or more back issues of *TV
Guide* were a library of paperbound Agatha Christie mysteries
and a number of Readers Digest Condensed Books. It was a
dwelling that camouflaged rather than betrayed her personality, and there was little for my searching eyes to rest on during
the meal. At one point, after a long silence, she looked up at
me appraisingly as she chewed.

"So your mother is sick, I hear," she said. I put down my idle
fork.

"Yes," I answered.

She nodded, and I tried to assess this small gesture of affirmation. Was this something she approved of, my mother's
illness? I looked away. The paperweight sat heavy and useless
in the midst of the plates, an awkward centerpiece.

We went to bed early after watching, or pretending to
watch, a crime drama on television. The old set's rabbit ears
were bent crazily, one snapped off midway, and the reception
was terrible. I stood from my chair as the credits rolled up and
said good night. In the guest room, I lay clothed on my bed
and listened to the sound of his mother's feet as she walked on
the floor overhead. Dulled by the long drive and the tense
dinner, I fell into a half sleep, not comfortable enough to relax
completely, not awake enough to rouse myself and dress for
bed. In the absolute night of the windowless basement room,

all noises took on an exaggerated effect, and I listened to the largeness of them. The darkness pulsed before my tired eyes; I heard a drawer open and shut, a rush of running water, the whine of a window being opened. Floorboards creaked, pipes moaned. I rubbed at the few dry scabs left from my case of shingles, my fingers finding the places out of habit. By now most of the blisters had burst and dried, leaving just a faint pink blush in memory of the skin they broke. Even the bigger ulcers on my shoulder and ribs were healing. It still hurt, though, and the nerves were raw and sensitive to every stimulus, even an imagined, or feared, caress.

Suddenly, I heard my father's heavy tread, his feet coming down the stairs. I sat up on the hard twin bed and hugged myself as the door to my room opened and admitted a wedge of light bearing his tall silhouette. He closed the door softly and approached the bed, knowing his way in the dark. My eyes burned but saw nothing. As I started to speak, I felt his finger on my lips, silencing me.

Upstairs there was a repetitive, percussive noise as if someone were beating dust from a rug, an unlikely nighttime occupation, and I found myself worrying obsessively about the source of the noise. Perhaps this grandmother whom I didn't know was an insomniac. Perhaps she cleaned the house at night when it was cooler. Perhaps she was angry. The noise grew larger and larger as I crouched very still, listening. It almost obscured the smaller but unmistakable sound of my father taking his pants off, the slow snarl of his zipper's metal teeth separating.

He kept his hand over my mouth and I could taste the salt of his sweating palm as he fumbled with my clothes.

After he left the guest room—the little bone buttons on my favorite shirt torn off and scuffed under the bed—and after I'd finally gotten up and put my pajamas on, I lay back down in the dark. When I couldn't sleep, I got up, turned on the light, and looked on the floor and in all the corners until I found each button. His mother was a good housekeeper: the room was very clean, no dust anywhere, not even along the baseboard under the bed.

I put the six buttons in an interior pocket of my overnight bag, and I folded the shirt so the torn places weren't visible, and placed it gently at the bottom of the bag, underneath the other clothes. We were going to spend only one night, we'll be leaving early in the morning, I kept thinking to myself—perhaps I even said the words out loud—and I set about preparing to depart. After going through my clothes and selecting what I would wear for the drive home, I plugged in my tiny travel iron and sat on the floor waiting for it to warm up. Using the cool linoleum as a makeshift board, I swept the flat metal palm of the appliance over and over the material and I removed all the creases from my black skirt, which I hung with a red blouse, over the chair.

Not able to sleep, I ended in ironing all the rest of my clothes and repacking them over and over. I thought of how Mommom used to pack for me, with two fresh sheets of tissue paper between each layer of clothing. Without the paper, the job wasn't complete. Finally I gave up and went back to bed.

That night, that morning, I dreamed of a baby conceived in the wash of my menses, disfigured by terrible birthmarks and able to converse and write at birth. It stood in its crib at the hospital and said unspeakable things to the nurses.

I never did sew the buttons back on. I kept the shirt as it was, torn. I have it still.

I have a dream. In it, Mother and I are looking through a photograph album together. I comment on a picture of myself as a baby in her arms. But she says no, that it is not me in that picture, but the one she lost, the one she couldn't save, the one that drowned.

Suddenly, then, we are at the beach in La Jolla—Shell Beach where we sunbathed so often. But the day is stormy and raw, the sea cold, brackish and unfriendly. I am intensely afraid.

Through the fog and the spray I see Mother in the dark surf, straining the water with her hands. She is trying to find the baby she has dropped, and I know, watching her, that the baby is me. I understand that I have been dropped inadvertently and drowned. With her I understand that I had been more than one, many, and that now I lived and survived only at the expense of others that could not be saved.

We are present to one another in the awareness of that loss, and sad. She is sad for having failed, and I too am sorrowful, sorry for her and sorry to have lost some of myself.

Sixteen years old, being fucked by David for the first time—his first time as well, two clumsy virgins—I was thinking of my mother. Seventeen, being fucked: Steve, Brad, Mark, whoever. Nineteen. Twenty. The whole brilliant unknown territory of sex traversed in somnambulance. Coming from the waist down, my mind playing over the same face, the same hands, childish fingers, so soft, round-tipped. Every time, my mother and I—we entered into sex together. I would see her lying under some man, was it my father? Someone faceless until after I'd met him. My father had sent me pictures all along, but she got the mail first and threw them away: hundreds of letters and pictures. Eighteen years' worth.

Men. I was untouched by their lovemaking, untouched by gentleness. I drove men to violence so that perhaps they could awaken me.

The first time I was sixteen. The same age as my mother when she and my father lost their virginity together. She told me about that night and about other nights as well; she told me about getting pregnant in her own girlhood bed. She felt herself get pregnant, she said. I remembered her saying that, and felt my diaphragm slipping. How could I concentrate on anyone else's flesh inside mine? I was too busy learning the curve and placement of that little rubber dish. Walking carefully afterward for the whole eight hours, lest it move and some one brave cell slip past the barriers of spermicide and rubber: a child I didn't want. I could see generations of myself before me, unwanted children.

When I was fifteen, my mother made me get my first diaphragm. She drove us to the gynecologist's gray-walled office on the fifteenth floor of a skyscraper in West Los Angeles. Through the tinted windows and the summer smog, the city below looked cool and elusive, half hidden under a blue shroud. Toward the ocean, where the pall lifted, I could see traffic crawling on the tiny distant freeway.

My mother was in the examining room when the doctor broke my hymen so he could fit me properly for the device. He used a series of graduated green plastic phalli. First a tiny, little boy–sized one, then larger and larger ones, until he withdrew one whose shaft had been discolored by a smear of blood. My mother leaned against the wall, watching. She stood just to the left of a poster that revealed that most intimate, cellular level of human communion, one triumphant sperm breaking through the egg's thin, eager wall.

I writhed on the table as the doctor swabbed my genitals with disinfectant. Then, after producing the correct size of diaphragm and instructing me on its insertion, the doctor left the room, taking my mother with him, so that I might climb painfully down from the table and try to put it in correctly by myself.

"I'll give you a few minutes, and then I'll come back to see if you've done it right. No point in using it if you're going to put it in wrong," he said, and he smiled benignly. The door closed. I put my shirt back on before squatting on the linoleum, the slippery little dish of jelly in my tense fingers. It sprang out of my grasp, skidding along the floor, twice before I got it in.

I kept that diaphragm in its white clam shell of a box and dusted it religiously with cornstarch to protect the rubber from dampness. I held it to the light and looked for imperfections. But I didn't use it. I thought of it as hers: she was the one who had wanted it. Later, when I needed one, I went to a clinic and got my own, identical, but in a pink case.

All the boys who fucked me, some reaching for me with love on their faces, some with anger, also reaching. One disgustedly. Finally he settled for front-to-back sex, his front to my back. I suppose then he might have convinced himself that I was participating emotionally, my hips grinding in feigned lust, the bed creaking happily in collusion, masking my silence.

The IUD didn't really help: I imagined a child born with a hook in its mouth, a fish dredged out of the sad amniotic sea, gills torn, gasping in the new world. It would wear a scar on its face that said to all that its mother didn't want it and had taken precautions, attempted prevention.

And still I thought of my mother every time it happened. So fearful that some force of imitative magic would cause me to have a girl baby that I did not want and would have to give to my grandmother. Had Mom-mom taken my mother into the linen closet as well? Had she told her it was all right to get pregnant? Had the force of her will and desire entered into my creation, an equal part to adolescent lust?

And yet, the constant message of my childhood: Do not make the mistakes that your mother did. Do not get involved with the Wrong Boy. Do not allow anything to stand before college. Do not Do not Do not be stupid and ruin your life. Do not.

I was so afraid. It was fear that squeezed my heart, not desire, fear that made me squirm and sweat and move faster faster to get it over with. I sat up immediately to give the sperm a harder climb. I used two tablespoons of jelly and we—whoever it was—slept in a puddle of it.

And for nothing, Mother. Whatever you did, when I was too small to speak out against you, worked. I shall never have a child, can never conceive or bear a child. But I didn't know that at seventeen or nineteen, or even for years after your death. I spent nearly a decade in a panic of unnecessary birth control.

Is it something about having grown up in Los Angeles? The earthquakes, perhaps—that inability to put a plate on the edge of a shelf for fear it will fall when the house tilts and bucks. Even my sweaters are pushed back against the wall, a full margin of eight inches of shelf. Every picture bolted to the plaster. That big one in 1971, it all came down then, books thrown from their cases, every last volume of the old Encyclopaedia Britannica.

I compulsively memorize fragments of possibly useful information, as though preparing for some new apocalypse. I rehearse data I might one day need to know.

There is a twenty-four-hour pharmacy at the corner of Sepulveda and Ventura. The automatic teller in the shopping center with the Safeway runs out of cash by midnight, but the one just three miles up the street should be okay for at least fifty.

Beverly runs parallel to Wilshire and to Olympic and the

other boulevard that begins with a W. Think B. W.O.W. Bow-wow, like a dog, that's the way to remember them. If you have to get to the airport during the morning rush hour, use Sepulveda instead of the freeway; if the flight is in the afternoon, 405 should be clear.

One ounce is equal in volume to 16 drams, 437.5 grains and 28.35 grams, and so a milligram is .015 grains.

Baking soda for kitchen fires, water just makes it worse.

There's another pharmacy that's open at least until midnight, maybe two A.M., and it's a little closer than the twenty-four-hour one, on Sepulveda before you get to the freeway.

Flick the syringe with your index finger, then squirt a little of it out and hold it under the light to make sure there isn't even one tiny bubble. Slap the vein a little if it won't come up.

A body falls at the rate of thirty-two feet per second per second.

Don't give her water if she's choking.

It came in a tiny bottle, one dose as an antidote to poisoning. And so much more of a punishment, because of the nausea. A horrible seasickness, a little bit dizzy, it was enough to make me nearly cry in discomfort. $1.39 per bottle; and I had to ask the pharmacist. It was not controlled by prescriptions, but was kept behind the counter.

"Excuse me, I'm putting together a first-aid kit, and I need a what-do-you-call-it, an emetic, in case of poisoning." I practiced my very casual delivery before entering the drugstore. In fact I knew what it was I wanted, had learned the name in Girl Scouts when I was twelve and had earned absolutely every badge, committing possibly useful information to memory.

"Ah, ipecac would be what you want," he said and reached for the shelf where I could see the little vials lined up.

"Three bottles, please."

He placed them on the counter and I bought them.

Of course I could not keep returning to the same pharmacy, but had to seek out a new one each time. Soon the words sprang naturally to my lips and I was not nervous lying to the next stranger.

It was so loathsome, this syrup of ipecac, that soon I could take less and less of a full dose to make myself vomit. Finally, all I had to do was unscrew the lid and smell it, deeply, the little glass neck to my nostril, and I would gag, an easy Pavlovian response without the twenty-minute wait, sweating and writhing from the illness it caused. It worked so well, in fact, that even now I cannot take cough syrup. The medicinal sweetness is too like the other's and I throw it up.

There was one year that I stopped eating almost entirely, subsisting on predigested liquid protein, another sweet, thin, red syrup, and Shasta diet cream soda, which tasted more substantial than the other flavors. But after my period had been gone for a year, after I believed, with a religious fervor, that I had broken myself of the vulgar habit of food, and had begun to wean myself from sleep, I suddenly became hungry and could no longer fast. I started eating again, ravenously, and solved the problem of calories by sticking my finger down my throat. True, I was no longer saintly in abstemiousness, but there was something new and quite seductive in the slyness of my reestablished relationship with food. I stopped avoiding any social event that included food: I ate and then excused myself to vomit, which I could do so very quietly. I especially looked forward to dinner out with my mother and with Albert, not because of the expensive restaurants and French food, but for the mean pleasure of throwing it all up afterward, while Albert paid the bill.

Ask any son or daughter who has had to accompany a single parent on a date: it is an experience that never improves. True,

I was fifteen, no longer a child, and Albert and my mother had been together for a year or more, but our outings still implied the reluctant forging—Albert's and mine—of our relationship, our little "family." And no longer was it the same hot embarrassment of being seven and sharing a date with my mother and the Israeli man with the greasy hands, the man to whose Pontiac I unwittingly referred as a "Grand Pricks," and later cried in humiliation in the backseat at the memory of my mother and this tall dark man collapsed in helpless hilarity on the hood of his long black car. And it wasn't as if Albert's son, whom as a teenager I despised, accompanied us. No one, least of all my mother, was that ambitious.

And Albert wasn't peculiar like some of the men Mother had dated before. Carlo, for example, lived in a big Spanish-style house, the red tiles dropping from the decaying roof into the mossy old swimming pool where he kept his river otters. He had an outdoor cocktail party around that pool, the wet little beasts running among the legs of the guests, cadging hors d'oeuvres. Everyone loved Carlo except me; he was so uncontaminated by bourgeois cares, such a free spirit; but I was the one who, too young to drink, was encouraged to swim with the otters in their murky unchlorinated pool. In the thick, green water they hung on to the end of my long braid like monkeys on a rope, and I was afraid to pull them off. Carlo had shown me the scars where one had playfully nipped right through his hand. All the adults laughed at their antics and wheedled and cajoled until I agreed to swim with the little animals hitching rides on my hair or my bathing suit straps. When I tried to get out of the pool with one still clinging to my swimsuit, it pulled my bikini bottom off and everyone laughed all the harder.

Still, even if Albert never tortured me the way Carlo did, I resented him, and with even greater determination after the one evening when he filched a potted plant I had admired on a bistro table, and presented it to me, silently, in the parking lot after dinner. Albert was the quietest man I have ever known. He spoke little, if at all, during those dinners; and in all the years we knew one another, we barely had one conversation. Even as Mother was dying, we never talked to one another about our loss. Our communication was limited to dosages and pharmacy bills and laundry.

The little plant was the first of many gifts. Albert was a kind man, and over the years he gave me innumerable tokens of what I now recognize as his affection. All were presented silently, or left where I would find them, with a tiny monosyllabic note attached. Like preprinted holiday tags, the notes read, "TO: Isabel, FROM: Albert," and they were all stuck with cellophane tape to presents carefully wrapped in the Sunday newspaper's comics section—picture books on shell collecting, hair combs, silver trinkets—all of them thoughtful purchases that showed he knew me and my likes and dislikes, that he had been watchful in his silence.

For years I was afraid of being contaminated by his gifts, made vulnerable by his affection. Like all his offerings, the flowerpot was too winsome to reject, and after the little begonia died I kept the pot grudgingly in my bathroom to hold my barrettes. The dinner, however, I disposed of, slipping away after dessert. I had an almost erotic response to my thinness and couldn't resist, if the restaurant's powder room was empty, pulling my shirt up after I was done to admire my rib cage, the shocking bump of my sternum, the disappeared breasts. On a hot evening, the ropy veins stood out like a road map over my abdomen.

Finally, however, I somehow hurt myself, despite being careful and washing my hands each time before. My fingernails were not short enough, and I grazed my throat. The scratch turned into an abscess, and within a week I was quite sick. My grandparents had to take me to the emergency room one night when my fever was high and my throat insanely sore. I leaned over the plastic emesis basin and a thin yellow stream ran over my tongue and out my mouth. In that sudden rush of pus provoked by the nurse's exploration with a cotton swab, I recognized a sweet, almost meaty taste of decay, one I had noticed building for the past few days, and in the realization that it had been the infection I was tasting, I retched and retched until my throat started bleeding in earnest and the doctor gave me a shot to make me stop.

As I fell asleep on the cool table, I saw my grandparents talking in the hall and it looked as if Opa were crying. He had his gardening clothes on, an old sweater with dirt and burrs caught in the weave, frayed trousers. He had to look up when talking to Mom-mom, which made him appear as an ancient child, and his confusion and concern made me feel briefly guilty—I had so successfully fooled everyone—so that it was a month before I bought the first bottle of ipecac.

It was the very punishment of the medicine that I wanted, that pink, sticky corrective, its intent barely masked by the terrible sweetness of it. A caution on the bottle warned that it ought not to be used if strychnine, corrosives such as lye, or petroleum products had been ingested. Those poisons must be diluted. The first dozen or so times I swallowed it, I would read the label compulsively while waiting for it to take effect. I would imagine the sort of tragedy—one quite beyond my panic over a piece of cake—that rightfully heralded its use. Parents wringing their hands over stricken children. Suicide attempts. Later, I hid one dose in my purse and went nowhere without it. The label carefully scrubbed off, I kept the vial sealed in a plastic bag against leaks.

I soon discovered that its effects varied, depending on what I had eaten. Fried food, anything greasy, guaranteed the most purgational nausea. What I believed about ipecac was that because it made me feel so bad for a half hour or so—so intensely ill—it might break me of this shameful habit. For I

188

did feel wicked in my wanton, wasteful narcissism and I remembered all the people who didn't have food and each time I truly did intend to stop. But I didn't. The medicine worked entirely too well; and if I couldn't stop eating again, not indefinitely, not for more than a few days at a time, I could choose what to eat, judging by how easy it would be to throw it back up. I was careful of my throat now, avoiding whatever hurt, so the old staples of my diet, green apples and popcorn, were taboo.

My mother rewarded me for being thin. She bought me clothes, took me out with her more often, fed me pleasant lunches in Westwood cafés. I was frightened that I might gain weight and fall from her favor, but the ipecac saved me from any return to baby fat. I never did get plump again, but her new interest in me was temporary nonetheless. Only when I stopped menstruating was she once again invested.

Clearly, my extreme thinness was something she liked, but Mother found its consequence, the loss of my period, intolerable. I'd had it for only two years before it went away, and she was determined to resurrect it. I followed reluctantly behind her, up and down elevators in various medical plazas. For the first time in years I felt simple and clean and unburdened. I didn't want it back, but she was a woman with a mission.

The only thing that worked, aside from weight gain and the only temporary half-effectiveness of hormone therapy, was acupuncture. So each Wednesday and Friday after school I went to the acupuncturist—it was close enough that I could ride my bicycle—and I sat in what looked like a dentist's chair while a Chinese doctor punched long thin needles into my knees and ankles. He attached them by wires to a little box which delivered a current to further "stimulate my meridians." When Dr. Wong turned the current up too far—to eight or so on the dial whose highest setting was ten—the large quadriceps muscle in my thigh started clenching and unclenching, a disturbing slow-motion twitch. As soon as he left the little room, I would reach over and turn the knob back to four or five. Then I'd do homework in my lap for the half hour of therapy. Despite my resetting the voltage, my period returned, accompanied by excruciating cramps and nausea, after thirteen sessions.

Satisfied with the bloodstains on my underpants—she wouldn't believe me without evidence—my mother let me quit the acupuncture against the advice of Dr. Wong, after four months. The next time I lost my period, I didn't tell her.

I dream of the Aztecs, beautiful people, brown and vital, long-haired priests high on their pyramids, a way to step closer to god, their braids matted with blood. They worship the sun, which is sensible. At appointed times they ritually excise the heart of a worthy sacrifice—a warrior perhaps or a beautiful princess—and offer it up from the highest point, appeasing some being so powerful and unlikely to be impressed as the sun.

Cortez arrives, with a seasickened crew of pale men, men who by some cruel trick of fate arrive from the East, where the sun daily rises, and who are white. The Aztecs take these shining pale men for gods and fall down before them—holy writings have foretold this event—and behold, the new gods hold aloft their god: a dead man on two crossed sticks.

How amazing to forsake the obvious glory and constancy of the sun for Jesus, thin and bloodied: not Moctezuma's gold, not the feathers of Quetzalcoatl but a crown of humble thorns on his bent head. Perhaps it was the blood which served to lead the Aztecs to this new faith, the power of life spilled.

I want to believe in that redemption, of blood and of love. I want to believe again that enough love saves, that enough blood cures. That love will save us all.

But now I understand that this is untrue. Some love makes the world less safe. And I have witnessed the cheapness of blood, seen the gift of life spill uselessly into a dying woman. I have squandered my own blood. Always, I fall back to paganism. I am impressed by the sun's presence and I want god to be just that burning and bright and mute, impenetrable and all-consuming.

And if I want my god to have a personality, then whose better than Athena's, who sprang from her father's head, from thought and knowledge, rather than from the terrible vulnerability of his loins, his passion.

How fine to be Athena striding into battle assured and unafraid. I am tired of Jesus and his aching humanity and want my gods invincible and unbesieged, untempted by human frailties.

I have done a terrible thing and I don't want to be forgiven by Jesus' great bleeding heart. Better to be immolated than to be forever grateful, humble and mindful of how base I am.

Sometimes I can't remember why it happened or how it began.

It began at the airport when he was returning to Needles after that first visit, ten days after my eighteenth birthday. When he kissed me good-bye, my father put his tongue into my mouth.

Did it happen also because I enjoyed the power I had over my father? I had that power possessed by the sexually desirable, control over those who were not wanted for their bodies, those whose bodies were not wanted. My father used to weep sometimes when I said no.

I know who he was. This is a story about desperate women and their unhappy destructiveness. My father was a man manipulated by women. His life was a long struggle to effect a shift in power, to disentangle himself from their terrible meddling.

In Douglas, Arizona, in 1948, the wind blew hard through the cottonwood and the air was alive with the seeds of the trees, seeds borne aloft on long silken strands. They glistened in the air when my father looked toward the sun; they made his eyes itch, his throat close. He couldn't breathe and when he lay on the floor and gasped, his missionary grandmother began to cast out devils. She used every trick she knew from her long, dusty training in Matamoros. She prayed over him and shook her Indian rattles; she mixed a burning poultice of hyssop and poke root and cayenne; she made him lie on a damp, mildewing pallet soaked with holy water and she bound his hands with her scapular and chanted him crazy; and when he could breathe again she told him his life belonged to Jesus, that he would grow up to be a man of the cloth.

My father, the smaller of a pair of identical twins, was delivered into the world by his grandmother. His brother, born seventeen minutes before, was dead. In the womb, the two had been bound so tightly together by the dead child's umbilicus that one had perished, and the survivor, my father, was forever marked by a slightly crippled right arm. The fingers of that hand never worked as well as the other's—they were stiff and short—and that elbow would not straighten. Unclothed, the arm was slightly womanish, smaller and with less hair than the other. Thus my father was made left-handed by fate rather than by natural predilection, and even on the hottest summer days he wore long sleeves. Still, as his grandmother told him, it was the mark of God upon him, he was saved for a purpose, and his disability was slight and certainly would not prevent him from his calling. The wandering eye, too, she interpreted as a sign of his vocation, saying alternately that it looked ahead into the next life, or behind him, for the approach of the Devil.

But my father never wanted to be a priest. During his brief enrollment in seminary, years after his divorce from my mother, he was subject to fits of rage and put his fist through the plasterboard wall of a cheap little church hall in Kingman, Arizona. The seminary board said that he would have to undergo psychotherapy before he could be ordained. But he refused. From the psychoanalyst's initial diagnostic profile he learned that he thought he wanted to be a priest only because his grandmother had told him that he owed his life to Christ: it was all in payment for an ancient debt, one which he was no longer interested in honoring. My father left the Catholic Church for a different mission, the life of a small-town politician. He traded texts, forsook the Bible for the civil code, but was no less a zealot. When I met him he was still delivering homilies but the topic wasn't the quality of Christian mercy, but rather air and water safety.

Love can be as basic as need, and people ripen toward that need. My grandmother's theory of weddings was that a person married when that person was ready to bond, an inner biological, emotional imperative having little to do with the chosen love-object. She was never much of a romantic, my grandmother.

But it was that sort of bond that I had with my father. Our needs were complementary. No, they were the same: he needed to hurt my mother, and so did I. I did have remorse, but not enough to withstand the force of his heavy, grinding lust, and my guilt was ultimately insufficient to combat my own passivity, the paralysis of despair.

My father was a selfish man, and greedy. And I was selfish, too, because I gave nothing; I made him take what he wanted. I allowed his sin because it was a vessel for my own anger. And I allowed myself the consolation of taking from my mother the only thing she said she had ever cared for: my father's love.

One night, sometime in the beginning of my junior year, my father arrived unexpectedly at my dorm room. Despite my earning only a few units as a sophomore, I'd reentered college with just enough credits, including those advance-placement ones I'd earned in high school, to stay with my class. After the shock of Mother's being diagnosed with metastatic disease the previous summer, it seemed important to attempt to normalize myself, so to speak, and carry on. With that purpose in mind, I had gone back to college with a determination to resurrect my old high school fervor, to reinvent my lost obsession with grade-point averages, that small arena of perfection for perfection's sake. Every evening that I wasn't with my mother I planned to spend in study, no exceptions. I thought I could not be derailed from this intent, but when my father came that night, after he had driven the 277 miles from Needles without stopping and had only just arrived, I agreed to talk to him. I hadn't seen him for several months.

I got into the sprung passenger seat of his car, avoiding the place where the coil popped through the upholstery, and we drove to the old Mexican church where they still left the door open all night. It was a place he and my mother used to go when they were in high school. They used to kiss in the pews, she told me, and once he took her underpants and stuffed them in the collection box.

"What is it?" I said. We were standing just inside the entrance and the tall double doors creaked shut. "Why are we here?" I asked.

By the hand he took me to the church's simple altar. It was after midnight, and the building was dark except for dim lights trained over wooden effigies of the saints. Francis of Assisi hung, as if arrested in the process of ascension, to the left of the altar. A battered brass box with a slot for coins was bolted to the wall under the martyr's sandaled feet. I remembered my mother's underwear.

"Promise me," my father said, squeezing my hand so hard that my old turquoise ring cut into my finger.

"Promise you what?" I tried to pull my hand away, but he held it fast. He worried the ring from my finger and it fell, striking the stone floor with a tiny chime and rolling beneath a pew. From his pocket he produced a little hinged velvet box.

I snatched my hand away, turned from him. There was a glass case to the right of the altar, illuminated like an aquarium with swimmy green light. Inside, an infant Jesus doll was dressed in a miniature purple robe and golden crown. A pile of new baby shoes lay under the case: tiny cream-colored shoes with pearl buttons, black patent leather slippers with bows, tiny red Mary Janes, even one pair of white satin christening booties. An old Mexican legend told that the statue walked from midnight to dawn, doing good deeds, performing miracles and mercies. The Christ child wore out a pair of shoes each night, and so parishioners made offerings of new baby shoes. It was ten minutes past two. I wondered if the people who brought the shoes ever checked on the doll, to see if it were truly out working after midnight. Probably not: such would amount to a betrayal of faith.

My father was standing in the half-light, holding the little box. "Don't you even want to see it?" he said. "It's quite pretty."

I shook my head no. We stood in the old building, not speaking, for some minutes. On the back wall, our shadows were huge and menacing, and, by watching my father's, I could see as he replaced the box in his pocket.

"All right," he said finally, and his voice was low and even. I listened for some thin fuse of anger but found none. His consistently bloodshot blue eyes were even more red than usual, and the wandering left one was curiously steady. "All right," he said again. "Let's go, then."

We left the church, Saint Francis, the Christ child and his shoes, a night's miracles delayed, and drove silently back to

197

campus. When we stopped in front of my dorm, he said nothing, just waited as I got out. I paused on the sidewalk for a moment, turned back. The car's old engine shuddered as he depressed the accelerator, and then lurched away from the curb.

I am dry, dry like the earth after a long period of drought. I am so light I shall soon be able to fly. The wind will come up under my parasol one bright day, like this day, and bear me aloft, like a seed, the dry seed of a dandelion, milkweed, airborne.

It is good to be so light.

Driving in the summer through the desert, the soil is so red that where the earth cracks, it looks like flesh—the lips of a woman dying in the sun: swollen, cracked. My own chapped lips.

I think of the lips between my thighs, and imagine them as dry, too, like paper. I recross my legs and I hear the sound of leaves of paper touching one another, the sound of a book closing.

My father steers the car very carefully, and we traverse the cracked face of the desert without incident.

199

Dr. Weinstein called me—he left messages at all my numbers: Mother's and Mom-mom's and at school—and asked that I come to the hospital for a meeting to evaluate my mother's "status." I skipped my eleven o'clock class to talk with him and with her primary-care nurses. I am not sure what I expected of this meeting, but I carefully thought of nothing as I drove to the hospital, allowing the cheap emotion of Top 40 songs, played at a deafening level, to wash my mind clean of all coherent perception. When I got out of my car on the top level of the tiered parking lot, I had a precarious feeling, not unlike vertigo, and when I looked up the blank blue sky seemed to be tipping. The whole skyline listed slightly, as if all the buildings in the city were slowly, inexorably sliding toward the ocean and would, one by one, drop into the water. But, then, I hadn't eaten all day, and a lack of food sometimes had such an effect.

I had long ago disconnected myself from my hunger, and it resurfaced in a number of ways: moodiness, headaches, and often this sense of slippage, like a film projected crookedly onto the screen.

I walked into the lobby and the receptionist paged Dr. Weinstein who appeared with unprecedented punctuality and accompanied me down the long, sterile corridors to the doctors' lounge where the nurses, ever obedient to schedule, were waiting. When we were all seated, he wasted no time with pleasantries and told me that my mother was terminally ill and that she had known this for a year.

"A year?" I said, incredulous. An unnaturally high pitch in my voice betrayed my shock, and the nurses looked down in embarrassment. We were gathered around a small, oval conference table in the tiny lounge. The walls were mauve, and there was a coordinating oil painting of mauve and purple flowers hanging over the coffee machine. It, too, looked crooked to me, misaligned. I wondered if other patients were so secretive. Mother had told Mom-mom and me that she was nearly well, that the tumors were smaller and she was approaching remission. She didn't seem well, or even better, but it never occurred to me that she might lie.

"We think your mother should be discharged," Dr. Weinstein said. "She no longer can benefit from hospital care, and what palliative treatment she needs is quite doable at home." He explained his use of the word *palliative:* the humane management of pain and anxiety while she waited. All that could be done, he said, was to offer comfort.

Mother had no health insurance and the bills, which Mom-mom had paid as long as she could, were rapidly mounting.

"I see," I said. "All right. I'll talk to her about it."

Mother was sitting up in bed when I got to her room. The big television, suspended by a slender metal bracket bolted just underneath the ceiling, was on but she wasn't watching it. It was a cooking show, a close-up of a big knife dicing carrots, then the camera panned the efficient kitchen which conveyed a perfect balance of clutter and organization, a tangle of shining stainless steel utensils next to a platter of spring lamb, blood oozing onto the white china.

"I think we should talk about this," I said, and when she didn't answer, I said it again, and she glared at me.

"There's nothing to talk about. What is there to talk about?" she said. Her arms were folded childishly, and while I felt angry with her, I was also mad at Mom-mom whose age and reluctance to consider death meant that she had deferred to me the management of yet another of her maternal obligations. The grandmother of my childhood, always able and acerbic, was gone, replaced by a passive imposter.

I thought for a moment, but the longer I was silent, the more difficult it became to speak, so tempting was it to yield to our habit of sidestepping delicate issues. Finally I said, "I just feel like we have some things to say to one another, you know. I mean, I never knew. You lied to us."

"What do you want me to say?" she snapped. "That I'm dying? Okay, I am. Soon I'll be dead." She looked at me for a moment, daring me to answer. When I didn't, she looked away and then spoke toward the window. "See," she said, "there's nothing to say, is there?"

"You could have told me and Mom-mom, that's all," I said, finally.

I thought there was a lot to say—a lifetime of conversations avoided, all those hundreds to come that she would neatly escape. I moved away from the bed and she turned up the volume of the television and the sound of the knife striking the cutting board filled the small room.

I didn't bring up the subject of her leaving the hospital again. I knew that she didn't want to go, that after weeks in that bed with the shining chrome rails and the daily visits from

Dr. Weinstein, the even more frequent attentions of the respiration therapist who counted and measured her breaths, her capacity to live just a little longer, she no longer felt safe in any other place. Home seemed a far less efficient and caring environment.

Two days later she had a fever of 106 degrees and was hallucinating. A kidney infection. Dr. Weinstein said this was it: She was dying. I signed a nonresuscitation order at the nurses' station just twenty yards down the hall from her high raving chatter. She was calling me, she was talking about Easter. I must remember to buy the lilies for the altar, she said loudly. Dr. Weinstein said he expected it to be over in a week.

But days passed, the fever abated, Easter came and went, and Mother came back to us. Mom-mom sat in the hospital room, a long, ghostly figure asleep in the yellow molded plastic chair by the bed, for days and nights. I bought the lily and left it on her unused rolling dinner table until its last flower was spent. I told her that I had given one to the church as well, but that was not true.

On Easter Sunday I did go to mass in her stead, and a crazy woman sat in the pew behind me. I wore a white dress with an abstract pattern of lines and arcs drawn on the material. In it the woman must have read some occult meaning, some cabalistic sign, because after the service she waited while I put a dollar in the box and lit a candle for my mother's illness, that it might be swifter or slower, more brutal or less so; I prayed for something, some resolution. When I turned around the woman started speaking in a high-pitched, rushed tumble of words. The church was empty, the priest outside with the stragglers, and her voice bounced harshly off the smooth cool walls. She told me never to dare to come into the house of God with that on my person. She said I was playing with fire. Immediately I thought of my father and backed away from her, a mad seer perhaps. I left her in the church and drove in my grandmother's long dark car to the hospital. I assuaged my nervousness by making a funny story of the encounter, telling Mother what had happened. She said the dress was fine, and we laughed a little about the incident.

Finally, it did come time to take Mother home, and as I had anticipated, she was frightened and uncooperative. One evening early in May, my grandmother and I broke the news to her together, and she started to weep and clutch at Mom-mom, saying, "No, Mummy, no Mummy, please." We had been cowardly enough to wait to tell her until the night before she was to leave.

The next morning when the ambulance attendants collected her from her room, gingerly placing her on the gurney, she was still weeping. She clung to the curtain that hung near her bed, the same that had so often drawn a soft circle around her and her doctor; she held weakly on to the door frame as she was wheeled out of her room; and she plucked at the white sleeves of the nurses as she left the oncology wing.

I rode home with her in the ambulance, siren off but still moving swiftly through the few cars on the noon-hour freeway. Another day of classes shot, but I could always skim by. If college taught me anything, it was how to make the grade with the least amount of effort.

We had equipment waiting at her apartment, a makeshift hospital room that Albert had helped me assemble. She hated it all. Lying in the electric bed in the middle of the room, she had us rearrange all the furniture and roll her from corner to corner, Albert straining to push the bed and I following like some absurd caboose with the big green oxygen machine. Finally, we found the least objectionable spot.

That night we had to give her twice the prescribed dosage of morphine and three Xanax tranquilizers before she settled down and we sank onto the couch exhausted. Having been trained by a visiting nurse, Albert and I had been practicing for the past few days how to fill the syringe and inject a dummy Hickman catheter. I'd practiced until my thumb was so sore I could hardly move it when the time came. It seemed as if it must have been my incompetence that caused the first shot to have no effect, but when I called the doctor, nearly hysterical myself, he said that it was Mother's anxiety that was escalating the pain and to simply overmedicate her this one evening.

Chemical solace notwithstanding, the situation at home quickly deteriorated, and Mother and I had a number of arguments about whether or not I should administer a lethal injection of morphine. If I made the mistake of asking what I could do for her, she'd clutch at me, my arm, my shirt, and say, "End it, end it, for Christ's sake. Just get it over with." Her eyes glittered with misery and morphine, the long dark lashes matted with tears. I couldn't answer, would just shake my head dumbly and try to pull away.

Her bed sores were deep and they stank of rotting flesh. I was frightened by the one on her left buttock; it looked as if there were something white in the center and I imagined it might be bone, part of her pelvic girdle, or, even more horrible, a maggot. I flinched whenever I saw it, out of fear, but I could see that she misinterpreted this as loathing. It did smell bad, and we were both embarrassed when I changed the dressing.

When I kissed my mother on the forehead, that most unobjectionably bland and chaste area of the body, I left the room quickly after my lips had touched her skin and got an alcohol prep—a tiny square of gauze soaked in disinfectant and packaged in foil which we used on the needles and the Hickman catheter—and I scrubbed the oily, stale smell, the soft feel of her flesh, from my mouth. Sometimes I cried because I felt so guilty, but the touch of her skin to my mouth was more than I could bear. My usually pale lips were an unnatural cherry color, chapped red from all the rubbing.

I didn't like her hands anymore; they were twisted and half paralyzed. Sometimes when she touched me I only just managed not to withdraw and I could not respond in love. I was torn constantly between my revulsion—my fear of her illness—and my hopeless desire for some sort of communion with her.

Tuesday or Thursday afternoons, freed from class, I went to the galleria, whose consolations I discovered one week when Mom-mom's car was being overhauled and I couldn't drive it aimlessly, amnesiacally around the city. My own car wouldn't do; it was too small and its ragged convertible top gave no sense of the enclosure and safety of Mom-mom's battered behemoth.

I gave Mother her morphine at two-thirty as usual and recorded it in the log. She took a number of Schedule II drugs—those deemed by the FDA to have the greatest potential for abuse—and it was legally imperative that all doses be accounted for; records would be maintained for seven years after death. But Albert and I screwed up here and there, made mistakes and falsified the entries later, before the nurse came by to check on Wednesday mornings. The afternoon when I stole some of the oral suspension of morphine, I refilled the missing inch or so with water. One week we found we had used far too many of the tranquilizers and had to lie when asking for a renewed prescription, saying we'd somehow misplaced the bottle. I think Albert was taking the pills occasionally; in fact, when all the medication disappeared so quickly after Mother died, I suspected him of hoarding it somewhere. At times his grief would melt away into a familiar blank sedated stare.

I would give her a big shot of morphine at two-thirty, as much as I could. I'd fill the syringe carefully from the brown glass ampoule, holding it under the desk lamp to make sure I'd got all the air bubbles out, and then I'd have to reach into the

bodice of her nightgown for the catheter, my fingers avoiding
her breast, trying not to touch her in a way that would embar-
rass us. Sometimes I'd bring a stool from the kitchen and sit
down as I was giving the shot. The slower you push the plunger
on the syringe the better. Sometimes I would be in a hurry to
leave, but still I did it so slowly that my shoulder ached with
the waiting. The plunger was easy to depress quickly, hard to
push slowly; but if the drug was introduced to the bloodstream
only a little at a time, it would be more generally distributed
to all the pain, and would last longer. Too, it was dangerous to
flood the vein because it was so close to her heart. The shot
took a full three minutes to administer. By the time I was
finished, her eyes were already rolling upward, the muscles in
her face twitching, and she would say something stupid or
unintelligible. I'd wait ten minutes to make sure the morphine
had kicked in completely and then go out. My grandmother
would be in the living room, sleeping; Albert in the kitchen,
either cooking or drinking, the only things that gave him pleasure. It was easy to slip away unnoticed.

The galleria was half a mile away from Mother's apartment
and I walked through the summer heat to its doors and on into
the six balconies of shops around the atrium filled with waxy-
looking plants and a matching pair of glass elevators. As my
body was transported up and then down, smoothly, silently, my
thoughts moved in a way that was also slow, smooth and me-
chanical. I'd get off on one floor or another; it didn't matter
which. I didn't stop in any of the stores, just wandered past the
endless shoppers, the limitless things to buy or eat. Sometimes
I didn't even get out of the elevator, just watched the shoppers
through its glass walls as I rode up and down from level to level.
I'd pick out one person in a particularly loud shirt or dress,
something easy to spot, and follow his or her progress from
store to store, accumulating packages, licking an ice cream,
sitting on a bench, moving on.

Over my head, through the great Plexiglass and steel sky-light, the heavens looked oddly green, as if the whole complex of stores and restaurants were under water. I would look up at the clouds—spread across the sky like a worn, threadbare shroud—and feel a pressure in my ears as if, somehow, I were fathoms under the ocean.

I dream that Mom-mom and Albert and I keep a vigil around Mother's bed—there are others there, but I cannot be sure who; we are all in a huge sort of hospital or institutional compound. Albert is very playful with me, his gestures carrying a sexual weight, as was often true in our waking lives. I have a sense of our all being there for many days. He comes to Mother's bedside; he has brought a platter of hors d'oeuvres for her, and bends over me to put them on a small table. I find myself tweaking his thigh in what I realize is an inappropriate advance, and he turns and says to me, "DON'T," in a very loud voice, his large angry face just inches from mine. I am frightened and hurt and I run from the room, away from the bedside.

I find myself, then, involved in other things; it seems that I am in a school of sorts. I am aware of books, papers, written tests. Although I am far from my family, I realize that the institution is the same one that cares for my mother. It is just that I am in a distant wing.

In a large public lavatory I overhear some women talking; they mention my name, my mother's name, my grandmother's. Unaware of my identity, they speak among themselves of my mother's recent death and of the family's concern over my absence. Everyone is looking for me.

I begin to run and run and run, down long corridors. I am far from my family but I know the way back. I keep hoping that the nurses in the bathroom have been mistaken, that mother is not yet dead. Finally I arrive at the big double wooden doors—like church portals—to Mother's room. I stand outside. For the first time in my memory they are closed, and I am concerned that this is an indication that she is truly dead.

I open the doors slowly and walk through a small antechamber to the room with the hospital bed. It is as I had feared: Mother is dead. I can tell this is so because she is on top of her bed linen, and naked. They have taken her hospital gown.

No one speaks to me: Mom-mom and Albert are silent, and all the other people are gone. I look unabashedly on my mother's nakedness. I see that her legs have withered away, wasted to bone and skin, and that her belly is huge and flaccid—the way she did look at the end of her life, distended with tumors. But as I am staring, she starts to move and to speak. I say to her, "Mother, are you dead?" She nods her head and whispers, "Yes." And I ask her, "How can you tell, are you sure you are dead?" And she nods and smiles as if she is faintly amused by my naïveté. She explains to me that she can feel it, Death, sitting on her stomach. I cannot understand what she means and I feel concerned that she yet speaks and feels, but I do believe her.

She sits up now, with her legs crossed like a fakir, and her face *has become beautiful, as it was when she was young and before she was ill. As I look at her I think that she must be telling the truth, and I remember that her gown had been taken away and that the doors had been closed to visitors, and I try to tell myself that yes, these are the signs that she is dead.*

It was so simple, the plate I ate from. It promised health and balance and freedom from cancer. In the center was a signature, in a gold color under the glaze: *Michio Kushi,* this country's expert on macrobiotics. The plate was divided into a simple pie graph, the kind I learned in elementary school. In each wedge was some writing. Vegetables 25%. Soup 15%. The rest was obscured by my food, none of it approved by Mr. Kushi. According to him, my diet would make me sicken and one day die.

Almost a year before, I had bought that plate with my mother. Two plates, to encourage us to follow the regime. I had been eating macrobiotic foods with her—as company and encouragement, and because I myself was always highly susceptible to faddish diets. My eating habits were so peculiar, so dictated by impossible, rigid and ritualized schedules, that I'd never bought a meal plan at college or even eaten in the dining hall with the other students. Just before I switched over to macrobiotics I had been eating nothing but tangerines and carrots, and only at certain hours. If I got hungry and it wasn't either nine or noon or three or six exactly, the minute hand on the twelve, I wouldn't eat. My palms and the soles of my feet were orange with carotene and I was feeling a little weak, so the diet that Mother found so harsh actually came as a relief to me. As long as it had rules and corollaries and was the doctrine of some zealot, I was happy.

For a while we subscribed to a local macrobiotic newsletter as well as to *East-West* and we read and reread Ohsawa's *Macrobiotic Guide for Living;* we joined a wellness support group and went together to obscure and hidden stores in ethnic corners of the city. There we bought distasteful imported vegetables which we pressure-cooked into mush and ate with our brown rice (also pressure-cooked) and gomasio and miso and tofu—but not too much tofu. We ate soba and udon noodles, with nori and hiziki. And for dessert we each had one Japanese umeboshi plum; pickled in brine for three years, it lay brown and wizened in a pretty cut-glass bowl. Increasingly, Mother used her good crystal and flatware, linen napkins, even candles to compensate for the Spartan, colorless food. On our dinner plates, however, remained all the checks and balances, all the strict proportions, lest we forget. Each Thursday evening, a thin blond homosexual who had studied in the East came to teach us new ways to prepare macrobiotic foods. Despite all the recipes and techniques, however, every meal turned out the same: overcooked and bland and slimy with seaweed. On Saturdays we went to a tiny restaurant in the Hollywood Hills, my mother painfully limping with her cane up a narrow flight of stairs, and ate macrobiotic food. The best in the city, it was no better than what we produced with the help of the polite young teacher.

After two months Mother threw the entire regimen over. Mealtimes had become ever more stressful, our faces set to conquer rather than enjoy our food. The seaweed we had to add to everything made the once-fragrant kitchen stink. Stacked neatly in the refrigerator were packages of tempeh and kombu and gargantuan daikon radishes, like severed arms, long and white and bloodless. There was no bread in the bread box, only bags and bags of tiny aduki beans, spilling forth from some undetected hole. I slipped on one that lodged under the heel of my shoe and twisted my ankle painfully. Mother sickened and embarrassed me with details of the physiological changes wrought by the regimen. *Mucus* was the watchword. When your body throws off mucus, it is cleansing itself with the help of wholesome nutrients. She blew her nose a lot and told me that even her urine was viscous and thick with mucus. Was I noticing a difference in my bowel movements? she wanted to know. It was inconceivable that my mother, who never had made reference to personal habits, was discussing excrement at the dinner table. I was too embarrassed to reply, just traced my fork along the lines of the pie graph on my plate.

Now my mother ate what she liked, and if one of us made the mistake of bringing her a snack on the Michio Kushi plate, she refused it. Chemotherapy had failed, and now that it was over, food became one of her greatest pleasures; she wanted no reminder of diets, of deprivation and self-discipline. Even I felt a little happy when I saw the expression on her face as she ate Swiss chocolate. There were yet a couple of things that made her smile for a moment. This was the first time in her life that she was not watching her weight, and there was something luxurious in this admission of defeat. After months of useless struggle, it was in a way glorious to lie back and succumb to elegant decay. Her collapse was complete and exemplary. Her limbs grew quite thin, the muscles all atrophied, but her belly, once invisible, was the one sign of her remaining pleasures. The waist that tormented me, twenty-three inches, vanished.

I wiped the crumbs from Mr. Kushi's signature plate and set it in the sink.

Opa is in the nursing home for several months before he dies, and I lie in the big electric bed with him and make the back go up and down. I peel an orange and share the segments with him. He is so thin, his pajamas seem empty. He is just a disembodied head speaking from the top of the bedclothes.

I am seventeen, a college girl now, but I climb into bed with him the way I did when I was small. I remind him of how he used to take my new Mary Janes from the Stride Rite box and scratch the leather soles with his pocket knife, scoring the slick glossy hide of the bottoms so I would not slip. Or of how every morning I ate a soft-boiled egg on whose shell he had drawn a face. Sometimes a goblin face, like the ones that came down the chimney and danced their sooty feet over the carpet; sometimes a man with a bowler hat. He'd take a butter knife and lop off the top of the egg, scalping the little man and letting yolk spill down his cheeks.

I'm scared feeling how little of Opa is left under the covers. At night I keep dreaming that when I hug him, he comes apart in my arms, dismembered.

Does he remember helping me with my schoolwork? "Mary Queen of Scots was superstitious, supercilious and punctilious. She walked and talked an hour after her head was cut off," he would say. "What does the first sentence mean, and where do you punctuate the second so it makes sense?" All my life I associate the bloody queen with chickens, because I didn't understand where the period went when I was just learning to write, and Opa once told me that headless chickens ran off from the butcher block. Around and around until they died in the farmyard.

They steal everything from his room, I don't know who, the crazy old women, the nurses' aides. It's all gone, the radio, electric razor, shoes, a mug, candy. They leave the get-well cards, though. Someone has taped them crookedly to the wall beside his bed.

Mom-mom comes to have tea with Opa every afternoon. She brings it in a thermos, with four cookies tied in a Baggie, two napkins, and a tiny container of milk. When they have eaten the cookies, drunk the tea, she puts the thermos and the little milk bottle and even the folded Baggie back into her purse.

Eight o'clock, late in August, nearly dark, Los Angeles could be almost charming. I left the air conditioner off and convinced Mother to let me open the big sliding glass door near her bed. The weekday traffic had subsided; the air retained a blush of the summer day's warmth; and the lights—the millions of lights from businesses, streets, homes and cars—came together gracefully. The radiant monoliths of Century City's two skyscrapers reached heavenward through the invisible smog, and the ridiculous palm trees on the boulevards, having escaped the sun's scrutiny, were now lit artificially and seemed believable as part of an elaborately staged scene. On such nights, the city was expectant, poised as though waiting for dramas yet to unfold.

Summer nights were windy, and every so often the curtain at the open door would fill with a great breath of air and reach toward my mother's fingers which rested on the stainless steel bed rail. I watched to see if she would move her hand away in irritation as the fabric brushed her knuckle, but she did not. Perhaps she could not feel it, the morphine was too high a wall for so small a sensation to scale.

Mother had been home from the hospital for months now, and we had settled into a schedule that was manageable, if draining. Albert, whose occasional work as a film editor gave him flexible hours, stayed with Mother while I was in class; and I came to sit with her most afternoons and evenings, often picking Mom-mom up on my way over.

It had been weeks since that night when my father and I had gone to the old church. I thought he might not return after my refusal even to look at his ring or whatever had been in that little box: his threat of ownership; but he did, willing me away from my books nearly every weekend. He never asked about Mother, although he knew she was dying; and my interaction with either parent seemed to presuppose the nonexistence of the other. Not having the courage to confess, I longed to be found out, accused, and would provoke arguments with my mother as I sat by her deathbed. But the conflicts were so unfocused and cowardly, so veiled in their intent, that neither of us knew, or admitted that she knew, what the other had implied; and so the disharmony was to no purpose.

I would sit near Mother's bed and place my chair in lazy reach of anything she might need: Kleenex and morphine at arm's length and the television's remote control in my lap. There were many stations from which to choose because my mother subscribed to almost every available cable service. While she was ill she became the consummate consumer of television entertainment and wouldn't let me turn the set off for any reason, not to play the records she used to love, not to talk on the phone, not when the vacuum cleaner had obliterated its voices. She turned it up and kept the volume

high, wouldn't turn it down during a conversation. Sometimes the television was our only means of keeping her calm.
The steady infusion of pretended intrigues, the characters'
remote movements on the bland screen, were often more ef-
fective than tranquilizers. So much violence and grief, so
many deaths per viewing day, so many medical dramas: perhaps the television minimized her own plight. Her limp hand
rested on the remote if we had to leave her alone for even
twenty minutes.

And I, who as a child wasn't allowed to watch much television and who was initially displeased by its intrusion, grew first
resigned, then increasingly addicted, to the calming noise of
the set, the illusory presence of other people. Sitting there
beside her, however, I could no longer watch in the usual,
conventional way. I didn't need a program guide, because I
didn't make choices but watched everything at once, switching
rapidly from one show to another, rarely staying with any
program for more than a single line of dialogue, an isolated
gesture. "Stop it, Isabel. It's bad for the TV," Mother would
say as I ran through the channels. But I couldn't. The manic,
random sampling of simpleminded plots, of endless commer-
cials and news bulletins, talk shows, game shows, documentar-
ies: they all mesmerized me; and my channel-hopping became
a way of remaining there beside her, of sitting still while satisfying my agitation.

Ultimately, the television became an unexpected catalyst for
our communication, or miscommunication, as it were: its
voices both provoked conversation and masked the silences
when we weren't talking. One night, as I punched the buttons,
we had an argument about my dropping a class. The set was
momentarily tuned to a PBS French lesson. *La piscine. Le
livre. La table. La voiture.* An earnest man with a waxed mus-
tache, beret and striped shirt mouthed the elementary vocabu-

lary, as he pointed to corresponding illustrations, pausing after each word for students at home to mimic him.

I told my mother that I had dropped French 403, articulating in a self-consciously correct accent: *"Français quatre cent trois."*

"Oh, no, Isabel," Mother wailed histrionically. She began weeping, a fairly predictable response, in that she'd been crying at almost any provocation for weeks.

I didn't need the credits for the course and was already nearly fluent in the language, on paper at least. More significantly, I had hated every French class I had ever taken, from first-grade baby French when we played translation bingo with Madame Durand—the prize was a sucker if, after filling in a row on your printed card, you could name the lollipop's color and flavor in French—through the previous semester's nineteenth-century novel class in which I'd had to slog, at half-speed, through books I'd already read in English. It had always mattered terribly much to my mother that I speak French: she and Mom-mom were fluent, and French was the language of crisis in our household; arguments often finished in a hysterical escalation of foreign epithets. Albert, who grew up in Paris, refused to speak his native tongue with my mother; and for years, despite my excelling in every other subject, I brought home D's or even F''s in French, which she correctly interpreted as a refusal to come of age into this language of female strife.

We sat for hours at the kitchen table, Mother drilling me in verb forms, I looking blankly into space until her temper broke and she started screaming, or, worse, slapped me across the face. Now, at the mention of my dropping a course for which I'd already missed more than the acceptable number of classes, she was weeping, her ragged whimpering breaths overlaying the absurdly hearty tones of the man in the beret. I switched channels and the antic Frenchman disappeared, replaced by a woman reporting the weather. The reporter held a microphone and stood at a deserted intersection in the Miracle Mile where a sudden gust of wind rearranged her carefully styled hair and flattened her white blouse against her chest. Her breasts were small and her nipples stood out dark and erect, visible through her brassiere. She clutched the lapels of her trench coat together. Storm warnings for the next day. I punched in a new channel: a talk show featuring overweight teens. They sat sullenly on a red couch, their fat thighs touching one another's, as the trim, hyperactive host asked them how they *felt* about themselves.

My hatred of French was finalized, made irrevocable, when I was plump and thirteen and my mother imposed a system on our telephone communication.

"I want to know when it's you calling," she said. We had this conversation in her car, stopped at the long red light at Sunset and Beverly Glen. She was inspecting her eye makeup in the rearview mirror as she spoke.

"Sometimes you're the only person I want to talk to," she said. "I don't want to answer for anyone else." She readjusted the mirror to reflect the road and continued. "So, if you call and let the phone ring just once and then hang up and count to ten slowly and call again, that way I'll know it's you and I'll answer."

One night I had tried to reach her, dialing over and over. Finally resigned to her wishes, I was trying to earn an A in my French class and had written an ambitious composition full of idiomatic expressions that I wanted to check with her. And, too, I missed her. At midnight, I called one last time, imagining the phone ringing in her empty apartment, the curtains drawn, the little living room dark. Sleepy, I forgot the code that last time. She answered on the third ring.

I had wondered all along if perhaps she wanted me to use

the code to *avoid* talking to me, but it had been one of those suspicions that I'd told myself was silly, paranoid. I'd never tested her before, not wanting to lend credence to such fears, not wanting to empower them.

"Hello?" she had said. "Hello?"

I used my finger to depress the button, disconnect us, and sat for some minutes on the end of my bed, the receiver still cradled between my cheek and shoulder. Finally, I walked over to my desk and tore up the composition. I stayed up until three that morning, writing a new, mediocre paper that included only those constructions I already knew.

French, that exquisite language of love and insanity. Verlaine, Rimbaud, Baudelaire. All the mad poets whose work I studied. All the mad conversations to which I'd listened, silently translating their anger into the language I spoke. Mother, and her mother, and her mother, and all the others before them. I don't know of any woman in my family who didn't speak French, especially when angry, out of control. The language of passion, vitriol. I dutifully earned my A's, learned to understand what was being said. But conversation? No, I never had any real intention of speaking the words aloud. French 403 had met six times and I had managed to miss all but the first introductory session.

Of course, Mother would interpret this only as a betrayal. She cried, and mucus and tears ran down the outside of the oxygen tube from her nose. She moved her hands vaguely to wipe at it. I ignored her, clicked to a new channel: a broadcast malfunction, the picture jumped and all the people appeared to be trembling violently, with rage? with fear? There was no sound, and the fretful click of my mother's rings against the stainless steel bed rail became suddenly loud and insistent. Two of the actors embraced, but it looked as if one were shaking a confession out of the other.

"That time with the phone code," I said, "That stupid thing

you made me do: dialing and waiting and dialing again. You tricked me."

I couldn't look at her, the tearful pink blotches on her pale cheeks, the way her long eyelashes matted together into starry clumps.

She didn't answer, and, childishly, I punched in 39, the scrambled reception of Channel X which aired porn films for those who subscribed. I knew it irritated her. Two bodies, perhaps three, twisted into the impossible postures of contortionists, moved together. Warped flesh undulated under black horizontal bands of snow while static obscured the voices. Their struggle seemed anything but erotic, and sadly familiar. I hated everything about my life.

"Code?" Mother said, finally. "I don't know what you're talking about." Her voice was low, controlled, the thin edge of a lie just audible under her words. "Turn that off," she said. "It makes me nervous."

I looked at her. "Why?" I said. "What about it makes you nervous?"

"The reception is all wrong. We don't get that channel."

"We get it enough," I said. "You can see what's going on, can't you?"

An arm moved beyond the obscuring black band. It fell languidly on some other piece of flesh. The sound of laughter, slow and languorous and drunken, under the hiss of static.

"If I wanted to see that, I'd subscribe," she said. "Turn it off."

I placed the remote on the bed: out of my hands, out of her reach. Unmistakable beneath the black bands, the livid close-up of a penis filled the large screen. Its purple glans bobbed malevolently.

"Isabel!" Mother's voice was shaking again, impossible to say whether with anger or exhaustion. "I don't want—" she began, and stopped. "I don't want—"

Silence opened between us, deep and vertiginous like a chasm, the television's static made small and incidental.

She closed her eyes, and I turned off the set. "What don't you want?" I asked.

"I don't want to look at *that*. I don't want it forced on me. I don't want to be reminded."

"About what? About sex?"

"About anything," she said, and she started to cry again. "Isn't this enough, Isabel? Isn't all this enough?" Her fingers, eloquent in their small movements, gestured at the room filled with equipment and medication. The art books that had filled the bookcase were stacked on the floor, replaced by little piles of sterilely packaged syringes, bottles of Betadine and rubbing alcohol.

I looked at her. But this isn't what I wanted, I thought.

She sighed deeply. "Turn the TV back on," she said. "And put the remote control here, where I can reach it." She frowned with the effort of raising her hand. I slipped the remote under her fingers, and she painstakingly selected the channel for the program she wanted: a hospital drama. She had the airtimes of all of her favorite shows memorized.

"Isabel," she said, and she had to raise her voice over the melodramatic score, "we're almost through with one another, and I'm very tired."

On the screen, a young woman was being rushed by ambulance to the hospital. A handsome young fireman slipped an oxygen mask over her pale, still face. For once, however, my mother was looking at me, instead of at the television.

"Don't tell me what *you* need to say," she said, "tell me nice things, tell me what *I* want to hear." She struggled to sit up against her pillows; her eyes met mine. "Tell me lies," she said.

The light over the long mahogany banister is extinguished, the sweet humid air of Shanghai, the smell of the river suddenly palpable in the darkness. Outside on the veranda, the grown-ups are drinking a punch of claret and lemonade and their voices are low and slow and distant. My grandmother's heart is in her throat, a feeling of delicious fear prodding it to beat faster, faster. In a moment she will scream. Where is Lilly? Her white dress must catch the light, but she is nowhere to be seen. A noise of feet on the stairs, the sudden howl of "Monkey Dark!"

My grandmother nearly falls as she runs, the Oriental rugs slip on the clean polished wood and bunch under her small feet. Where is Lilly? She can hear but not see her and she falls screaming behind the divan. The fear is turning from good to bad, the monkeys are all about. If only her father would hear and come get her. Lilly's mad cries come from a high place now. "Monkey Dark!" she shrieks again and again and she makes a terrible high chattering and then falls, never laughing, onto my grandmother, her little sister, and begins to tear at her clothing.

It started out as almost fun for the little sister, but now there is something awful about it. My grandmother, Regina, or Rina, as she was called in 1904, is screaming and kicking at the monkeys—how many are there on her?—at their horrible little hands all over her, at their teeth and nails and hot monkey breath. Her father doesn't hear or come to stop them and she starts to cry. "Monkey Dark Dark Dark" screams her sister. She is pulling off Rina's knickers.

A hundred million monkeys swarming and screaming and their fur is black their tails are long. They have ugly faces and they want to do bad things to you. My grandmother has nightmares about the monkeys, somehow not remembering in her sleep any better than awake that the monkeys are Lilly, a little girl only three years older than herself, a little girl who likes to play tricks. In the dreams the monkeys are big and they are everything that is wrong with the strange country she lives in, the place she waits to leave. They are the beggars with typhus, the dogs with rabies, the old women with opium. It is against them, somehow, that you go to bed each night, no matter how swelteringly hot it is, with a band of wool flannel girdling your waist—a cholera belt—wrapped tight, itching. It will protect you from them.

The monkeys are the threat of sex, inarticulable at the age of six but present in the form of Daddy and his size, in the feeling, not completely unpleasant, but wrong, of the carpet on her bare bottom, in the sensation of Lilly pulling off her pants, in the terrible heat of spankings and the better warmth of the brandy she is given by her tippling nanny.

The monkeys are black, they are evil, they are exciting, but *they hurt you. They come in the night and Lilly unlocks them and lets them get you because she can reach the gaslights and is allowed to turn the key and dim the flame.*

Mistress of the monkeys and of the lights, Lilly has power over darkness. On Chanukah, it is her privilege to light the candles, one by one, another each evening after sundown, until on the last night there are nine burning and she catches her hair on fire, the holiday's dramatic conclusion. All the presents and candies are forgotten; the doctor is called; Lilly's head is wrapped in salve and bandages.

Convalescing in her canopied bed, in her white turban of gauze, Lilly asks for and receives a terrible gift, something she has seen on a trip with the governess to the open-air market: a marionette, a puppet monkey whose black limbs she animates. Excused from lessons, she has little to amuse her all day besides practicing with her toy, and soon she grows adept at manipulating the crossed sticks which move the strings. It is not long before the little monkey, whose tiny hat and coat she has removed, can dance and curtsy on the floor near the bed. Her nimble fingers make the black furred arms reach out, the little mouth chatter.

My mother was always excessive in her material generosity and gave an embarrassing flood of presents for every birthday or Christmas. For a few years before she died, and certainly long before I ever suspected that my mother was dying, I saved one or two gifts. I would rewrap them in their pretty paper which I had been careful not to tear and save them as if they could provide some protection—like canned goods—against famine, a future dry season. I have all those presents, some still wrapped. I am unsure of the contents of the boxes; the paper is faded, ribbons are missing or frayed. Some I opened, on a birthday, perhaps, invoking her presence. Two cashmere sweaters, one blue, one gray—never worn, but in the drawer now with the others—a nightie, a porcelain dog, a bottle of my favorite perfume sealed with a pressed medallion of wax and a gold cord. The perfume is on my dresser, undoubtedly spoiled from the strong morning light that floods the bedroom. No matter, I would never open it, despite Sam's irritation at the mere sight of that bottle, stoppered against the leakage of an old love.

Cosmetics, too. It was years after her death that I opened and used a bottle of German shampoo that my mother had brought home from an import store when I was still in college. I had put it away, carefully, remembering its presence, not just forgetting I had it. I moved four times and packed that bottle of walnut bark shampoo, unpacked it and put it in a bathroom cupboard. I washed dust off that bottle. Finally, I opened it when I was bathing for a New Year's Eve party. I had run out of my usual brand of shampoo and, pressed for time, knew the nearby pharmacies were closed.

I used to steal my mother's makeup, a lipstick or an eye pencil, the wrong colors for my complexion and not becoming. Rarely used, they sift up from the depths of a bathroom drawer every now and then.

There is another, similar sort of contraband in the apartment: items I always assumed were Sam's and then suddenly discover once belonged to his ex-wife. We have not lived together for very long, and it's not surprising that this should be so, yet I feel a pang when the serving bowl that holds my salad is suddenly revealed as Lisa's. Likewise, Sam feels betrayed at such revelations as, say, that the tweezers he uses to pull out a splinter were my mother's. Like a past lover, her smell is everywhere in our house. She's been dead for years, he never met her, but her presence is yet among us.

Had I only prepared by saving something important, a recording of her laughter, for example, the redemption of that wonderful sound, high and sweet and uncontrolled. Why do I not have it taped somewhere, like that last bottle of perfume, unopened, a talisman against my loneliness, that I might always hear it one last time?

I used to love making my mother laugh inappropriately, in a quiet gallery, or theater, at the movies, anyplace that told a story not our own, where we could be, briefly, friends. In church her laughter would ring out, the awful torment of Christ for a moment forgotten. We had to leave the sanctuary one Easter Vigil, having broken the solemnity of the occasion with my sad mother's lovely ringing laugh.

Everyone who knew us said we sounded alike in laughter, she and I, that infectious trill which had us both, albeit years apart, thrown out of class so often. But I cannot hear her in my mirth, nor in my mind, as she used to laugh when I teased or manipulated that unwieldy ever-growing cast of imaginary characters designed especially by me to make her smile. The extraordinary adventures of her docile cats, the absurd vision of the fat one, Mike, in the red truck we pretended for his travels. How delightful she was for that instant when she forgot herself, and me, and who we were to one another. If only I had preserved the sound of her happiness, to balance just one iota the memory of her sadness.

Which time would I have chosen, which laugh? Once, I tried to teach my mother how to drive a stick-shift car. After an exhausting afternoon of hundreds of shuddering stalls, it seemed as if she finally had it. She let the clutch out slowly, we slipped gracefully into a busy intersection—and then suddenly leapfrogged straight into the back of a pool-service truck. On impact, a precariously balanced bag of chemicals fell off the tailgate and onto the hood of my car; an avalanche of brushes and leaf strainers followed and the bag split open, white crystals blowing everywhere. The pool man, who spoke no English, danced a furious jig of irritation around our locked bumpers, swearing in Spanish and slapping our fenders to punctuate his incredulous anger. I'm sure we never laughed so hard again. We sat, weak with mirth, still clutching at one another, as he jumped up and down in his truck bed, trying to free his pickup.

If only I could hear that sound again, the breathless mix of her laugh and mine.

In Los Angeles, everything happens in cars. They provide such perfect, self-contained stages for personal drama, for revelations, proposals, confessions, for fights or reconciliations. People sit behind their closed, tinted windows, fumes rising. Opera plays in the background, or heavy metal. Or the radio is off and there is silence. On the other side of the protective glass, the shatterproof windshield, the noise of surrounding traffic is distant and meaningless. Emergency vehicles with their flashing lights and sirens pass unnoticed.

Opa had his first heart attack in my car. We were coming home from a flower show in Long Beach, navigating the cloverleaf between the Santa Monica and San Diego freeways. I hadn't been a driver for very long, only four months, and I thought his gasps were in response to some blunder on my part. I kept yelling, "I did use the turn signal, I did use the mirror," until I saw that his eyes were on the ceiling, not the road, and that his hands were ineffectually grasping at the seat belt as if to free himself. I parked and ran the quarter-mile of shoulder, dodging broken glass, to the yellow emergency call box. By the time the ambulance threaded its way through the traffic, Opa looked much better, was passing off his discomfort as indigestion.

"There's someone out there who's having a real heart attack," he said to the medic. He gestured at the crowded freeway with one hand while holding tightly to his tie with the other.

"Am I going to have to cut it?" the medic answered. He made a snipping motion at the frayed silk paisley, and Opa let go reluctantly. He insisted on walking from my car to the ambulance, wouldn't allow them to transfer him on the gurney.

"What do you take me for!" he said. The medics followed him into the back of the ambulance. "No sirens!" I heard him say just as they shut the door.

All the major fights that I had with my father began in a car. Sometimes, driving his old sedan, he would reach across as he maneuvered through traffic and force his hand deep and hard between my legs, hurting me, daring me to cry out. I never did.

One afternoon, my father ambushed me in the parking lot of the art building at college. His car was covered with pink dust from the long drive west from his desert home. He opened the passenger door and I got in before he could reach across and yank my arm, his usual invitation to go for a drive. We took his long blue Oldsmobile with its rusted rocker panels and worthless suspension back into the desert, heading northeast for hours until we were deep in the dry center of the state, past Victorville and Barstow and the Calico mine ghost town, past the Soda Mountains and north almost to Death Valley: a long trip, relieved infrequently by the barren terrain, the occasional snarl of the ocatillo's eerie, twisted arms.

When my grandfather was a younger man, in his fifties, he used to drive into Death Valley and fill the trunk of his car with the beautiful rocks he found there: heaps of rose quartz, chalcedony, petrified wood, fool's gold, moss agate and, once in a long while, a broken geode. Sometimes he took my mother with him. She wore a sundress and hat and carried a tiny pick and a pail. I have a picture of her as a little girl, prospecting up near Boron where you could chip jade out of the rocky hills, small pieces and poor quality but, still, real jade. The back of Opa's car would sink with the weight of the rocks, some of them big, almost too heavy to lift, until he'd have to stop and turn around, head back to Los Angeles. At home, he piled the rocks into strange, colorful cairns in the garden. Visitors sometimes asked what they meant, what they were for, these curious monuments, but Opa would only smile and shrug off the question.

My father had no air conditioner in his car, so we kept the windows rolled all the way down, and the dry wind teased tears from my eyes. We didn't speak, just continued in silence until we were too stiff and uncomfortable to sit still any longer. He pulled off at a roadside stop and we got out and walked around its faded asphalt perimeter, pausing at one of the sandy picnic tables. My father sat on the warped bench, and, cautiously, I perched on the opposite end. The wood table was splintering and gray; and, like a child, I peeled long slivers off the surface. As so often happened when we were alone together, I started to cry.

For a month my father and I had talked about my unhappiness, how everything was wrong. I didn't usually say much about him or his relentless pursuit of me; we never spoke of the desperate, awful sex—had never acknowledged it in words. I talked about other losses, though, about my mother dying, and about Opa's death. My grandfather died years before he could see me graduate from the university for whose admission I'd worked so hard: the honors program in history that he told all his relatives in England about, shouting over the wires. He never learned to speak quietly on an overseas call. Opa wanted me to be a television anchorwoman: he wanted to turn on the six o'clock news and have me read the stories to him.

One month before my eighteenth birthday, my grandfather died. Mom-mom and I went to have tea with him in the nursing home, and when we got to his room, he was lying very still in his bed, his right hand cupped behind his good ear, as if he were trying to hear something, a faint voice.

Mom-mom had already unwrapped the cookies, poured tea from her thermos, when I took her hand and said, "No, no. No tea." I pointed at his slack cheeks and blue lips, his still chest. She didn't answer, but sat down, gently, as though afraid to wake him, on the empty bed next to his. As the attendants were sliding his body onto a gurney, to take him away, she sipped his cold tea from the thermos's red plastic cup.

I'd shown my report cards to Opa for twelve years, from first grade on. He signed them, and gave me a silver dollar for every A. I never spent the money; I still have the coins stacked in my sock drawer. After he died, I found it hard to care about grades. Now I was on academic probation, failing my few classes. I'd been dropped from the honors program long ago, but my adviser knew the situation with my mother and had convinced the university not to expel me just yet.

It was Opa's death that marked the end of my childhood and the last of my innocence. He was the only person I had loved without fear, and although he was very old, I had believed, with the dumb trust of a child, that he would always be there, that he would come home from the convalescent hospital and re-plant his garden. That he would draw faces on my eggs, put a saucepan on his head, dance a jig in the parlor, chase me with string, score the soles of my new shoes so I wouldn't, couldn't, slip. But that was many years ago.

I looked up from the peeling table. My father had a beautiful head, overly large, a little grotesque, like those ubiquitous visionary heads of Constantine multiplying over the territory of Rome in her decline: that same gaze, staring past its object, his cold eyes made passionate by their terribly bloodshot whites. I've known you since I can't remember, I thought. You with the blue tights, big chest, bullets blazing from your fingertips: superhero. Confused somehow with other invented fathers before I'd ever met you. It occurred to me suddenly that, of

235

course, it was Opa who had been my only father. This man I didn't know: he was a stranger who had crept past the preoccupation of my grief, promising solace.

I felt I couldn't endure it any longer, lying on the floor of some motel room. He rested on his good elbow when he fucked me, his big hands over my ears, and dribbled my head like a basketball on the floor. Staccato: faster than the tempo of the fuck. When he rolled off, my eyes had been closed, my head rumbling on the floor for so long, it seemed, I couldn't speak, a train ride to someplace from which I couldn't return. I'd think about any crazy thing while it was happening. While it was happening I was far far away.

My grandmother took the Trans-Siberian Railway from Harbin to Paris in 1908. The train stopped on the steppes and she and her sister Lilly got out. Wearing fur bonnets, the two little girls played in Siberia's beautiful and empty purity, a white canvas for their fantasies. They rolled in the snow, ate it, drank it, threw it until it fell down upon them like dust dropping from the skirts of angels. Mom-mom remembered that when the train tracks changed gauges—several times during the journey—the wheels would scream and rattle until the engine came to a slow labored halt, and then they would tumble out of the black car to play. Their faces would be covered in coal dust and grime from the smoke, the occasional pink showing through where the snow had washed a spot clean. Back in the compartment, her mother took a handkerchief and cold cream and rubbed off the soot. When they arrived in Paris they had very bad sore throats and were taken to a Doctor Billelius—a noted Greek throat surgeon—to be cured.

"I can't live like this," I said.

My father said nothing, shifted his weight on the bench.

"Don't you understand? I'm very unhappy. I want my life to be normal."

"You've gone beyond that," he said. "Your life can never be

normal again. It wasn't normal from the beginning. What is normal? No one's life is normal. It's a mathematical concept, inapplicable."

"You know what I'm saying. I'd like to have a husband, children, a family like other people have. To be loved like other people are."

"What people?" My father took his sunglasses from his breast pocket and put them on. The desert light reflected off their lenses so I couldn't see my father's dishonest eyes. The wind kicked sand across the asphalt.

"You know what I'm saying, just an average life, different from this. I want it to be five years from now. I want to live in another place and have you be like everyone else's father, a letter now and then. I want you to leave me alone."

"Isabel," he said, "it's too late." He smiled the way I imagined he must have when he campaigned back in Needles—an easy, ready twisting of his lips. "You'll never be able to get close to someone other than me, because you won't be able to resist telling them what we've done. That's just who you are, a bad liar. And once they know, they'll leave you, all of them. No husband would stand for it. He'd have to kill one of us, either me or you."

I believed my father that day, and for years after I had escaped him. Spoiled meat, unclean. I was something he had used and now I wasn't fit for another purpose. His reasoning, self-serving as it was, made sense, and I felt myself damned. Even if I couldn't bear my life, I didn't have a chance at another.

I stood up from the table and started running. Across the hot asphalt, past the cinder-block restrooms, into the desert. I cleared the low fence in one desperate leap and tore the skin of my ankle as I went over. Into the dry dry desert, sand in my shoes. One came off and I kicked off the other and felt the sharp stones, thorns and brush under my feet as I ran farther and farther from the highway and the long black car.

The luxury of hysteria. Men have the gift of rage: they can bellow and threaten without any fear of being ridiculous. And women can leave reason behind and in doing so more fully and exultantly embrace their gender. I was crying as I ran, like an animal, a child. I was saying over and over and over, Mother, Mother, Mother, like a mantra. My mother was dying in the city and I was running through the desert past the weird sentinel forms of the saguaro, the dry beautiful yucca arms reaching out. I tore my feet on their sharp spines; the lower buttons on my shirt came undone and its tails flapped and snagged on brambles; my hair tangled and caught as well; and my cheeks stung from scratches.

For the first time since I was very small I sobbed until I gagged. My chest was burning, and my feet were bleeding and I coughed with asthma and let myself fall into the ground screaming Mother, but hoarse now and silently.

I lay on my back and looked at the blank blue sky like a bowl inverted over all our heads, impenetrable and inscrutable and not like heaven at all. My father's old sedan approached and I thought tragically, tragicomically, of hurling myself beneath the tires. But I was played out and just lay there as he cut the engine and got out of the car. He handed me my shoes which he had picked up along the way, and I put them on, forcing the creamy leather flats over my bloody swollen feet. I got in the car and leaned against the door.

The tires spun in the sand for a moment before they held, and we moved off, back toward the highway.

MotherMotherMother. Of course I could never have hated my mother so much, enough to allow her husband to fuck me, had I not loved her so desperately. I would have done anything to get her attention. For soon after her unkind ministrations during infancy and childhood came the worse deprivation of

238

her cool detachment during my adolescence. The years in which I ached for her touch.

The hate has burned itself out, nearly. Still the occasional shaking rages. But the love remains like a vast cold ocean. A physical longing, a sickness. Whenever I am tired, anxious, rundown, I catch it again, this lovesickness for you, Mother. All problems, every injury, seem to grow from the lack or the fact of you.

Ever since I can remember, each hurt has gotten lost in Mother-hurt. When I was yet in grammar school, any pain, physical or emotional, would lead me back, drop me into an older, more basic agony, and in privacy I would hold myself and rock myself and say MotherMotherMother over and over and over, the way you repeated your secret mantra: an acknowledgment and prayer to the central truth of my existence.

That day in the desert, I said your name reflexively, not thinking. I said it because your name is the one I have always called when I am frightened, I said it because I had finally seen my father and his cool clever cruelty and because in trying to take some love from you—since you were so miserly with it—I had lost what little I had. Your love was precious for its smallness, for the yawning lack of it.

I am learning that there are two kinds of value in love. Yours was the tiny winking gem, too little to use before it was all used up. For many years, that was the only kind I understood, and I sought out other people whose love was notable for its limitations. I loved those best who clearly had less than I needed in return. One drop of balm for an acre of dry need.

The other is remarkable for its abundance and its ordinary nourishment, like milk or air. Sam knows who I am, he dislikes my past and it pains and angers him, but his love is a sloppy, generous flow, evidence of it all about me. He is, of course, like Opa. I met him in his garden, the gush of water from his big aluminum can splashing mud onto his shoes. I was dressed for our blind date, but I put my hands into the soil to set a pepper plant into its place. A little test, he later admitted, that sort of thing important on a blind date. When I took the little seedling from him and put my manicured hands into the earth, I passed.

Oh Mother, I still call your name. I still am stricken, sick and speechless, by the memory of our loss—our huge and miserable failure as mother and as daughter—and cry at any small disharmony between people who love one another. I had a fight, a very minor quarrel, with Sam the other day, and when I could escape I went into the bathroom and turned out the light and closed the door. I pressed my face into my bathrobe hanging there, a gift from you some ten Christmases ago—I had only just cut the tags from it the previous week—and I whispered, so he could not hear me from where he was standing in the hall, MotherMotherMother.

I think that I will do it all my life, call out to you. I still want you so. It is the one great continuous fact of my existence, lending constancy. No matter where I am, this is who I am, the one who wants you so badly.

In the gas station's restroom, above the cracked white tile, the filthy porcelain, is a luna moth. Each wing is the size of one of my hands. And they close and open slowly, as if caught unaware and undecided, not committed to either an attitude of prayer or one of offering.

I stand eye level with the moth and its wings are open wide against the dirty screen of the window; wide, wide with the opening beat of my heart, and then they shut with the closing of it. This pale creature which lives only a week or a day, its rhythms are magically those of my own full heart. I reach my hand toward it—it is so large, like a bird—and feel it struggle for a moment between my hand and the screen, leaving a faint green dust on my palm. When it flies away, it sinks a little in the air; some of its ability to fly has rubbed off on my hands.

When I return to the car I do not tell my father but keep my hands pressed tight together between my thighs, the magic power of flight and escape caught tight in my grip.

On the eve of my mother's funeral, at ten minutes before midnight, on the uncomfortable mattress that folded out from the old sofa in the den (a bed directly below my grandmother's in the room above), and, as was habit, in complete silence, my father fucked me for the last time.

It had been months since I'd seen him, since that day in the desert. Perhaps he had taken pity on me, for he never again arrived unannounced after that day, and the few times he called, I hung up on him. But I felt that I had to tell him of her death, and ask that he be present at the funeral. For "closure," I thought, that neat psychological trick by which grown-ups do their emotional housekeeping. With the help of antidepressants and weekly therapy, I was relearning, or being taught for the first time, how functional adults were supposed to behave. My shrink was one of the kind who says nothing, and when he nonreacted to my sounding out the idea of having my father present at the funeral, I chose to interpret it as a good idea, or at least not a dangerous one. I had some dumb expectation that we could then bury it all, that it would be truly over. But Mother has never really died to me; I have kept her living, fed her on the blood of my sleep, my nighttime vampire mother. Oh, you are alive in my dreams, so much more vital than I. And just as you thus lived beyond your death, so did the complex of desires that you spawned.

Can I tell you a secret? On the morning of your funeral we divided your clothes. My father, your ex-husband, took what he wanted—dresses, sweaters, shoes, a jacket. I kept the rest, ultimately giving most away, but I saved the things you wore closest to your skin—your bras and camisoles, slips—the slippery soft silk that smelled of you and your perfume. I kept them in three plastic bags, one inside another, and when I was very lonely, when I was frightened, when I ached, I took the bags from my closet where they were hidden behind the shoe rack; and I opened them, one, two, three, and smelled you. For a time I kept one of your slips under my pillow and touched it as I fell asleep, when I fell asleep.

It was two days after you died that he flew in from Needles. When he disembarked from the little Cessna—a friend's private craft—he didn't come to where I was standing by the exit door, but walked slowly to the stainless steel drinking fountain. He took a long drink and then wiped his wet mouth with the back of his hand. He looked at me, and then approached.

"You're thinner," he said. A physical observation, an almost proprietary comment. Body as metaphor. Over the past couple of years my once rangy father had grown steadily larger—not fat exactly, but bigger, stronger—and I smaller, less substantial, stripping my sexuality away, returning to the guiltless child body. It was as if he had consumed me, or what he wanted of me, my womanhood. Looking up at him, I felt a cool edge of fear thinking that we would have to leave the little municipal air field and its travelers, its witnesses.

In the car he put his hand on the back of my neck and I felt how large it was, the fingers curling toward my throat. How many times had he taken my neck in his hand, and guided my head to where he wanted it? How many times did my lips bleed from biting them shut? At least there had been some point at which I had refused: one increment away, perhaps not meaningful, certainly not commendable, from utter debasement.

At home, in my grandmother's house, he read for an hour or two after the late dinner. Mom-mom had gone to bed. I still had the living room to vacuum, several spots to scrub from the dining-room rug, food to prepare, windows to wash—a night's worth of chores before the fifty or so mourners descended after the requiem mass. I knew that without attempting escape, it would be over in a matter of minutes; whereas if I were to protest, to squirm from his grasp, to refuse, he would argue with me, follow me about as I polished the silver, chopped vegetables. He would weep, and feign chest pains. Finally, he would threaten me. He wouldn't go to bed and to sleep but would squander the last of my energy on argument and steal away the remaining hours of solitude and accomplishment. There was something, too, about the antidepressants, those four Deseryl tablets that I took every night before bed. They made it easier, even possible to get up each morning: to shower, dress and behave like the next person. But I was also flattened by them into lassitude, as unable to laugh as to cry, and likely to take the path of least resistance. If, for example, I were walking along the street and were knocked down, I might not get up. I might just sit on the pavement, watch others go by. I wasn't depressed, not exactly, but I had succumbed to an absolute fatalism and sensed no control over my environment. So, for the sake of expediency, I acquiesced that night. It seemed, ludicrously, like just one more chore.

Under his body, his flesh heavy and damp with lust, I braced myself, each foot planted, to keep his weight and thrust from pushing me off the lumpy mattress. I closed my eyes as I felt his hand on my nipple, his fingers like those of a safecracker twisting the dark knobs of flesh. I let myself shrink and fall into the usual, practiced vision in which I became ever smaller, until in my mind I saw myself as no more than a black spot, an insect caught under the pink expanse of his body. His hands were on my head then, and when he came, I felt the force of each finger as a separate tight point on my skull. Finished, he rolled off, and I slipped out of the bed. I pulled the blanket over his shoulder so he wouldn't wake later from the chill night air and I closed the den door very softly.

That first time my father raped me—when I was not even nineteen, that time in his mother's basement guest room—I had met her only three hours before. She didn't like me or my mother or my grandmother, and she told me so at dinner. His mother loved my father—her son—and told me that, too. There didn't seem much point in calling for help from her basement.

He did it and then he left the damp guest bedroom and went upstairs and I turned on the light and sat up on the narrow bed and looked at the cinder-block walls. They were painted white and fishing poles were displayed on them, five poles and one big blue marlin mounted on an oak board. I sat very still and looked at its eye, trying to discern from a distance whether or not it was real. It looked plastic.

My grandfather, the one I never met, had been a sport fisher. When he was alive he went to Ensenada, Mexico, for months at a time, living on a boat. These mounted fish were all that were left of that life.

Like my mother's beauty, my paternal grandfather's charm

and sexual appeal were fabled, the subject of a hundred family tales. It was said that women followed him down the street like bitches in heat and that he could hardly help his unfaithfulness.

My father told me a story on the day that we met. My father did most of the talking during that dinner; he was making up for lost time, filling in the blanks, and he told me stories about his childhood. Once, his attention entirely taken by the stealthy progress of a woman stalking his father who walked before him on the hot sidewalk, my father, eight years old and not very tall, knocked himself unconscious on a parking meter that he did not notice in his path. The woman was blond, very, and heavily perfumed. When my father opened his eyes he could see the sheen of perspiration gathering into a slick runnel that disappeared into her deep, fragrant cleavage and ended in a cherry-colored stain on her dress's tight pink bodice. The woman comforted my father, whose head was in her lap, while making a date to meet my grandfather the following evening. After she had stood up from the pavement, displacing the boy whose head still ached in silent amazement, she left them, and father and son continued together, this time hand in hand, to the hardware store.

I kept a tally. Five times at my mother's—when she was in the hospital and Albert was there with her. One time at his mother's. Once in my grandmother's den. Four times in my dorm room when my roommate was out of town. Thirteen times in motels. And on seventeen nearly consecutive Saturday evenings in the back of his old car, parked in some abandoned place. My mother, lying in the hospital, Mom-mom, my room-mate, they all thought I had some secret boyfriend who spirited me away each Saturday. They asked to meet him. Thought it was "healthy" that I had this outlet, this release.

Forty-one times and each time the same: silent and accomplished with an economy of movement as well as of sound; missionary, semiclothed. He wore a shirt and socks only; I wore whatever I could leave on.

Those feverish afternoons when he arrived suddenly and took me for a few hours, stole me, then drove all night back to Needles, back to his city council office—one time it was on the eve of an important speech he was to give, a bid for the mayoral candidacy. He arrived home just before he was due to appear downtown. Who knows what his wife, his family, friends and associates thought of him; perhaps they thought him some sainted madman, raving in the desert like John the Baptist. Having eluded the formal church, he'd yet to completely escape his grandmother's ordination. And he continued to make failed bids for the mayor's office by running on some ill-conceived moral platform in a town of desiccated old desert ranch hands and sorry-looking prostitutes, who worked the truck stops, tuning their patrons in on the CB radios in their rooms at the Glass Slipper Motor Court. There weren't many churches, or churchgoers, in Needles.

My father said that my body gave him inspiration, that my beauty let him touch God. Sometimes in the motels he would yell at me afterward and say he didn't like to be *tolerated*, he wanted to be passionately made love to.

One time after the motel room, we went to a coffee shop for dinner. We were passing through Lake Havasu City—we never had anyplace to be when we were together, my father and I; our unnatural partnership began in an airport, a restaurant, a car, and found temporary shelter in rented rooms, roadside stops, tourist attractions. Thirty miles south of Needles— through which my father drove me without stopping the car, once shoving my head down below window level when he thought he saw someone he knew—Lake Havasu City is noteworthy as the resting place of the London Bridge. Disassembled block by block over the Thames, it was painstakingly put back together at the mouth of a dammed-up bend in the Colorado River. The man-made lake was slimy and stagnant and lividly green, and on the underside of the bridge I could see numbers still etched into some of the stones, evidence of a cataloguing system for keeping track of the order in which they were taken apart. Some rich eccentric bought all the pieces and had the nursery rhyme bridge reconstructed in the middle of the Mojave Desert, complete with turn-of-the-century gas lamps and a fake Tudor village featuring a fish-and-chips shop and a few depressing little souvenir stores. I bought a postcard of the bridge standing alone in the desert, blue skies above, Union Jacks flying. It would have amused Mom-mom, perhaps, but of course I could not give it to her without arousing suspicions.

I would not eat at the double-decker bus hamburger stand, so my father took me to a nondescript diner along the highway. In line at the salad bar he pulled my plate out of my hand and let it fall to the floor and shatter, cherry tomatoes rolling between my feet. When he thus had the attention of all the diners, he said loudly, "You're a slut just like your mother." One entire family turned around in their seats and looked to see who I was.

When I fell in love with my father I dropped heedlessly into the arms of a madman. After nearly two decades of unsuccessful attempts at reconciliation with my mother, my father returned to Los Angeles. Angry with her and with my grandparents who had exiled him after my birth, he returned with the intention of settling scores. A repetition compulsion, perhaps. In any case, the form this settling of scores, this drama, would take was the capture and enslavement of me.

I didn't believe or understand any of this at the time.

I was eighteen, just. Opa had died a month before. Only three days earlier I had broken up with Matthew, a law student who fascinated me, and whom I loved, an unbalanced boy-man who hit me occasionally and who forced me into acts of sexual compromise. Having all my life bent my will and broken it under the desire to please and secure the love of my capricious mother, it was easy to slip into relationships of sexual submissiveness and degradation. My very body and blood understood subjugation to a loved one. My mother taught me to hold very still under her dangerous hands.

Matthew played a game with me. On Friday nights—the rest of the weekend being reserved for study—I was his sexual slave. I wasn't allowed to speak or wear underwear. I was often blindfolded, but I experienced my blindness as a relief rather than the discipline intended. I didn't want to see what was coming. Matthew had a predilection for anal intercourse, and he would stop only when the blood ran. I had always believed in the value of pain and passivity, the arts of gentle Jesus, and mistook my debasement for sanctification.

That first spring evening when I put on my mother's dress and opened the door for my father—having seen him only three times before, and briefly, when I was two and ten and twelve—after dinner, he spent the night at my mother's apartment. I slept over, as well. It was too late to drive back to school, to wake up my roommate, a conscientious student who retired early and rose at dawn to work on her physics. That night, I heard my father pay a visit to my mother in her bedroom. Then he crossed the hall to the living room where I lay on the convertible sofa, saving the guest room for him. He sat at the foot of the thin mattress and watched me, assuming that I slept. Only once did I dare to open one eye, and just a crack. I saw the streetlamp glint coldly on his open fly. For a moment I thought he had a knife in his lap.

He lived hundreds of miles away, with his family: a wife, children. Ten months later, he came to see me at school, leaving his office in the care of a young male secretary. He drove through the desert to Los Angeles, rented a cheap guest room in the kind of hotel that my grandmother called a flophouse. He learned my body and called it his own flesh.

He had the fearful energy and seduction of the mentally ill. He spoke and called himself a prophet. He told me that I was God's gift to him, fruit of his loins, his to relish. Between his anger and madness and my anger and desire for revenge, I allowed it to happen. I was mad, too.

I stopped going to school, spoke to the dean and convinced him that it was in my best interest to take a break. In the basement apartment of a graceless brick building just one mile from campus, I stayed in bed until noon each day, avoided my friends and dropped acid too many times. After I started to trip and was sure I was capable of responsible driving, I got in my car and drove until I reached the dry gold hills that I loved. Slowly and rhythmically I shifted the gears of my car, and then I entered the freeway and nimbly moved among the other drivers, keeping in my lane. Driving my car in such a state of grace, I was an angel and maneuvered as such a creature, exactly between the lines, exactly in control of the direction I took. The experience of driving was so full and engrossing I could not spare attention to the radio, I could not sing a song and drive, and so was silent. I heard the terrible slow language of my heart over the road; it beat as the dashed white line spun by my tires, three dashes for each diastole. Or was it three pumps, three surges of blood to each stripe of paint? I lost all sense of time and was freed. I became known as an eccentric, which in my junior year of college, when all are so desperate for distinction, seemed an honor.

What did it mean that I allowed this profane thing to happen, that my father, my mother's mate, was for two years, and until the day that she was in the earth, the only man who fucked me?

Two things are true: My father was violent and forceful, and my father articulated things that had never before been said. He was mad, he was crazy, but he was also honest at times, and, born of a family of liars, this attracted me. For years I had interpreted questionable acts in the best of all possible lights. I made better excuses for my mother's negligence and cruelties than did she. My father did not. He told me that she had wanted to abort me and that it was he who had defended my life. He said that she had always hated me, whereas he had burned with love for me from afar. All my life, my mother had not touched me—with her hands, that is—unless the occasion demanded it. She parceled out stiff hugs at airports and holidays and birthdays; I felt her flesh shrink from me when she was not steeled for an embrace. He fucked me, yes, but he held me afterward, and for brief moments I believed that for one of my parents my existence had not been a trial.

Of course, I was miserable. I neither liked nor understood my father. I felt sympathy for him, that his mind had been bent by unhappiness and reversals, by the Bible and his missionary grandmother, by my mother, and her rejection. And his arm, which he finally showed me one night, gingerly unbuttoning his shirt cuff, made me sad. It looked not deformed but ghostly and like the limb of a gentler man, one who wouldn't hurt me. I wondered that my mother had never mentioned it. Now he was remarried; in Needles, there was another wife and children, guns kept loaded under the bed. He was dangerous, but he loved me, or so he said, and I was a slave to the affection of others, no matter its form.

And I did think I loved him. Although I knew I never wanted to be fucked by him, I thought that I let it happen out of my sacrificial love for him. I thought that was true until my mother was dead and I realized that I didn't love him anymore.

I knew she suspected. She sensed it right away. But then, in the beginning, and long before I had any idea that she was dying and that I was losing her, I didn't want to be found out. She took me to her psychiatrist—we went for three joint sessions—and in his presence she accused me of incest. I denied it, for once lying cleverly and coolly, alluding to Freudian psychoanalysis. I was glib: I said that I was retroactively working through the stages that every girl-child experienced, and that the appearance of sexual involvement, the acceptance on my part of an inappropriate public caress, the palpable attunement of flesh united in sin, all this was merely the result of a latent phenomenon. The doctor believed me—I could see credulity in his compassion and admiration: my words were so perfectly articulated, my voice halted and convinced in just the right places. But my mother was not for a moment fooled. She had taken me to her doctor, enlisting support, and she ended in losing her ally.

I lied to my mother when she said that her suspicions were destroying her, literally. Once, before she was too sick to drive, she and I got stuck in a traffic snarl at the Los Angeles International Airport. We had just dropped off an ancient cousin of Mom-mom's at the Air France terminal, the end of a visit prompted, no doubt, by the almost telepathic network of family gossip which had informed the extended and dispersed relatives that Regina's daughter was dying. The old cousin, a tiny desiccated man in suspenders that kept his antediluvian trousers hiked up to his armpits, jumped spryly out of the car, and disappeared with his suitcase into the crowds. Once he was gone, Mother and I circled slowly and silently around the terminals and, finally deciding to park and wait out the jam, we bailed out. She decided we would kill an hour or two having dinner in the silly theme restaurant, an unlikely spot for her to choose, that 1950s concept of the space age, its lunar module legs planted in the parking lot. A perfect place for us, however, in its synthesized graceless awkwardness: a place as clumsy as we were with one another. I knew that evening she was trying to ask me outright about my father. "Adam," she called him. My father had been named by his missionary grandmother for the first to fall.

"Adam," she said. "Your father," she tried twice, perhaps three times, before she continued. "Adam is, has not always been, a very, uh, normal, balanced man." She aligned her cutlery on her paper napkin and, when I made no response, continued. "I'm not sure his intentions are, uh, honorable." This last word came out like a question, lilting at the end. *Honorable?*

A big jet rose above the Pan Am terminal framed in the blue-tinted picture window behind her. All the little things on the table—the salt and pepper shakers, her sunglasses and the stand bearing a card advertising some blue drink—vibrated in the wake of its ascension.

"What are you saying?" I asked.

"I'm not saying anything," she said. "I'm just saying that he . . . your father loved me very much once upon a time." She stopped and looked at me.

"I know that. I've heard that," I said.

"He gets confused sometimes. He might feel something for you inappropriately. Something that he thinks he feels for you, but really feels for me."

"Like love, you mean," I said nastily.

"I didn't say that," she said, and looked away. Then she said, "Why are you always accusing people of not loving you enough?"

The jet had lifted beyond the frame of the big tinted window, but its whine persisted, a thin sob.

"Because they don't," I said. "You don't."

A waitress approached with menus and stepped back confused as my mother stood abruptly. She put her sunglasses on. Eyes concealed, hair stylishly cut, clothes more self-consciously fashionable than mine, adolescently thin, my mother looked very young. She *was* young, thirty-eight.

"Let's go," she said. She picked up her keys and started walking toward the elevator, her limp almost imperceptible to anyone not already aware of it.

I stayed in my chair. I was crying, but for once I kept my tongue, was able to speak through my tears. "What's the matter with you?" I said, and I said it loudly enough that she heard me, as did the waitress and the only other diners, a couple two tables away who interrupted their own argument for a moment to stare at us. My mother paused, her back toward me.

"You always miss your cues," I said. "You're supposed to say 'Of course I do.' Even if it isn't true, as a mother, you're supposed to have the sense to say, 'Of course I love you, Isabel.'" She didn't answer. I looked at the waitress, who looked away. For a long moment, nobody spoke, nobody moved. Then slowly, almost as if she were intending some stealth, my mother continued toward the lobby.

I looked at the stricken waitress and shrugged. I pointed at the little card in its stand. "I'll have a blue zombie," I said. The waitress flipped her order pad in her hand, nervously fanning its leaves. A little square of blue carbon paper fell out onto the floor. She didn't pick it up.

"Do you have any ID?" she asked. She looked past rather than at me.

"I left it in the car."

The waitress hesitated and then, evidently incapable of any other response, went to get my drink from the bar.

I could see my mother standing, waiting, by the elevator in the lobby. The dining room was a round spaceship of windows looking out onto the airport, with the lobby and the cashier in the center. When I didn't come out, Mother eventually turned around and lifted her sunglasses and looked in my direction.

She stood a moment, her face turned toward mine, expression unreadable at that distance. When she saw the waitress bring my drink, she walked slowly back to the table.

"Oh, for Christ's sake, Isabel," she said. "You make everything so hard." Her sunglasses, which she wore habitually indoors and out, slipped down her nose and she pushed them back before I had a chance to see her eyes. She looked around, at a loss for a moment, and then opened her wallet. She left a twenty on the table and walked stiffly out.

From the window behind her empty seat I watched her make her way slowly to the tiered lot where we had parked. She looked so solitary, as if she belonged with no one: she certainly did not look like anyone's mother.

I drank my stupidly sweet drink and watched the planes land and take off, and when the sun went down, I left and took a bus back home to the stop nearest Mom-mom's house. I had left my car parked in my grandmother's driveway, but when I walked over and picked it up I didn't go into the house, just sat in the comfort of the small, familiar space behind the wheel for a moment and then drove back to school to finish a paper in my dorm room.

That night I had avoided the truth, skirted the issue. Out of fear and revenge I lied when my mother said her cancer was feeding on lies.

It had seemed exciting for a little while, to transcend, simply step beyond and outside conventional rules: a taste of immortality in a way, and I felt grown up by my sin. Until later, when I felt stripped again, impoverished by abuse. Then I would have given anything for her accusations, her forcing my confession.

I wasn't with my mother when she died. I went away for a week, to a retreat, an unusual place for me, but I had needed to get away, to collect my thoughts. In a nonconversation with my psychiatrist, we decided it might be good for me to leave town, think about my life in a different environment. So, I flew to Denver, to a vegetarian yoga camp in the mountains where I stretched and ate lentils and rice and hiked and said nothing for a week. In retrospect, it wasn't very much different from what I did in L.A., just prettier and at a higher elevation from sea level. I thought that week at home would pass like all the others: Mother would consume her drugs, watch television; Albert would drink; Mom-mom would doze by Mother's bed until late afternoon when it was time to go home and feed her cats.

My mother died very slowly. Oddly, it was her heart that was too strong to let her go, and she outlived the predictions of her oncologist by nearly a year. Despite my dishonesty with her, I had hoped that the threat of death would force some resolution between us, some understanding, but as my mother grew more ill and yet survived, whatever "relationship" we shared fell further into ruins and threatened to leave me with nothing when she was gone. The night before I left for Denver, we had the same old quarrel over the morphine. "Please, Isabel, please, at least you could leave the syringe and the ampoules within reach," she said. She was picking at the blanket with her good hand, pulling fibers out of its smooth nap and rolling them into little balls of wool. Even though she had only limited use of one arm and hand, she thought she could manage, if in sufficient desperation, to inject herself. I would not allow her the opportunity.

We cried together on the night before I left, and I let my head rest on her chest for the first time since I was a child. I was surprised by the heat of her flesh, feverish and dry under her thin nightie, and by the strength with which she could sob. Her ribs bounced under my head as she cried. I was leaving her in Albert's care, but had arranged for an extra pair of hands.

In the morning a young Mexican woman would come in to help turn her while he changed the sheets; her name was Anna and she would come every day except Sunday.

It was the week before St. Valentine's Day that I left, and I mailed an embarrassingly large selection of cards to Mother from the mailbox in the terminal. That day had always been a sort of truce for us, ever since I was a little girl, and we had exchanged hundreds of stickily inappropriate valentines that promised immortal love.

On February 13 my mother went into a coma, and she died before I could get home. She was still alive when I left the camp in the mountains for the city of Denver—I took a bus at dawn and wound my way down from the clouds—but when I called from the airport, Albert said she was gone.

I hung up the phone; there were fifty minutes left before my flight. Well before boarding I started to shake, not unpleasantly or violently, but nevertheless a thin tremor that I couldn't control, and an attendant feeling of thirst. I bought two pints of orange juice at the snack bar and gulped them down; on the plane I drank some more. Within minutes I was wrenchingly and extravagantly sick, in the tiny bathroom near the galley, a place where one can vomit only standing up. And I did, over and over, my hands braced against the doll-sized stainless steel counter. At one point there was a polite, hesitant knock on the door and someone—a stewardess?—asked if I was all right, surely having heard me retching and coughing.

I answered in a bright voice, "Oh, yes, *fine,*" and waited for whomever it was to go away. I looked up as I spoke, and in the mirror I saw a woman, white-faced, mucus and orange juice running from her nose. She looked like no one I had ever known. She looked then a little like my mother: eyes wide and sad and uncrying.

My head was on fire, stomach acid forced into every tiny

recess of my sinuses. Finished, empty, I was too frightened and humiliated to go back to my seat. This was the first time I had ever been ill on a plane—I have always been one of those irritating people who enjoy turbulence, who smile as the trays bounce and the drinks spill, as other passengers tighten their seat belts and their grimaces. But now I was sick and there was orange juice, soured and stinking, everywhere. My fingers were shaking in a puddle of it. I could see bits of pulp drying on the mirror, on my chin, my shirt.

It took perhaps a quarter of an hour to restore order to the tiny lavatory. I washed my face and hands and neck and arms with the play-sized soap and mopped the mirror and the sink and the counter and the floor and even the walls with wet paper towels. Then I sat on the closed toilet lid and, with my feet braced against the door and my head on the cool edge of the sink, I fell briefly asleep. I woke with a start and felt more weary than I could ever remember feeling.

When I left the bathroom a stewardess approached me shyly and to my horror asked if I needed help: I couldn't answer. With my eyes set determinedly forward and away from her concern, I made my way back to my seat and fell asleep almost as soon as I sat down. When I opened my eyes perhaps an hour later I was covered with a blanket and there were two little packets of Alka-Seltzer tucked with an airsickness bag under my hand.

The body was gone when I got to Mother's apartment, and in the five brief hours since she had died, Albert had managed to rearrange the furniture and have the medical rental companies come to pick up all the equipment, everything. The bed, with its shining steel rails against which her hands had rested for so many hours, against which her rings had clicked as she fretted with the bedclothes, had been dismantled and removed. The oxygen machine and the big green emergency tanks, the little Scandinavian add-on shelves I had bought to put all the medicines on; they were all gone from the den, and the table and chairs that had been stored in the garage were back in place.

Albert and my grandmother were sitting on the couch. She had looked radiant at the end, they said, beautiful, like when she was a girl. She had been at peace. I couldn't imagine how this could be true: it seemed unlikely to me that the ravages of the last year might have been undone in some last transcendence; but Albert and Mom-mom were the lucky sort of people who believed what they needed, who had the ability to experience what comforted them, whether it existed or not, and so I went upstairs without comment.

Mom-mom had asked me to choose what dress and which underclothes and shoes Mother would wear in her casket. Hunting through her drawers, I came upon an old black cashmere sweater with a hole in the elbow, and I pressed it to my mouth and closed my eyes and breathed in that smell of her which I knew so well, that slight musky sweet smell of a life now mysteriously gone. I was charmed by that sweater. Mother never had holes in her clothes, or stains, hardly ever a loose thread. Her one pair of blue jeans had a knife-edge crease in each leg from the dry cleaner's. I found myself unable to replace the sweater in her drawer and so I put it on over my thin shirt, and continued with my chores, collecting underpants, bra, slip. A blue silk dress, quite formal, and matching pumps. I took the crucifix off the wall above her bed and slipped it into the toe of one blue shoe.

There were two days to prepare for the funeral. During those days I went to the mortuary three times to visit my mother, her body. Each time I had to call ahead and the director would have her wheeled out and laid in a visitation room, a small, frigidly air-conditioned chamber absurdly decorated to look like a tiny library, with a large wing-backed leather chair and ottoman, and a shelf of unlikely-looking books; I briefly wondered whether they were even real volumes, or rather just a stage prop, spines with nothing behind them. I never checked, though; I didn't care. The walls had a paneling of the thinnest oak veneer and the light reflecting off them lent a sickly yellow glow to everything.

I couldn't stop touching her, the incredible putty feel of her chin, the frozen sleep of her eyes. Despite cosmetic manipulation, one eye remained slightly open and I tried to slip the lid up to see her eyeball, but the flesh was firmly set in place. Similarly, my finger could not slip between her teeth to explore her tongue. She was all locked up.

I was furtive in my examination of her corpse, sure that the funeral director would be shocked by my peculiar attentions.

Someone had painted her face with makeup she never would have used: pink frost lipstick, which I scrubbed off with one of the Kleenexes they thoughtfully supplied, ten or so boxes of them tucked into every corner of the room, until finally her lips looked chafed and bloodless; and a strange pancake tint, undoubtedly supposed to impart some color to her cheeks, only made her skin look plastic, doll-like. Her eyes were left modestly understated, just a smear of blue shadow—to match her dress, no doubt—but I wiped that away as well.

I had brought a pair of scissors with me, wanting to take a lock of hair. But when I bent to cut it, I realized that she no longer had the hair I wanted: the lustrous, almost black hair of years ago, the hair that I reached for as a child, shining and thick and curling around her long neck. That hair was gone, and what was left was thin and dull and almost gray. I couldn't bring myself to take the piece I had selected and tucked it back behind her ear.

She was visible from the waist up, only. The lower half of the casket that I had picked out with my grandmother was shut over her, apparently for good; I couldn't find any release catch.

Still, I was unable not to explore with my hand down her legs, reaching underneath the oak lid as far as I could, to make sure, I suppose, that she was all there. I pulled up her dress to see if they had put her slip on, and I had a dreadful time getting its skirt tucked back over her thighs. There wasn't much room to work with under the closed half of the lid, and there was no way to get to her feet. I wondered if someone had stolen her favorite Maud Frizon pumps, which I had included in her little suitcase.

Her hands had been artfully arranged around her crucifix. Once I undid her curled fingers, I couldn't get them back in place and her hands kept slipping down the incline of her slightly distended silk-clad belly into her crotch, where they looked very vulgar, and worse yet when holding the crucifix, which I could manage only to tuck between her right thumb and forefinger like some strange fork. I panicked at the thought of any intrusion by the funeral home personnel and gave up trying to fix the damage I had done, leaving the crucifix demurely on her chest and her hands forced to her sides. Perhaps they would think that I had become distraught and embraced her too violently.

The last time I visited her, on the morning of her funeral, I kissed her good-bye. I let my lips rest on her cool forehead, her white cheeks, as I never had when she was ill. My own tears ran down her face and I put my mouth to her ear. "Love me," I whispered. "Tell *me* lies."

I have a dream and, for the first time in many years, the first time since my mother's funeral, my father's final departure, I walk in my sleep.

        I dream of poltergeists, vengeful spirits that take posses-sion of the appliances in my home, turning them against me.
    I am not a heavy sleeper. In truth, I am not a sleeper. I would like to be, but the hours I spend in bed are few and often tormented. Bedfellows report that I whimper, tangle the sheets, plead with an unseen assailant, weep.
    For a few hours I curl against the solid breathing comfort of Sam's broad back, a hand tucked beneath his ribs to know his weight and presence as I rest. For a few hours I am at peace. But then I wake and turn and settle into a different and troubled sleep. Spirits are all about me. Childish and petty, they fill my

house: they enter the iron, the toaster, the clock radio. Fuses blow. Smoke rises. The kitchen becomes a dangerous place.

I sit up and walk from my bed to the answering machine which, like the other appliances, is haywire, the tiny cassettes spinning, random beeps and fragments of messages disturbing the black early-morning silence. The words resolve themselves, suddenly, into coherent messages: the landlord returns my call, a friend says hello, a sigh is recorded before the sound of the receiver being gently replaced. These are all reasonable communications; I remember them from the past few days.

Then another voice intrudes, musical and very feminine, a message from my mother asking that I please return her call. This is a very old message, I think, and I wonder for a moment how it is that it was never erased. Then I remember that it was years after she died that we purchased this machine and its little tapes. My mother's voice continues, but I am too afraid to listen to her words which mingle now with a message from my grandfather. The message is short, utilitarian, but his voice cracks as if with emotion.

Suddenly I understand this visitation—the machine has become a medium to the underworld and the shades are all speaking to me. All the dead begin to speak now at once, all who I have ever loved and lost.

I do not want to hear them and I begin to push the various buttons on the machine, sensibly at first, and in order, but soon I am pressing two, three at once. I try STOP and REWIND, RECORD, PLAY, FAST FORWARD, but nothing will silence these announcements from the dead. It occurs to me that I can take the tape out; perhaps then they will stop talking.

When Sam wakes me I have the cassette in my hand, its long malicious tongue unwound and tangled on the floor.

I still have a file of photographs which I saved from the brief time that I knew my father. They are pictures that he gave me, snapshots of his family, ordinary fragments from which it is possible to reconstruct a life: his children, their mother, the dog, his car parked in front of their house, birthdays, holidays. Together they make an unremarkable collection, moments stolen from an average family.

One night Sam and I went through them again, not intentionally. We were cleaning out some papers: magazines we could now part with; brochures for small appliances long since broken, forgotten or given away; junk mail that escaped the garbage and traveled piggyback downstairs to the studies, wedded for a moment and then for months to some legitimate correspondence—all the terrible tyranny of paper that breeds in every well-meaning bourgeois basement.

The file of pictures suddenly emerged. One of those packages that has some life and urgency of its own; never sought out, it every so often insinuates itself into our midst. Not that it is malicious, just that it partakes of the past and that the past always resurfaces.

On a trip upstairs to the kitchen for garbage bags, it somehow traveled to the living room under one of our arms. Soon we were taking a break from our chores, Sam with his Coke and me with my coffee. It was suddenly dark outside, past forgotten dinnertime, and we spread the pictures out over the table before the couch, I on my knees stirring with one finger, Sam collecting the pictures of my father and placing them with distaste facedown and apart from the others.

"He has a mean face," Sam said, holding one photograph under the reading lamp. It was one taken many years ago, perhaps when he was courting my mother. "Skinny lips."

I shrugged, unsure whether we should embark on the subject of my father. Some of our conversations about him have lasted well into the night. They turn a corner at some critical instant and we are no longer speaking rationally and coming to terms with an issue. Typically, I am weeping and apologizing for the liability of my family—especially in the company of Sam's wholesome clan—and Sam has become fevered and entertains wild plots of revenge: midnight rides to Needles, underworld hits, blackmail.

"Doesn't he have a mean mouth?" he says, holding the photograph under my nose. "And what's with his eyes?" Sam never met my father and when he looks at photographs, he looks carefully, learning all he can, like an agent being briefed for a dangerous mission.

The animal, the tribal, the ritual self who dances and screams in the dark is never far: all of us perform a thousand rites each day, invoke deities, stroke talismans. I am not much surprised by the things we do. Sam and I seem quite ordinary, but our hearts thud to the same beat as the hearts of savages.

There was a pair of scissors lying on the coffee table and I had picked them up while we were talking and looking at the pictures. Idly, I trimmed a few threads from my sleeve. Then I picked up a picture of my father, his good arm aloft, making a dramatic point, a campaign photograph, no doubt, as he is standing behind a podium. I snipped off the hand. Then the arm. Severed his head from his body.

"Hey, give me those," Sam said, reaching for the scissors. His head was just over my shoulder and he was laughing, wanting a turn. I held the picture and the scissors away, out of his reach; he lunged and I clamped the photo and the scissors in my two hands between my thighs. The little head and hand fell onto the carpet near the couch and Sam grabbed them. He took an X-acto knife from the desk and, kneeling before the coffee table, excised the tiny eyes and mouth and nose from the face.

We attacked the photographs in earnest then, cutting up every last one of my father, some carefully, others into random bits, until there was a little confetti-like pile on the table. A blue eye, an ear, or, worse, a tiny predatory mouth, sifted up out of the heap and we looked at what we'd done. Dismembered, his features had strangely more life than they had when all of a piece in the photos.

"Now what?" I said. Sam was sweeping the fragments into the clean ashtray. He shrugged.

"I know—let's burn them," I said. I picked up the remains of the photographs and carried them into the kitchen to look for matches. The ceramic ashtray was a pretty one and unused, so I transferred the fragments to an old pie pan. A tiny eye glinted and I shuddered in giddy recognition that we were embarked on a barbaric game.

"Don't light it in here, the emulsion always smells when it burns. And besides, it's dangerous," Sam said, watching from the kitchen door. I couldn't read his mood: indulgence, enjoyment, bewilderment? Certainly I inspired all of those. But he was now a part of this; he followed me outside.

I placed the tin on the bare dry winter ground and then, when Sam grunted in distaste, moved it from the tomato bed onto the path where nothing grew. The little pieces of paper didn't want to light, but there was no wind and the match, having caught, continued to burn evenly. I blew into the pan, slowly, and the fire crept from the tiny stick into the paper.

Emulsion does smell when it burns, acrid and oily like plastic, and the fragments made a sullen little glow and then went out, leaving a black tarry mess in the ruined pie plate.

We stood looking at the smoking sacrifice; the moon was up and gleamed dully on the old pan. Sam nudged it with his foot. It didn't seem that we were finished, quite.

"Pee on it," I said.

Last summer we had shared an apartment owned by a cross old churchy widow who didn't like us much. She harassed us at every opportunity, and Sam had pissed on her flowers at night in revenge. I had understood this and it seemed like a satisfying and reasonable exacting for her tediousness, her querulous fussing over how we bagged our garbage (in paper sacks) or picked up our mail only weekly, or kept plants on the mantel. I had approved of Sam's canine response; dogs aren't dumb: they do a lot of things that humans would.

I nudged Sam with my elbow, pushing him toward the pan, and he unzipped his fly. This was the first time I'd ever really watched him take a piss, frowning slightly in concentration, aiming. The stream splattered in the pan and onto the dirt; the burning remains of the photographs sizzled for a moment.

"Now you." Sam zipped up and stood back, challenging.

"Forget it," I said, "girls don't do that sort of thing."

"Do it," he said, "you have to."

"I can't. I can't aim like you can, it isn't easy or natural, you've been doing this sort of thing for years."

"Isabel," Sam said, and then he didn't say anything, he just waited: and I realized that he was right, the spell would lack symmetry if I didn't take a turn at desecrating the remains. And so I squatted down and urinated very unevenly over the pan, wetting my shoes in the process. Anyone could have looked out their back window and seen us, I remember thinking, and not really caring. After all, it had been years ago that I had stepped out of the expected and into the taboo; now I was returning home.

We took a sturdy old tomato stake and drove it through the wet ashes and straight through the bottom of the pan, using as a hammer one of the rocks that marked the corners of the basil garden. Without saying anything we went back inside and continued to clear the basement, bundling old magazines and papers and carrying them like good citizens out to the curb for the recycling truck's weekly pickup. I sealed all the remaining photos—those of my father's wife and children—in a manila envelope and put them away.

The pan, with a stain of black sticky ash, stayed in the yard all winter, periodically frosted over with snow, the stake standing firm in the frozen soil. Sometimes I would look out the back window and see it, and it would seem very mysterious to me, that whole evening and its souvenir there in the yard. When we replanted the garden the next spring, we took up the stake and the pie pan and threw it all away.

I have a dream that I am pregnant, impossible but true. I have fooled all the doctors and thwarted their hopeless diagnoses and, not yet heavy and clumsy with child, I am happily, perfectly full.

Suddenly, with that clairvoyance possible only in dreams, I know that the baby wants to tell me something. That it may do so, I swallow a tiny golden pencil. Inside, the fetus writes me a letter on the wall of my womb.

Before term, I miscarry, and after the child is born, still and white and lifeless in the flow of blood and water, the afterbirth is delivered. I keep the gory membrane, proof of my fertility, and dry it like parchment.

Held before the light, transformed from flesh into some magic document, the writing is revealed to me, clear and beautiful, very legible. But the message is written in some ancient hieroglyphic code which I cannot read. Frustrated, I begin to weep.

. . .

Sometimes I daydream that we have children who are born deaf, and we send them to special schools and learn a language of hand signals so that we might speak to them. Or blind, and we spend endless hours telling how the sky looks from the available clues: the smell and sound and feel of the day. Or they are deaf and blind and mute as well, but always we break through every barrier. We love them and they know it.

Our persistence makes it impossible for us to lose: we find them, we reach them, in any void. They recognize our affectionate hands and signal to us their love.

We never leave them to find their way alone.